Awake, Awake, Deborah!

The rise of a new leader in Israel.

by Nancy Rita Myers

Awake, Awake, Deborah!

The rise of a new leader in Israel.

ISBN: 978-1-6781-6438-6

Cover art work by Gabriel Myers Prunty

Author's introduction

It was shortly after 1200 BCE, in the Ancient Near East, that major world powers collapsed. The Hittite empire, primarily in modern day Turkey, and the Mycenaean empire in Greece, crumbled. Egypt lost its hegemony over the land of Israel. International trade routes broke down. There was drought and subsequent famine causing many to go hungry. It was a dark age in a time where barely any history was recorded. People were on the move across the Mediterranean Sea, westward from the Jordan, and up from the coastal plains to the hill country of Israel. These voyagers and soldiers were in search of food, water, security, land, and life for their children and livestock.

It was during this time of tumult and challenge that the ancient Israelites came into history. Merneptah, an Egyptian Pharaoh, in his stele of 1209 BCE mentions that Israel was, "laid to waste and his seed not." This is the first time the people of Israel are mentioned in any extra biblical source. While Merneptah boasts of defeating the Israelites and laying them to waste, their seeds, nevertheless, took root in the hill country, west of the Jordan River and grew like weeds. At least, this is where the tribe of Ephraim lived.

As the Israelites struggled for survival they had to contend with differing groups of Canaanites and the Sea Peoples from Greece, who invaded the land. This was the time before the great kings of Israel reigned, Saul, David, and Solomon. Instead people called, "Judges" led the people. They were administrators and warriors who sought to protect the people and help them survive.

The book of Judges in the Bible mentions men of skill, strategy, and might, but there is only one female listed among their ranks, This is Deborah, who has two whole chapters, four and five, devoted to her leadership in a time of great danger to the Israelites.

How did this woman's achievements come to be recognized and even more importantly recorded in our Bible? She must have been an incredible judge and her victories were undoubtedly widely known at that time. I have always been intrigued by Deborah. Her wisdom and ability to guide her people had to be hard won. Utilizing my fascination with early Iron Age and my imagination about Deborah, this novel strives to weave Biblical elements, archaeology, and my imagination to make Deborah come to life.

I am first of all grateful for my sabbatical at Temple Beth David for giving me the time to write. My brother, Nathan Myers, assisted me enormously through the initial draft stage. He proof read every chapter, no matter how clumsy, and offered advice and encouragement. I'm sure I would've given up, if it weren't for his help. Thank you to my professional editor, Susan Leon, and her wonderful advice throughout the next few drafts. James Myers, my father, was helpful with formatting, dates, and general edits. Thank you to Jane Prunty for spelling corrections, Laurel Jarrick for grammar, and Anne Katz for her great editorial feedback. I am also grateful for my friends, family, and congregants who believed that I could do this.

And lastly, thank you to my readers. It's hard to make time to read and I am grateful that you are willing to give my book a try. I hope you will find this novel entertaining and insightful. May it awaken lively conversations.

This book is dedicated to my children, Gabriel and Shane.

Theodor Herzl, the 20th century visionary of the state of Israel, wrote, "If you will it, it is no dream."

Always work before you play and you can accomplish anything.

CHAPTER ONE
LAST DAY OF FESTIVAL OF SUKKOT
YEAR 1123 BCE

That night Devash struggled to fall asleep. Her thick date brown hair was tangled from flipping over so many times. So much seemed not right. What was her life going to be? Must she follow in her mother's and grandmother's footsteps? Was she destined to marry a man chosen by her father from the nearby Ephraimite hills? Devash struggled to picture herself spinning wool, chopping vegetables, and caring for children but the image wouldn't come. With a long exhale, Devash turned onto her right side and finally, finally fell asleep.

She is standing on the hills with prickly wild grass growing beneath her feet. A black vulture flies through the air overhead. Its wings spread out as it glides through the clouds. The day is peaceful, even pleasant. Suddenly, the ground starts to shake. Devash feels the sway of earth beneath her feet.

"Oh no, not a land tremor!" she exclaims.

The earth begins to jerk more violently. Devash stumbles forward and struggles to remaining standing. In the distance, she sees a young woman in a beautiful azure dress teetering on the edge of a cliff. The red hair is unmistakable, belonging to her best friend.

"Watch out Yael! Watch out!" Devash yells.

The earth shakes again and Yael falls off the precipice screaming into the abyss.

"No! No! Yael!"

Devash runs toward the cliff. As she peers over the edge, there is only blackness. Devash turns toward her village and sees structures collapsing. Stone walls are crumbling. Her chest tightens. She can't even scream. Then the jaws of the earth open up and into the chasm, animals and people fall shrieking. Devash sees the wooden beams of her home swaying. Clay bits break off the walls and then the stone pillars crack. The roof looks like water boiling and then it caves in. Devash hears her father scream from inside of their collapsed home.

"Aba! Aba! Where are you?" She yells but no sound comes from her throat. She struggles to cry for help.

Panic rises within her. She can do nothing to help. She can't even scream.

Bees begin to swarm around her. There are so many that she can barely see the sky above.

"Help!" she croaks. "Help!"

"Wake up! Wake up!" Shlomi shook his sister.

"You are having a bad dream. Wake up, Devash!"

Opening her eyes in surprise, Devash could see the light streaming through the window. It was well into morning.

"What hour is it?"

Her brother said it was time for the morning meal and that they had to go soon because today was the last day of Sukkot, the last day of the harvest festival.

Devash winced with the memory of the images. It was just sleep, she told herself. All is well.

Devash stood up hurriedly and put on her one and only pretty garment. She was glad that it was green because Savta told her that it brought out her emerald eyes. The deep crimson corded belt cinched the flowing material in perfectly. Even with such a pretty outfit, Devash was reluctant to go.

She certainly didn't want to run into Noah. However, she and Yael agreed that she should look beautiful, enjoy herself, if only to spite him. She knew everyone was coming out for this final day.

Her family dressed their best as well. Savta, her grandmother, put on a robe with the orange red hues of the sunset. Even her mother Tamar decided that for once she would wear her hair down. Despite years of hard work and having two children, her hair had little gray to it and was still a rich brown. Its thickness flowed over her shoulders.

When her husband David saw her, he remarked how lovely she looked. He also made sure to wear a perfectly clean white tunic and outer robe as he proudly dressed his son in one similar. Then they began the journey to the gathering site.

As they arrived, friends greeted them. David was speaking with the Israelite leader Gibor about preparations for the winter. It was a good growing season. They had produce and grains in abundance and were better prepared than in previous years.

Devash found her friends Shifra, Yael, Zack, and Dan standing together talking. They were happy to see one another but sad as well because it would be some time before they could enjoy each other's company again.

"Yael," said Devash as she studied her appearance. "You look very pleasing! The blue of the dress makes your hair seem even more radiant!"

"Thank you, Devash," she replied. "You look lovely as well."

Even Zack and Dan had groomed themselves for the last day of Sukkot. Zack wore a sand colored robe that matched his inner tunic. Dan's shoulders looked wide and strong as his tan robe draped majestically from his shoulder. Shifra's black curly hair was tamed with olive oil and she wore a flowing violet dress.

More and more people arrived at the gathering place. Israelites, Edomites, a few Midianite traders, and a number of nomadic peoples came out for the final day of Sukkot. Shifra elbowed Devash in the side.

"Look who's here," she pointed out to her right.

Sure enough, Devash could see light haired Noah with his father, mother, and younger siblings along with some of their tribal members. They had left their salt tables to watch the sacrifice.

"Let's walk to other side," Devash said to her friend. Devash and Shifra moved far enough away so she wouldn't see him anymore.

The priest wore a mauve robe with blue sapphire, green amethyst, and yellow topaz stones sewn into the breastplate. He stood before the crowds of people and proclaimed gratitude to God.

"Thank you, Adonai, for the wheat, barley, fruits, and vegetables of this season. We praise you and your holy name."

He placed his hand on the neck of a lamb. It was tied up and couldn't move. The lamb lay limp in resignation as the priest lifted up the blade. The knife sliced through the thick skin and blood started to trickle out.

Unexpectedly, a scream pierced the air.

The people looked around in confusion. The priest stopped with his knife still in the animal's neck. Hollering and screaming grew louder and louder. A couple of the men sprinted over to the side of the hill to look down. More Israelite males followed them as time appeared to stop.

The air felt thick and it was hard to breathe. In alarm, the men ran back to the baffled people.

"Peoples of the Sea! Peoples of the Sea!" They yelled. "We are under attack! Run, hide, or prepare to fight!"

The lamb was on the altar, lying lifeless, as people began to scatter. David ran to the edge of the mountain summit and was shocked by the sight. Down below were hundreds of men with shiny chariots. The sun reflecting off the iron was almost blinding. The soldiers had spears and round shields and were yelling as they ascended the mountain heading directly towards the Israelites.

David ran back to his family yelling, "Get to the cart! Get to the animals! We have to run!"

Devash was shocked. She looked at her friends. Yael looked back with eyes wide. Dan reached down to grab a wooden staff. Shifra ran towards her family's cart. Zack stood frozen in place. Then Yael began to cry. The people around them panicked as they sprinted away from the summit. Men grabbed wooden boards, bronze utensils, or anything that could be used as a weapon. Some retreated into their tents. Others started running down the mountain on the other side. Carts and animals choked the main pathway out.

"Oh, God of Abraham!" Devash exclaimed as the first soldier reached the top. His face was glistening in sweat and grimacing in anger. And then another one came up, and then another. Every one of them had a spear, dagger, or sword raised. Some of the soldiers wore kilts and others loin cloths. The most terrifying thing, though, was the metal helmet with horns on their heads. The men looked like beasts and then they shrieked. Gushing over the mountain ridge, they began their murderous rampage.

The first soldier came upon an elderly man. He could barely stand as the man from the sea approached him. The soldier lifted his iron blade and stabbed it into the man's neck. The old man's eyes grew wide in shock. As the soldier pulled the sword out, blood spurted from the gash.

Devash ran fast. The closest concealment she could find was a deep thicket of trees to the east. More horned-helmet men were now racing through the encampment.

Gibor, the one who only one day ago, proudly waved the ritual lulav with its palm, myrtle, and willow leaves, stood to meet them with a wooden plank. He swung it with all his force. The plank hit one of the soldiers solidly in the chest. The man crashed to the ground and his helmet flew off. Gibor raised the wood aiming to smash his face. Just as he was coming down, a different soldier pierced his belly with a spear. Gibor wavered, dropped the timber, and collapsed on the ground.

Then a fighter came over the crest riding in a chariot. His eyes blazed like coal and he was in full armor with a polished horned helmet.

An Israelite man exclaimed, "Whoa! Sisera of the People of the Sea!" In terror, he speedily fled in the opposite direction.

Shouting towards his soldiers, the leader of the Sea People ordered them to grab animals, grain, and to set fire to the tents and even the sacred altar. Smoke was rising up, blackening the sky. Horned men leapt over rocks, ripped open tents, and turned over carts in search of people.

One of them came upon the tent of the traders from the Salty Sea. Noah's father stood in front of his teen son and protectively pushed him back. Then Noah's father swung his bronze sword at his opponent. Hitting the soldier's face, blood oozed over the man's cheeks.

"Get out of here!" his father roared to Noah.

Noah and the rest of his family scattered but as they looked back they saw Sisera approach the brave Edomite. The Sea People's general raised an iron tipped spear and hurled it through the air. The sharp point impaled right through Noah's father shoulder. He was now restrained against a tree. The older man writhed in pain as Sisera descended from his chariot flanked by two of his soldiers. Approaching the immobilized man, Sisera took out his dagger, and traced his blade over the man's scalp.

Then with a quick movement, he sliced off his ear. The man yelped in anguish. Then the commander cut through the material of his victim's robe exposing his nakedness underneath. The poor man's shoulder was still pinned to the tree and blood was oozing out of the wound. With the tip of his blade, Sisera carved his initials on the man's chest as the man writhed. He then lowered his dagger and cleanly sliced off the man's genitalia.

"Aaaahhhh!" screamed the poor man as blood rushed down his thighs.

There were hundreds of soldiers and they attacked anyone who stood in their way. A few of the men killed just for pleasure and others pushed women against trees or over boulders and took them by force. Anyone who protested was instantly killed. The people shrieked as many tried to escape, a few tried to fight, and others hid in crevices, behind trees or rocks.

Devash was at the edge of the trees as she lowered herself into a ditch. Covering herself with branches, she decided that it was safer to conceal herself rather than run. She peered out from the twigs.

Before her, it was complete chaos. Smoke rose from the burning tents, carts, and altar. People cried. Soldiers continued their rampage of stealing, hitting, killing, and raping.

In the distance, Devash could see the commander Sisera. He stood surveying the work of his men with his bloody dagger at his belt with his chariot stationed behind him. Some of his soldiers brought to him a girl in a blue dress who was yelling and struggling to get away. Her hair was red.

It was Yael! Devash noted fearfully. Sisera looked her over, as the girl struggled against the arms restraining her.

"Hair like fire," he stated as he touched it with his hands.

Yael moved her head away but he slapped her hard in the face. Her cheeks were now inflamed and tears streamed down her face. Devash had to rush to help her. She had to do something! But then, a man came running towards Sisera.

He yelled, "Leave my daughter alone! Let her go!"

Yael's father had only a sharpened flint stone in his hand. It was nothing compared to the gleaming iron spears of the Sea People. Sisera looked amused at the man racing towards them. Taking one of his men's spears into his hand, Sisera raised it up over his shoulder and aimed it at the man approaching him.

Yael's father didn't even have time to evade it. The spear came at him like an arrow strong and swift. It went right through his chest. Stopping, he tried to yell, tried to walk forward, but instead stumbled and fell.

"Nooooo!" hysterically shrieked Yael, as Sisera's men held her back.

Devash was devastated. There was nothing she could do. She had no weapons. If she ran out, she would be killed or captured. Devash silently hid as she crouched deeper under the branches.

Sisera took hold of the hysterical girl and punched her so hard, her face began to immediately swell. He ripped her dress, the color of the sea, down the middle with his bare arms and threw her to the ground. Yael just laid there in disbelief.

Sisera pulled up his loin skirt and descended on top of her. His legs pushed hers apart. He thrust his erect yerech into her.

She screamed and cried. Holding her arms down, Sisera pushed with all his might puncturing through her maidenhood. Yael screeched in pain.

When Sisera did his final plunge, he quivered, took a deep breath, and then pulled out of Yael. Standing up, he wiped the blood and seed from his yerech on to the remnants of her dress. Looking at the girl sobbing in the dirt, he told his men to take her with them. They pulled the violently shaking girl off the ground as blood dripped down her legs. A robe was thrown over her and she was thrown into Sisera's chariot.

By this point, many people had escaped. Others were murdered, taken captive, or lay on the ground so wounded they couldn't get up.

Sisera's men put women and grain into the chariots and led the animals back down the mountain side. The ground was rubicund with spilled blood. The smell of death permeated the site. The sun was setting. Devash closed her eyes that were swollen from crying and fell asleep under the brushwood.

CHAPTER TWO
SEVEN YEARS EARLIER-1130 BCE

Two young children in the Judean hills were playing by the cistern. Devash ran over to the reservoir and leaned over with her two long braids almost touching the liquid. Today, she could see billowing clouds reflected on the surface. Most entertaining though was her smile. The young girl frowned, studied her appearance, and then smiled again revealing gaps between her teeth.

"Shlomi!" she joyfully yelled. "Come!" Her brother, younger by only a year and a half, clamored up the embankment towards her. He was two heads shorter than his sister and his cheeks were round with the fullness of boyhood. Shlomi's golden brown hair was cropped short.

"Dee, Dee!" he said happily.

"Look," Devash pointed below. "The water is blue today, like the sky."

"Water! Water!" Shlomi declared as he leaned over the rocky rim. Devash grabbed his tunic to prevent him from falling in.

"Devash and Shlomi," yelled a stocky woman in a long russet brown tunic. "Get away from the cistern! You know you aren't allowed to play in it. That water is for drinking."

Looking up towards the stone wall, the children could see their mother, her head covered in a beige linen cloth.

"Ohh!" called out the girl, "Sorry, Ima!"

Both Devash and Shlomi moved away from the water. Devash took the hand of her younger brother and led him up to the courtyard. From this height, they could see much of the valley below, and other homes clustered along the mountain ridge. As the children walked past a hastily arranged rock wall, they could see a number of houses with rough white stones plastered with lime. In between the rocks was mudding and some of the structures had a second floor. Their relatives' dwelling were only thirty cubits away from one another.

Their mother looked at them austerely and waved her hand towards their home.

Devash and Shlomi entered through the door and passed a long rectangular room separated only by a splintered wooden railing. Behind it, sheep and lambs bleated quietly.

"Savta," Devash called out to the elderly woman in a faded pumpkin colored shawl. Their grandmother had just pushed more coals to the center of the fire pit.

"Ah, Devash and Shlomi," she said, glancing up from a big pot in the fire. "Here, scrub these leeks for me. They are for our evening meal." The older woman tossed some yellowed parsnips into the pot.

Within seconds, Shlomi grabbed a long green leek and hit his older sister on the arm.

"Stop that, Shlomi," said Devash as she shoved him away.

"Now you two," reprimanded Savta, "You don't want your mother to see you behave like this."

Devash took the leek from her brother and cleaned the dirt from its folds in a bowl of water. Savta chopped up the leeks and carrots with a bronze knife and threw them into the simmering liquid.

"Welcome brother!" a bellowing voice called from outside. The excitement in their father's words made the children run outside to the courtyard.

"It's Isaac!" They both screamed in delight and ran into his arms. The tall lanky man smiled and nuzzled his long nose into their necks provoking greater squeals of joy.

“You are indeed as sweet as honey, little girl!” said the lanky man as his hand circled over her stomach. “The bees would love you, buzzzzz.” His hand struck at her tender belly while his other hand poked Shlomi. Both children rolled on the ground laughing.

Ima walked over. “It’s good to have you back. We’ve all missed Uncle Isaac.”

“Tamar!” His smile widened as he embraced her. “It is always good to be at Beit David, the house of David, my brother.”

“Come inside.” She waved her hand towards the doorway. “After our meal, we will hear of your travels.”

David stepped inside right behind his brother. “Savta,” he called out to his mother-in-law. “Let’s add some lamb to that stew. My brother is here with us. We haven’t had meat since the Festival of Unleavened bread. I’ll slaughter the one with the wounded leg.”

David was a lofty man and only in recent years did his belly begin to protrude. However, he still had the strength of three men gained from his daily plowing of hard earth. Walking over to the fenced-in animals on the side of the room, he easily carried the lame animal outside. He raised a large rock and struck the animal’s head, immediately rendering it unconscious.

Taking a rust-colored knife, David carefully slit the animal’s throat with one stroke. Blood streamed out from the lamb’s neck, saturating the earth beneath it. When the flow of blood subsided, he sliced the animal’s belly from neck to bottom and pulled out the stomach, intestines, heart, and liver. Blood stained his arms as he severed the legs, removed the skin, and brought it to the older woman by the fire.

"This will make for a hearty stew! We haven't seen my brother Isaac for two winters. We'll celebrate tonight," David said. "Isaac! Come! I'll open one of my jugs of wine for you!"

From the ledge of the second floor, two heads peered over the side.

"But Aba, Uncle Isaac is playing with us. Ahhhhh!" Devash and Shlomi screamed as they were pulled from the edge.

"Okay, no more laughter with uncle," Isaac said. "I have to speak with your father."

"Augh!" groaned the children.

"But tomorrow is another day, I promise," said their uncle as he climbed down the rope ladder to the first floor, walked past the sheep, lambs, and goats penned up by the side, and towards the older woman cooking the fresh lamb with the savory vegetables.

"Hmm," Isaac said, inhaling deeply, "That smells fantastic!"

His brother David unsealed one of the pottery clay vessels and poured fermented grape juice into small cups decorated with bold black horizontal lines. He dripped some date honey into the cups and handed one to Isaac.

"To my brother," he said and smiled. "Welcome back to Ephraim."

"To life," Isaac replied. Both men gulped down the contents.

The two men sat down outside the pillar house on small boulders, watching the sun set in the distance.

"David," said Isaac, "did you hear that brave Ehud finally died?"

"Ehud, that left-handed old man?" David inquired. "I thought he was going to live forever."

"There are some rumors that things may change," Isaac warned.

"What do you mean?" David asked as he looked at his brother. "We are a simple people living off the land. You remember how we moved up into the hills when we were little to escape the Canaanites. They've been in the land as long as we have. I always thought the land was big enough for both of us."

David drained his cup of wine and thoughtfully continued, "However, other peoples have invaded. The Moabites were beasts! Fortunately, once the judge Ehud killed the cruel King Eglon of the Moabites, all was peaceful, at least in Ephraim. What else have you heard?"

"Well," Isaac replied, "I hear that the Canaanites have been wanting to increase their land holdings and are now collaborating with the Sherden of the Sea Peoples."

"What? Those uncircumcised bastards! What do they want with the Canaanites?" David's voice deepened as his anger grew. "They come to our shores and take our land. What more do they want?"

Isaac shook his head. "I'm not sure, but there's been talk about the Canaanites and Sea Peoples making an alliance now that Ehud is dead."

"That doesn't make sense," exclaimed David. "What about Shamgar, son of Anath? Isn't he the judge over our people, Israel? I heard he killed hundreds of Philistines wielding only an ox goad. I'm sure they'll keep far from us."

"Yes, maybe," said Isaac, "but he was finally seduced by a Philistine woman. She had long dark hair and breasts the size of melons. They say that as Shamgar was sinking his erect yerech into her sweetness, another Philistine came in and was horrified. With a spear, he perforated not only Shamgar's back but it went all the way through the woman's belly! It's what the priest Pinchas did to the Israelite man and Midianite woman."

"That reckless Shamgar!" David exclaimed in disgust as he kicked the ground. "Why must our heroes be so unwise? I think any leader should have his yerech removed. It's the only way we'll have a good judge over Israel again."

"Maybe it's time for a woman to lead our people," laughed Isaac. "She can cook them all into a coma."

"Or badger them into exhaustion," added David. "Well, hopefully the memory of Ehud thrusting his blade into the fat belly of King Eglon of the Moabites will continue to keep the Sea Peoples and Canaanites far, far from the tribes of Israel."

David looked out towards the setting sun. The sky was darkening as orange and scarlet streaked across the horizon.

CHAPTER THREE
DAY ONE OF FESTIVAL OF SUKKOT
YEAR 1123 BCE- SEVEN YEARS LATER

Four youths carrying pottery jugs surrounded the large water reservoir in the hill country. The sun was a quarter high in the sky, just a few hours after sunrise. Three grassy hills converged into a valley where a rock lined cistern collected the runoff rain.

Zack, a slender male with tiny eruptions on his face, grinned as he said, “As the fly would say, you can’t go wrong with donkey dung.”

Shifra, with her wild pitch black hair, laughed, “That is the most abominable thing I have heard!”

A brawny youth with a square chin, put down his rimmed jar with a sigh. “Water, water,” he said, gazing at the sun reflecting off the surface in the cistern. “Without rain from the heavens, what would we do?”

“Well,” exclaimed Zack, “I guess we would bathe in wine, simmer our meats with wine, and know the secrets of women in wine!”

Shifra smirked. “Oh, the constellations will never align in that way. You’ll be the last one knowing a woman with a face that looks eaten by ants.”

“Keep on giggling, Shifra,” Zack said as he proudly stuck out his bony chest, looking as regal as possible. “Before you know it, I’ll be the most sought after man.”

A teenage girl with bright crimson hair stood by smiling.

“I think Yael will be the desirable one,” said Dan half-jokingly as he pointed towards her.

The red-haired girl declared, “Watch out!” as she pointed to her tresses. ‘If you touch the flames, you’ll get burned!”

As Dan reached out to pull one of her locks, Yael slapped his hand forcefully.

"Ouch!" Dan cried. "That hurt."

"Sissss," said Yael with pursed lips as Shifra and Zach began to laugh even more.

Yael looked out through the woods of sturdy Terebinth trees. Even though they weren't tall, they were wide with branches full of shiny oval green leaves. Yael's eyes opened wide when she spotted a young woman moving aside the branches. The approaching girl had long brown hair, braided into two sections, eyes as green as the leaves of a fig tree, and skin tanned to the shade of walnut brown.

"Devash!" called out Yael. "You are late today. The sun has moved several cubits higher in the sky while I've been waiting for you."

With a sigh, Devash lowered her jug off of her shoulder and set it on to the ground. "Ima needed more help with the ram skins. She's worried that the cold months are coming soon."

Yael nodded her head knowingly. "Yes, we are also preparing the hides. Sometimes, we need an outer robe as soon as the fall festival is over."

"I know the work is important," Devash said with another sigh. "But I really don't like staying at home during most of the daylight. Ima is training me to sew, wash the clothing, and cook." Devash looked up at her friend and then a little mischievous smile crossed her face.

"On the other hand," Devash uttered. "Aba promised me he would continue our shooting lessons. Now, that is rousing!"

Listening intently, Dan exclaimed, "Maybe you'll be able to shoot an arrow into King Jabin! Even though he's not fat like King Eglon, I'm sure his innards would pour out like pigeon guts."

"Eeew!" Shifra cried out.

"All right," Devash said sadly, "I can't tarry, Ima is expecting me back with this jug filled to the brim with water. Lots of work to do."

"Tomorrow night will be the start of the harvest festival," stated Zack with a big smile. "We'll have time for wine, women, men, and song."

"The sun cannot set and rise quickly enough for me," Devash answered wistfully as she immersed the collar-rim jug into the cool water of the cistern.

Devash took leave of her friends. She didn't see them often. They all had to work hard helping their families. There was always earth that needed tilling, vegetables to pick, animals to care for, and clothing to wash.

There were a few times a year, though, when all the families in the hills gathered together for a festival. In the fall, it was called the Feast of Ingathering or Sukkot. That summer the wheat and barley grew tall in the hills, the trees surged with olives and dates, and terraced crops were full of cucumbers, melons, and leeks. This was going to be a great festival.

After an hour, Devash returned to the family compound with the full jug balanced carefully on her shoulder.

"Devashi! Honeyed one!" called out her father affectionately from the courtyard. He had just stepped away from plowing earth on the side of the hill, and his forehead glistened in sweat.

"Let me have a sip of that water," he beseeched. She lowered the jug and his hands cupped the cool liquid and brought it rapidly to his mouth.

"Ah…that's better," he sighed in relief as he wiped his forehead with his arm leaving dirt streaks on his face. "Devashi, I need a respite anyway. Why don't you bring the water to your mother, then we can practice with bow and arrow," said David with a wide grin that revealed a couple of stained, discolored teeth.

"That sounds wonderful, Aba!" Devash exclaimed as she ran with the jug sloshing with water inside their house.

"Dee! Dee!" greeted her brother, Shlomi, as she came inside. He was eleven and could certainly pronounce her name but still called her affectionately by her nickname. The girl set the jug down by the cooking hearth and quickly turned towards the door.

"Where are you going?" he asked as he looked up from cleaning a black and white speckled goat skin.

"I'm going to do some shooting with Aba," she said glancing backwards.

"I'm coming too," erupted Shlomi as he stood up, checking to make sure mother wasn't around.

All three of them gathered on the other side of the grassy hill.

"Ah! I see I have two warriors with me today," their father said, smiling. "All right, let's work on our aim." David pointed to an oak tree with a thick trunk. Lifting up a wooden stick, he bent it into a semi-circle, quickly affixed a cord to it, and gave it to his daughter.

"Feel the tautness of the string," he instructed, "If it's not enough, tighten it some more."

Devash eagerly grasped the bow.

David continued, "It's critical that it be pulled tight or the arrow won't go far." He plucked at the twine causing it to hum with vibration. "Here is an excellent arrow." He lifted a slender wooden stick with a small bronze triangle at the front and bird feathers tied to the end.

Shlomi looked jealously at his older sister.

Noticing him, his father said, "You'll get a chance next, my son. First the older one."

Devash struck her pose. Her two braids draped over her left shoulder as she positioned the arrow.

"Good, good," David commented. Devash pulled the arrow back as her arm muscles strained, aimed, and then let the arrow fly. It landed in the trunk of the tree.

"Very good!" smiled David. "This comes easy to you."

"My turn, my turn Aba," exclaimed the boy.

David passed the bow and another arrow to the round cheeked boy and said, "Make sure you close one eye, it will help you aim."

"I know. I know how to do this!" Shlomi stammered. His golden brown hair was messy with a little clump standing up at the back of his head. He pulled the string back and released. The arrow fluttered woefully from his bow and landed just a few cubits away in the dirt.

"I detest this! Why can't I shoot like Devash?" he yelled.

"You only need patience and to be open to instruction, Shlomi," said David gently. "Shooting may not be your talent."

"Devash! Devash! Where are you?" hollered a woman from the stone fence of the courtyard.

"I'm here, Ima!" Devash called back. The woman stepped beyond the stones. Her hair was tightly pulled back into a bun, exposing a face already finely lined with wrinkles.

"Why do I always have to call for you?" she said in exasperation. "I expect you to be here working by my side."

"Sorry, Ima," Devash replied dejectedly as she walked over to her.

David called out to Tamar. "There's a lot of work getting ready for the festival."

She looked at him wearily and replied, "There's also a lot of work getting ready for winter."

Devash could hardly wait for the festival tomorrow. Even though she was tired that night, she couldn't sleep. She was going to wear the nice garment that Savta gave her when she turned twelve. The sage green dress was a little big at that time, but it should fit her perfectly now that she was a year older. Everyone from the hill country and beyond were going to the festival to celebrate their people's journey to Israel.

Sometime between the setting and rising of the sun, Devash did indeed sleep.

At the first morning light, she poked at her brother on his straw bed.

"Is it today?" he inquired sleepily.

"Yes, Sukkot is tonight," she exclaimed excitedly. Devash scampered halfway down the rope ladder and leapt the remaining distance, landing solidly on the ground. Her mother was already by the fire with Savta, her grandmother, making a flat bread for the meal offering.

"Here," Tamar said as she handed Devash a bright orange persimmon and a chunk of seeded bread for her breakfast. Her mother looked more refreshed today, with a pink hue to her cheeks.

"Are you looking forward to the festival tonight?" her daughter inquired in between mouthfuls of sweet juicy fruit and bread.

"Yes," smiled Tamar. "Our harvest has been good, better than it's been for years. We have a lot of grain stored." She pointed to the full jars lining the wall. "We have a lot to thank God for tonight."

Devash's grandmother was sipping some hot water steeped with mint leaves. She chimed in, "Yes, this has been a good growing season. Too bad we can't trade as freely as we used to. King Jabin disrupted many of the merchants from reaching the hillside."

The older woman's gaze grew wistful. "I remember how the caravans would come through non-stop. We saw colorful fabrics, painted pottery, and the most fragrant of oils. There was an Egyptian trader with a jar that had a red painted lion on it. Can you imagine someone taking the time to paint pottery like that?"

Savta smiled broadly and continued, "Oh, and the musicians that came through. I heard flutes, drums, and timbrels. Now those were glorious days!"

Tamar shook her head in resignation as she said, "Well, we can't go back. We can only do what we can, with what we have. This year, thank God, we have enough."

The morning went by quickly. In the early afternoon, after splashing water on her face, Devash put on her dress.

Tamar was already dressed in an ankle length lemon colored robe. When she spotted her daughter, she declared with a smile, "Devashi! Your eyes look as serene as the great sea. You will make a beautiful bride."

The teen's cheeks flushed and instantly matched her pink corded belt.

Shlomi stepped forward wearing a clean amber tunic as David hoisted a sheep, fruits, and vegetables onto the cart.

The house of David walked for over an hour to the nearby hill as the sun began to set. They arrived at the central gathering place at dusk. Smoke billowed from the wooden altar as three hundred people gathered around it. On the perimeter were ten huts made with oak wooden planks, lush branches with leaves, and palm fronds draped over the ceilings. Persimmons, apricots, dates, and grapes dangled from the tops.

David inhaled deeply. "Ah, the roasting meat smells delicious!"

One woman walked in front of them, giggling and stumbling. She handed Tamar a skinned pouch filled with wine. Taking a short sip, Tamar grimaced and then took a deeper gulp.

One man with a full grown beard was laughing loudly. As he spotted David, he exclaimed, "David! It's been many months." He stumbled closer and stared at Devash. "Ah, who is this peach?"

"Lanar?" David said tentatively. "Yes, Lanar, I remember you. Aren't you the one who is collecting animals and produce for the offering?" As Lanar stumbled closer to Devash, she could smell his rancid breath.

David stepped in between them. "I've got two sheep, a bundle of wheat stalks, and three grape vines for the festival."

Lanar looked at David in disappointment, scratched his beard, and pointed towards the altar. "Yes, over there."

Leading Devash away, David said with a smile, "It was a bountiful year. This is going to be a great holiday."

After the produce was delivered to the priest wearing a long purple robe, Devash went in search of her friends.

It didn't take Devash long to find fire-haired Yael.

"Yael! You look so appealing," Devash exclaimed as she gazed at her friend in a deep indigo colored dress.

"How did you get fabric dyed that color? It is so rare." Devash touched it and was surprised by how smooth it felt.

"Oh," said Yael as she shyly twirled her skirt. "My Aba has trade connections from a few years ago. He exchanged olive oil with a nomad for this material made from silk worms. It's from the Far East. When dyed, the colors are so bright. My aunt says when Aba marries me off, no one will be able to resist the pretty redhead in the lapis lazuli colored dress." Yael giggled.

Devash nodded her agreement. "Yes, my Ima is talking of weddings too. I am not in haste."

As she looked around, Devash spotted her other friends. Zack, Dan, Shifra came over until they were all standing in a circle. They could hear the chiming of timbrels and some men began to sing.

"Let the heavens hear what I will say.

May the earth listen to my words

May my utterance come down as the rain.

May my words distill as the dew,

Like showers on young growth, like drops on the grass.

For I call out in the name of Adonai; Give glory to our God!" (Deut. 32:1-3)

Devash took Shifra's hand and spun her around. Yael swayed her hips and clapped. Zack drank deeply from a wine pouch before passing it to Dan.

Dan took a few swigs of wine and said, "Did you hear of what happened in Gezer?" The other youths looked confused. Gezer was on the coast and Israelites from the tribe of Dan had been living there peacefully for many years. "It's Sisera!"

Yael looked confused.

Dan shook his head impatiently. “Sisera is one of the Sea People. They say he’s of the Sherden sect and that he has become King Jabin’s commander.” Dan’s voice became quiet as his friends looked on with fear. “My Aba told me that Sisera invaded Gezer and slaughtered many people.”

Zack blurted out, “When did this happen?”

Dan, with a hushed voice, continued, “A month ago. People fled their homes. Most of the tribe of Dan was forced to abandon their tribal land. They hurriedly grabbed their belongings and animals and headed north.”

Devash and Yael looked at Dan in horror.

Dan kicked the dirt in front him. “My Aba also told me that Sisera brought in other people of the sea.”

“The Philistines!” cried out Devash.

Dan jerked his head, “Yes, Sisera gave them the Danites’ homes. Some of the hearths still had hot embers.”

Zack’s face reddened as he bellowed, “How in Sheol could he do this? He never would’ve dared during the rule of Ehud or even Othniel. We need a leader now more than ever! Someday, I’ll be the next judge over Israel and I’ll get revenge and bring peace to our land.” Zack shook his fist in the air and then accidently let out a loud belch. Shifra, Yael, and Devash laughed.

“Well, Gezer is far away from here,” Shifra responded. “We are safe in the hills. Let’s return to the festival.”

CHAPTER FOUR
DAY TWO OF SUKKOT

The night was long and joyous. David and Tamar returned home with Savta, Shlomi, and Devash. Later that evening, the thirteen year old girl lay down on her straw bedding reminiscing about a boy she encountered. His name was Noah and he was tall and attractive. It was after the offerings that this young man with daffodil colored hair approached her.

"Shalom! In all the gatherings," he stated with a smile. "I don't think I've seen a girl with eyes like the sea." Devash had looked down at the dirt beneath her feet. She felt warmth radiate from her cheeks. "I'm from the Salty Sea," he added. "I've come to the festival with my family and some traders."

Devash thought of this encounter as she stretched on her bedding. She had never met anyone from the Dead Sea before. Noah seemed different from the other youth she had known. His eyes were welcoming and she just couldn't stop thinking about him. With a smile, Devash turned on to her side and drifted to sleep.

The next morning, Savta made a barley bread sweetened with honey and gave the children a cup of fresh goat's milk.

"Savta," asked Devash. "How many years are you?"

Savta, a kind looking woman, with deep lines on her face, thought for a few moments.

"I'm not sure, sweet one. Maybe, I'm a jubilee."

Shlomi looked astounded. "You mean fifty? You are fifty complete sun cycles?"

Savta chuckled. "Oh, it's possible. I ceased keeping track some time ago. But I hope to live to the age of Moses, one hundred and twenty years."

Popping the last bite of honey bread into her mouth, Devash inquired, "Savta, tell me what happened to you in your youth? Did you…did you ever love a man?"

The young girl looked eagerly at her grandmother.

"Love! Bah!" responded the old woman. "Love doesn't fatten the sheep nor cause the wheat to grow high."

Shlomi slurped his goat's milk.

Savta stared at them thoughtfully for a few moments.

"Well, maybe you are old enough to hear. I lived through Joshua's war."

Shlomi interrupted, "Oh, war! How exciting!"

"No, no, war is not something anyone should desire my little Shlomi." The old woman looked lovingly at her grandson.

"But the one you are named for," she continued, "thought war was a great adventure. His name was Shalom and he was so handsome."

The old woman looked wistfully past her grandchildren towards the wall behind them. "His hair was wavy and the shade of wheat. All the girls said he was prettier than any of them. The boys, however, made jokes of him. They said he would make the most beautiful bride."

Savta grew pensive for a moment.

Then her eyes lit up and she whispered, "When we met, there was this spark. Shalom told me, 'Efrah, your eyes are like emeralds and your spirit is as free as a bird.'

"I thought my heart would burst at these words. After a long walk, he went to my parents. They were so eager to have me married that they started to make the arrangements. I was so happy to be in his arms."

Savta closed her eyes and smiled.

"We were married for only a month, when word came of Joshua's campaign to conquer all the land North to the cedars of Lebanon, East to the Jordan River, West to the coast of the great sea, and South to the Negev."

The old woman clenched her fist as her voice grew resolute.

"When Shalom heard of it, he wanted to enlist immediately. This was his chance to showcase his virility. All those who thought him too feminine would have to swallow their words. He was going to be the fiercest warrior of all!

"I told him, 'But Shalom, you have nothing to prove and you have no obligation to fight, especially within the first year of marriage. Stay with me. Don't go.' I pleaded."

Shlomi and Devash sat riveted as they listened to their grandmother.

With a sigh, she continued, "However, he was just sixteen and full of pride and conviction.

"He said, 'Do not worry my dear bride. Before you know it, I'll be back with some silver and fine linens, and I'll dress you like a queen. When I come home victorious, we'll have lots of strong sons!'

"I hugged him tightly, afraid that it may be the last time I would see him. Savta's eyes began to redden. "Sadly, I was right."

She coughed loudly into a rag. With a deep breath, she relaxed. "Just as Joshua and his army crossed the Jordan River, a band of Amorites attacked. Joshua was completely unprepared. He thought he would get to choose when and where the battles would take place. He was wrong. Seeing Amorite men sprinting towards him and his soldiers, Joshua ordered them to fight. My beautiful husband, Shalom, was the first one to sprint towards the enemy.

"According to one of his comrades, he raised his dagger, ready to kill a huge Amorite soldier when he tripped over a rock. As he turned over, my dear Shalom must have been shocked to see a giant Amorite towering over him. One of the Israelite soldiers told me that…" Savta's face cringed in pain. She stuttered, "he…he…slit Shalom's throat, laughing as he did."

The old woman fell silent. The children's eyes widened. They had never heard this before.

Savta grimaced and continued.

"The battle went terribly and Joshua and his soldiers ran away and sought shelter in the ruins of Jericho. This defeat was so humiliating that Joshua feared for the well-being of his campaign. How would they conquer Israel? If their enemies knew how easily they were routed by the Amorites, then they would be attacked from every side. He needed a plan.

"Surveying the burnt walls and damaged buildings around him, Joshua stood transfixed. And then the idea came to him. No one knew when or how Jericho was destroyed. Looking directly at his men, he declared, 'You, my fellow mighty Israelites, destroyed Jericho!'

"They looked at him in confusion. Was Joshua mad? They wondered.

"But Joshua continued, 'It was you…you who blew the ram's horn and the walls of Jericho collapsed. You…you fierce Israelites, killed every person who approached you and every animal that stood.'

The Israelites slowly began to comprehend Joshua's words.

"'You mighty Israelites. No one can stand against you. You burned the city to the ground and now all fear you. Those who died, died heroically, in the battle of Jericho.'"

Savta stared momentarily at the stone wall with her forehead creased. Then turning back to her grandchildren, she weakly smiled. "When I heard of the story, I didn't care about the ruse. I only cared that my dear Shalom was gone. By the age of fifteen, I was a widow with nowhere to go. My father refused to let me move back home. He said I was a cow that had already been milked and no one would want me.

"I was forced to beg from house to house for a full year until Shalom's older brother, Avi, was willing to marry me. Avi was at least ten years older, had an enormous growth on his nose, and already had two other wives. Even though there was no love between us, I was grateful not to have to beg by the roads any more. He faithfully consummated our marriage on our wedding night and miracle, of all miracles, I became pregnant with your mother."

Efrah looked at her grandchildren tenderly, "Devash and Shlomi, I did everything I could to give my daughter Tamar as many blessings as possible. I taught her how to take care of a home, procure food, and ultimately helped her to find a husband at the right time. When your mother was a couple of years after getting her first blood, I encouraged her to take notice of David."

"You mean Aba?" Shlomi said excitedly.

"Yes, his family was farming the land in the hills of Ephraim. David was eighteen, thin as reed, and had a kind smile. During the barley harvest in late spring, I saw how David looked at Tamar as she danced. He wasn't the only one; other men would watch your mother as her long hair would fly through the air with every spin she took."

"Ima danced?" said Devash incredulously. She couldn't picture her mother happily moving to music. Her mother was always full of worry and anxiety. Was it possible that she was young once?

"Oh yes," the old woman continued, "but youth doesn't last long, not for any of us. I asked Avi to procure David for Tamar. He was uncomplicated and I knew he would till the earth and provide for the family. I was confident that if war came, he wouldn't be the first one to enlist. Your father is a good man, but adventure doesn't appeal to him. David, just as I thought, was a good husband for Tamar and became an excellent father to you both. Don't you agree? By the end of the summer your parents were married."

Shlomi was nodding his head as he listened to Savta. "And then what happened Savta?" he eagerly asked.

"Your parents did grow to love one another but life wasn't easy. They moved to the hills and took me with them. We lived for years close to your father's brothers and sisters."

Savta motioned her hand as she pointed beyond the walls of their home. The children knew she was referring to the houses close by on the hill.

"The soil here is hard and it requires hard work to plough it. In the beginning, there were winters so harsh that food was scarce. We were so hungry that we boiled shrubs and thistles into a foul tasting stew. Those were the hard years.

"However, David and his brothers' efforts paid off. A few seeds took root, and your mother and I rejoiced in seeing the small green leaves fight their way through the soil. With our first harvest, we were able to buy a goat and then a sheep."

"Wow!" exclaimed Shlomi. "Now we have at least twelve animals."

"Yes," continued the old woman. "In a few years, our goat and sheep doubled and we finally had grain for the winter.

Instead of grass stew, I could make barley and wheat cereal, breads, and puddings.

"It was during one of those short days of light that your mother became pregnant. We were so excited! Finally, a child. Hopefully a boy. Tamar grew round and heavy. After nine moons, she went into labor. David's aunt Sima, a midwife, stationed her between two rocks to support her weight and as she stood screaming in pain. Sima knelt under her with massaging oil as she gently stretched the way to her womb."

"Yuck! I don't want to hear this!" bellowed the eleven-year old boy.

"You are right, Shlomi," the old woman said, nodding, "but I realize that it's important for your sister. Why don't you step outside for a few moments? You can even pick another melon and bring it to me."

The boy stood up and quickly ran outside.

Savta looked at Devash. "You are getting older. You need to know that childbirth is wonderful but also very hard."

Devash gazed at her grandmother intently without moving.

Savta continued, "Your father David went as far away from the house as he could. Hearing his wife shriek like that ripped out his heart. Your mother panted, gripped the rocks until her fingers bled, and pushed through the excruciating pain. I did everything I could to help her. I gave her sips of water and told her that her son would be as mighty as Abraham, Isaac, and Jacob. My daughter screamed and screamed. She said it felt like a sword was cutting her open."

Devash's eyes were wide in terror. "Why would anyone want to go through that? It sounds horrible!"

Savta placed her hand on her granddaughter's shoulder. "It's because it's the ultimate blessing. To be a mother and then a grandmother, it's the best that life has to offer." With a sweet smile, the old woman continued her tale.

"After a full day of straining, your mother was able to push out the baby's head. Sima was able to draw it out carefully. But... there was only silence. We could only hear your mother's panting. I looked at the baby." Savta's eyes began to tear up. "He was a beautiful boy but he wasn't breathing! Sima pressed gently on the baby's chest but…there was no movement."

"Your mother called out, 'How is he?'

"Looking at the dead baby cradled in her arms, Sima said, 'I'm sorry Tamar. The baby has been in Sheol for some time. God took him while he was in your womb.' Tamar screeched. With blood still running down her legs, she shakily stood up. I grabbed my beloved daughter and hugged her.

"'I am so sorry. There will be others. There will be others.' My tears flowed like a river as I held your mother.

"That's terrible!" declared Devash as she clenched her fists. Her fingernails dug into the palms of her hands.

"Yes, it was," replied Savta. "But that wasn't the end. Over the next few years, your mother got pregnant twice, and both times, babies cried so loudly that we laughed. You and your brother were healthy and alive.

"Not only did your parents gain children, but I," the old woman said with tears streaming down her cheeks. "I became a Savta!" As she finished, she stood up, pulled her granddaughter to her, and hugged her tightly.

"I hope you live to one hundred and twenty, Savta," murmured Devash as she was engulfed by her grandmother's soft breasts.

CHAPTER FIVE
INTERMEDIATE DAYS OF SUKKOT

That night, as on the previous one, hundreds of people gathered together on the flat summit in the hills. The family of Beit David, the house of David, made their way back to the festival site. David brought a goat along with the branches of green leafy myrtle, palm, and willow, and a bright, yellow citron.

As soon as Devash saw her friends Yael, Shifra, Zack, and Dan, she ran to them. After they shared a few jokes, Shifra pointed to a few teens in the distance and declared, "Look! They are from the valley by the Salty Sea."

Devash glanced over and saw a towering young man whom she immediately recognized as Noah. "We just met them last night. Let's see how they are faring."

There were two males and a petite girl standing with Noah.

"Blessing to you," said Yael as she approached them. "You live very far from here, right?"

The small girl called Sera, responded, "Yes, our families are nomads who work by the lifeless sea. We extract the salt from the water and sell it when the roads are safe."

Dan scrutinized them. "Are you one of the tribes of Israel"

"No," replied Noah running his fingers through his straight hair. "We are from beyond the Jordan."

Devash inquisitively looked at Noah, "What brought you here to the Harvest Festival?"

Noah replied, "Just as you would think. This is a perfect time for our parents to sell salt."

He pointed to the wooden carts in the distance. "They are all full of minerals. My father anticipates our journey back home will be much lighter."

In the distance, a ram's horn shrieked. Yael exclaimed, "Oh, it's time for the Sukkot offering. Let's all go and watch."

The nine young people joined the gathering in front of the burning wood.

A man, in a purple linen robe with bells dangling from its hem, stood to the side of the altar. In front of him lay a tied-up goat, jerking against the rope.

He declared, "Here we offer to you, our God, this goat. We say thanks for our ample harvest."

The priest lifted up a rock and slammed it down on the goat's head. It smashed the animal's skull and its body lay motionless. Taking out a long bronze knife, the priest quickly sliced the skin at the neck. Blood trickled out and ran down the rocks. The priest immersed his fingers in the warm flowing blood, stood up, and flicked it seven times into the air. He then bent over the animal and cut it wide open.

With arms soaked in gore, the priest took out the heart and placed it in the flames. The organ hissed as it contacted the fiery wood as smoke wafted from the altar. Next, the priest removed the liver, kidneys, and then the intestines. Those too, he tossed into the fire. He cut the animal into parts, separating the hindquarters as he put them on a metal grate over the fire. Smoke ascended, and the smell of roasted animal meat permeated the gathering.

Devash breathed in the aroma and declared, "Praise God, tonight, we will all eat well."

Once the meat was roasted, it was removed and sliced into portions. Two women in azure and honey colored robes passed the tender meat out on platers to the people below.

Noah was standing next to Devash as a plate of goat's meat went by. He easily grabbed a few oily slices. Handing some to Devash, he commented, "I think this will taste as good as it smells." They both bit into the moist meat as the juices ran down their chins. It was succulent. They shared the meat with the other youths and then passed their wine pouches from one to the other.

After feasting on food and drink, they walked into the huts decorated with the grains and vegetables of the harvest. Shifra picked up the myrtle, palm, and willow branches. As she waved them through the air towards the sky above, a dangling pomegranate hit Noah in the head.

Devash chuckled, "You have the curse of being tall. I pity you, Noah."

Noah looked down at her smiling, "It's not a curse." He reached up and picked one cluster of black bulbous grapes dangling from above. After handing some fruit to Devash, he popped two into his mouth.

Biting into the ripe grape, the sweetness filled Devash's mouth. She acknowledged, "I can see height is indeed a blessing."

"Come walk with me," invited Noah as he led Devash out by the hand. She walked with him, leaving her friends behind in the hut. As Noah and Devash strolled out by the palm trees far enough away, they could barely hear the people in the huts or by the altar.

"I haven't seen a girl with eyes like yours before," Noah confided. "Where did you get them?"

Devash smiled mischievously. "There once was this cat who didn't want to chase mice anymore. And there was a woman, who didn't like being human. They had an arrangement. They agreed to trade their bodies for a while.

After drinking from enchanted waters, the cat was transformed into a woman with these eerily green eyes. The cat loved being human so much that she refused to go back to her life. Fortunately for her, the human who became a cat was happy sleeping all the time, so their destiny was fulfilled."

Poking a finger playfully into her side, Noah exclaimed, "Oh, so you are a cat woman, are you?"

"No," Devash laughed. "The cat is my grandmother. I'm the granddaughter of the cat."

"So you are a story teller, I see." Noah turned to face her. "Tell me, if you could change places with any person or animal, what would you choose?"

Devash was surprised by the question. As she shook her head, her deep brown hair swayed over her shoulders. "I haven't thought about that before. I do like being human, however sometimes I wish I wasn't a female. Then I could do anything I wanted."

"Well," replied Noah as he looked intensely at her. "I'm sure glad you are a female. I don't think I would do this if you weren't." He then lowered his head and lightly touched his lips to hers.

A warm tingling radiated through her body. Startled, Devash jumped back.

"I'm sorry," said Noah. "Did I offend you?"

Devash looked at him with a mystified expression. She had never kissed a boy before.

Taking a step closer to him, she said, "No, far from it."

She lifted her face up towards his, silently beckoning him.

With a smile, he lowered his head to hers and they kissed as the stars shined brightly above.

CHAPTER 6
INTERMEDIATE DAYS OF SUKKOT

That kiss, what a kiss, thought Devash as she rested in the loft later that night. Looking at the crevices of mud brick in the ceiling, she lay there wide awake. A few cubits away, Devash could hear her brother snoring. Her parents and Savta were already in deep slumber as well. Inhaling deeply, Devash stroked her fingers up and down her neck. As her fingernails grazed the soft skin, she shivered. Imagining Noah caressing her, she thought, maybe marriage wouldn't be so terrible. She smiled as she imagined having sons and daughters with him.

With sweet thoughts and warm sensations enveloping her body, Devash fell into a deep sleep.

In the morning, Devash awoke to a fragrant smell. She bounded down the rope ladder and saw her mother cooking pudding over the fire.

"What is that Ima?" she inquired as her stomach growled.

"I thought I would try something different," said her mother. Her hair was held back in a sky blue scarf. "I put in some eggs, goat milk, dates, cardamom, and last day's bread. I think it will be good."

Ladling some of the bread pudding, Ima gave a bowl to Devash. The aroma was amazing. Taking a spoonful to her mouth, Devash savored it.

"Where is Shlomi? Where is Aba for that matter?" Devash asked after she quickly devoured her morning meal.

"Your father has taken Shlomi to the letter drawer. He needs to practice writing the alphabet." Ima stirred the pot.

"Why does he need to do that?" Devash asked.

"We have many hopes for our Shlomi. Plowing a field, you don't need to read or write, but if he is to become a record keeper or a leader, he is going to need to identify spears, pottery, and to keep track of trade. He will need to know the twenty six symbols of the Phoenician alphabet and the sounds of Aramaic as well."

Devash frowned, unsure of what to say next, but then blurted out, "Why am I not learning to read and write Ima? You and Aba always tell me how intelligent I am."

Tamar put down the stirring spoon, stood up, and wiped her hands on her skirt.

With a puzzled expression, she stated, "Devash, there are other skills you must learn. I never had any need for reading."

"But, but," Devash protested. "What if I don't want to do those things?"

Tamar shook her head. "It is the children of Jacob's way," she said sternly. "This is what you must do. This is your place and future."

The girl's eyes reddened as she glared at her mother.

Her grandmother entered the room and glanced from mother to daughter.

Placing her hand on the teen's shoulder and pointing beyond the door, Savta spoke, "You must understand honeyed one, look around at the country side. What do you see the women doing? They are having precious children like you. This is what you must do."

Savta's eyes softened as she consoled, "You will in time gain understanding. Being a mother is the greatest gift of all."

Devash felt her chest constrict. Without looking at her mother and grandmother, she walked deliberately to the door. Once outside, her legs moved and she found herself running through the courtyard to the nearby fields. Only when there was distance between her family and fate, Devash stopped and stood still. With deep breaths, the cool autumn air filled her lungs.

The rest of the day was filled with chores. Devash removed the hay filled with sheep and lamb droppings and replaced it with fresh grasses. The animal pen smelled better immediately. The women scrubbed clothing, soaked them in water, and hung them out to dry. They separated the wheat germs from the stalks. Devash's hands were well calloused and used to the work. Uncomplaining, the teen girl dutifully did her tasks. As the sun began to move past mid-point, she saw her father and brother coming up the hill.

"Look, Dee, look!" proudly exclaimed Shlomi as he approached her. He held out a piece of pottery with at least ten different symbols.

"I'm writing now!" He smiled with cheeks rosy from the sun.

With a shy glance to her father, Devash said barely audible, "Aba, I want to learn to write."

David was carrying a large cloth sack over his shoulder. He moved it to the other shoulder with a grunt.

"What would you want to do that for?" His forehead creased and then he set his sack down with a thud.

"I just want to, Aba. I know I can do it. Please?" she implored.

"Well," the man looked toward the house with a worried glance. After a few moments, he said, "You know reading and writing is not for girls."

Then with a little nod and a quiet voice, he said, "However, if perchance your brother here decides to 'practice' with your encouragement. No fault could be found with that."

Devash's eyes opened wide.

Turning to her brother with the ruddy cheeks, she said with a whisper, "What do you say? You can practice with me. We can do this together?"

The boy shrugged his shoulders, "Sure, why not."

"Thank you Aba!" Devash hugged her father. He stood there as she hugged him saying softly, "Shhh, quiet now."

Later after Shlomi cleaned one of the plough irons and Devash repaired a leather sandal, they scampered to a big oak tree outside the courtyard. There Shlomi showed Devash how to form the letters of Aleph and Bet.

"This is just the beginning of the alphabet," he instructed. "Aleph has an 'a' sound and Bet has a 'b' sound."

It took time to master the curves and angles of the letters, but the girl was eager to learn. When Shlomi finished teaching her letters up to Lamed, Devash proudly pointed to a spear the family had for at least one generation. It was attached to Shlomi's rope belt. Lifting it up, she correctly noted the letters inscribed on it.

Night was coming. The family packed up for the intermediate days of the Feast of Booths. Aba hoisted another sheep on to the cart for the offering of thanks to God. Shlomi added a basket full of melons, pomegranates, and yellow squash.

An hour later, they arrived at the flat hill top. The crowd of people had thinned compared to the night before but there was still over a hundred people. David's family and those who lived close by went home every night. Those who had to travel a distance, though, spent the night in tents for the entirety of the week.

David looked over at one of the tents and recognized the families of the Salty Sea. There were three big tents covered with the taupe skins of camels. Outside one of them was a wide plank of wood resting on two large rocks with many fist sized cubes of white salt. A couple of Israelites and nomads were inspecting the quality of the dried mineral.

Extending his hand in their direction, David said, "Let's go over and see if we can trade some vegetables for a square or two of salt."

The people from the Salty Sea wore cream colored scarfs wrapped multiple times around their heads. Their bleached robes billowed in the wind. In the heat of the valley, white was one of the few protections from the blistering sun. Behind one of the men, Devash spotted her fair haired man. Noah noticed her and grinned. As Savta was inspecting one of the squares, her eyes inquisitively went from her granddaughter's face to the youth behind the grown men. Pursing her lips knowingly, she continued with her purchase.

The daylight passed quickly. It was already dark when Devash and Noah stole away. As Noah and Devash strolled through the oak and pine trees, they could see the brightest of stars filling the nighttime sky.

Devash really didn't know much about Noah. She knew that his family harvested salt from the Lifeless Sea and that they traveled to sell their goods. That was all.

"Noah," she inquired. "Who is your patriarch and your people?"

Noah was holding her hand and looked down at her as he spoke. "Well, who is your patriarch and people?"

Devash shrugged her shoulders. "Isn't it obvious? Joseph was my patriarch but we identify through his son Ephraim."

Noah smiled. "Yes, that is indeed obvious. I can see the good looks of your great grandfather Joseph has been passed down." Squeezing her hand, he grinned.

"Noah, truthfully, who is your family? I want to know."

Releasing her hand, they walked side by side. "I am of the Edomites. My great grandfather was Esau. We have lived in the southern land of Seir for three generations. My father is Teman, first born of Eliphaz, Esau and Adah's son," Noah stated matter of factly.

Devash in surprise said, "You mean, your great grandfather is Isaac and Rebekah's son, Esau, the red haired man?"

Devash had never met an Edomite before. She heard stories that even though Jacob and Esau reconciled, their relationship was still strained. To this day the descendants of Jacob were not allowed to travel in their lands. But here was a real, live Edomite.

"Do any of your people have red hair like Esau?" she asked.

"Very few," Noah responded. "You would think we would all have his hair but we don't. Most of us have dark hair, eyes, and skin. But once in a generation, a child is born with hair of crimson, and it's said that Esau's spirit has returned."

Devash nodded. "It's rare for us to have light or red hair too. It is only my friend Yael. Maybe she has some Edomite blood in her? I wonder?"

Noah looked at Devash as they stood facing each other. "Speaking of rare beauty..." Noah paused, his eyes transfixed on the young woman before him.

"So...," Devash looked down embarrassed. "Would you trade all your salt for a bowl of red lentil stew?" She said with a raised eye brow.

Placing his hand on her shoulder, Noah laughed, "No, but I would for a kiss from you."

The tall youth lowered his head until his lips touched Devash's. It was that same energy. Her lips eagerly kissed him back as his arms wrapped around her waist holding her close to him. She could feel the heat of his chest against hers. Draping her hands around his neck, she moved her fingers through his soft hair and their kisses deepened. With Noah's arms around her, she felt warmth and belonging.

Perhaps it was only a few minutes, but it felt like hours when Devash heard cheers erupting from the crowd in the distance. Breaking away from Noah, she reluctantly said, "We'd better go back. They will be looking for us."

Hand in hand, they came out of the forested hills. Devash encountered Shlomi, her brother.

"Dee! Where have you been? They are getting ready to wave the four species together." His cheeks were flushed red from running with other children.

Noticing the tall youth by his sister's side, he asked, "Who is this?"

"Oh, he's a...well...." Devash let go of Noah's hand.

"Come on! Down there, by the main sukkah!" Shlomi pointed to a large hut framed in wood and decorated with green palm fronds.

Devash and Noah accompanied Shlomi to the hut that was big enough to hold forty people. There were pomegranates, figs, cucumbers, and grapes dangling from the roofing beams. As they looked up, they could see the bright moon in the night sky.

One of the prominent men of Ephraim, a strong man in his forties named Gibor began to speak.

"Here, we bring to you, God, branches of palm, sweet myrtle, lush willow with this ripe Etrog to thank you. We thank you, Adonai, for the fruits of our harvest with which we have decorated this sukkah. May we all have ample food this winter and may we have peace and prosperity."

Gibor held together the four species in both hands and shook them in the four directions of wind and then to the sky and earth below. The people cheered and heartily said to one another "'*L'chayim*, to life!" as they drank to celebrate the festival.

'Devaaash! There-ere you are!" called her father. His face was beet red from drinking wine and his white robe was stained with drops of red liquid.

"Hi, Aba," Devash replied tentatively.

"I know your friends." David stumbled and then stood upright again. With blood shot eyes squinting at the unknown teen, he asked, "but who is this young man here?"

"Sir, I am Noah son of Teman." Noah stated stiffly as he tried to look directly at Devash's father. "I'm with the salt traders. Peace unto you, sir."

"Son of Teman, son of Teman," muttered David confusedly. Then he looked down at his hands. "Ach! My cup is dried out! I must save it." The inebriated father went off in search of more beverage.

Devash nodded her head smiling, "Well, I'm glad Aba is feeling the joy of Sukkot."

As Devash and Noah exited the sukkah, they found Devash's friends Yael, Zack, Dan, & Shifra standing in a circle.

"It's quite a celebration! Isn't it?" gleefully stated the pimpled youth Zack.

"So," Dan stuck out his chest as he turned toward Noah. "What's it like living in the South by the Lifeless Sea? I imagine you don't eat a lot of fish."

"No," replied the lanky youth. "I don't see much of it here in the hill country either. However, my family and I don't live all the time by the Dead Sea. We are there only long enough to dry out the salt and then we travel throughout many lands."

Shifra's hair was especially frizzy and she added, "That must be an interesting way of life. I've only lived here." Wistfully, she continued, "I would love to see the other side of the Jordan River. I'm told that it is lush."

"I've been there," replied Noah. "In many ways, it's similar to life here. They farm the hills in tiers like you do. They shepherd goats and sheep and they speak the same language. However, there is a place that is different."

The teens became quiet.

"Where?" Zack asked curiously.

"If you go west, as far west as you can," Noah explained slowly. "You come to the coast and you meet people unlike any other. They came on boats via the Great Sea. They have the most beautifully painted pottery and they eat a juicy meat that is different from any you have ever tasted."

Dan commented, "What do you mean a different meat? What other animals are there? Is it monkey?"

"No," Noah explained. "The animal's hide is pink and has a snout. It rolls in the mud and its meat is tender and tasty."

Yael listened closely and then said, "I think you are describing pig. That's not suitable to eat. My father said it's an abomination."

"Well," replied Noah, "If all abominations are this delicious, I guess you can call me abominable."

The teens laughed but Dan added more seriously, "Actually, I hate to say this but you may be considered not suitable. You're an Edomite."

"Dan!" angrily yelled Devash. "That is offensive! You are disrespecting my friend!"

"It is no insult," answered Noah. "I am not ashamed of my people or heritage. Dan may be right. The children of Esau haven't lived with the children of Jacob for generations."

"It's time to change tradition!" cried Devash as she turned away.

"Devash!" Noah called after her.

She had just passed one of the great oak trees, when Noah caught hold of her shoulders. Facing her, he stated, "Devash! Please don't be angry with me. You know as well as I do that what is between us is only for the duration of the festival."

With her eyes wide open, she roared, "What? I don't understand. I hoped we would marry!"

He shook his head. "I…I… believe I could love you but my family would never accept it and frankly I don't think yours would as well."

"You don't know what you are talking about!" Devash exclaimed angrily. "My family doesn't define who I am." Defiantly, she stood facing him.

"You say that now." Noah softly replied. "But as you get older you realize that you are part of your family. There is no changing who we are and what our parents expect us to be."

"You are indeed a pig!" screamed Devash as she ran away from him.

With ragged breath, Devash scrambled up one of the nearby hills. She walked steadily placing one foot in front of the other. It was dark but the light of the stars provided enough lumination.

She didn't get far until she realized that someone was following her. Even in the moon light, she could tell it was her friend Yael.

"Devash!" she called out. "Wait! Wait for me!"

Devash stopped climbing and sat down on a rocky edge. Yael, nearly out of breath, sat down next to her.

"I'm sorry, Devash. I really am. I could tell how much you cared for him," consoled Yael.

"I detest him!" Devash spitted out. "Why did he even approach me? He only wanted a festival whore!"

The red haired youth sat quietly by Devash's side as her friend cried.

"I never felt this way before," said Devash through her tears. "What if this is my only love?" And Devash covered her face with her hands.

"You don't know this, Devash," softly said Yael, "But there was one I cast my eye on. At the last festival of unleavened bread, I took a liking to a Bedouin boy."

"Wait," Devash said slowly, "Was it that dark haired boy? The one who sat with you at the Passover sacrifice?"

Nodding, Yael continued, "His name was Manoah. I immediately felt love for him and I could tell he took interest in me too. He was sweet and good looking. We spent the first three days of Passover together. You remember?" Yael saw Devash nodding her head in agreement.

"Well," Yael continued, "I wanted to be with him. I asked my father to arrange for us to be together but he said no. He told me that I had to marry within our tribe. He told me that I would be marrying Gibor's son, Micah, within two years. The arrangements were already made. I was deeply distressed."

"I remember the boy you are speaking of but I didn't realize the depth of your feelings," Devash remarked.

"I was very upset but I knew that I had to accept my father's wishes," Yael conceded.

"Weren't you to tempted to fight your fate?" asked Devash.

"Yes, no, I couldn't defy my family. I didn't want to let down my father. While I was sad initially, with the passing of a couple of months, I thought less and less of Manoah. Now, I'm excited that, in time, I'll marry Micah. I'll have lots of sons and we'll live here in the hill country next to you."

Yael put her arm around her friend.

"Hmmm, maybe our future will be blessed after all," wistfully added Devash.

The two friends walked down the hill together.

CHAPTER SEVEN
DAY AFTER SUKKOT RAID

The joy of Sukkot seemed so far away, like a dream. Was it just two days ago, that Devash was waving the lulav, drinking wine, and feeling the pangs of love lost? Maybe it was a year ago? Through her eyelids, Devash could tell it was morning but she didn't want to open them. She laid in the dirt with her right arm bent under her head. Lifting it hurt. It wasn't a dream. It was a nightmare. Who were those horned beasts? Images of blood and lifeless bodies filled Devash's thoughts. It didn't happen, she told herself. I'm not going to get up. I will stay here.

Her body was stiff and hurting more as she remained motionless. Reluctantly, she opened her eyes and saw sun light streaming through the branches above her. Looking at the yellow fuzzy light was calming as she lay in the ditch with wooden kindling above her. Her sukkah of refuge sheltered her however she knew that when she got up, it would be anything but peaceful. Devash slowly moved her arm and wriggled her shoulders.

Dread began to fill her. What happened to Yael!

No, she pushed that thought away. It was too terrible.

What about her parents, her little brother, and Savta?

"Please God, let everything that happened only be an awful dream," she muttered. Devash remembered the earthquake and how the houses crumbled. Yes, those were only images from sleep, she told herself. She shuddered, it was a dream. I'll wake up in my home and see the cracks in the wooden beams of our ceiling. My family is safe and my friends unharmed.

Let it be that I just hit my head and everything is as it was.

Devash felt this wave of dread wash over her. She knew the truth. She knew it was real and hoping that it wasn't, a futile prayer. God doesn't undo what has been done. What could she do? She couldn't just stay there. She must get up. It was completely quiet except for the chirping of birds. Sisera and his army had departed many hours ago. She had to get up.

Get up! She steeled herself and pushed away the branches above her.

Climbing out of the ditch, she felt her muscles cramp as she struggled to stand up. Thick oak and terebinth trees surrounded her. Placing her hand on the bark, she touched its roughness.

"Oh tree," she said. "Give me your strength. You have seen so much over the years. Give me the strength to withstand what I must."

Devash walked through the edge of the woods into the flat encampment.

Before her were overturned carts. The wheels turned upward facing the sky. The earth had deep brown stains almost everywhere. Devash realized that it was dried blood. She came across a small body on the ground. It was a boy about nine years old. He was just a little younger than her brother Shlomi. His hair was matted with blood and his eyes were wide open frozen in terror. As she looked over his body, she saw he was missing his middle. The fabric of his tunic was torn and underneath, his skin was missing. There was a dark hole and his intestines hung out like a bundle of little snakes on the rocks.

Devash felt her stomach twist. Clutching her belly, she turned away from the corpse and threw up on the ground. Crying, she backed up, unable to avert her eyes from the little dead boy.

"Oh my God!" She cried out still with some vomit dribbling down her chin. "How could you let this happen? This boy did nothing wrong! And Yael! Yael, she was such a good girl. She had a future. She was going to marry Gibor's son, Micah, and live in the hills."

Devash looked at the sky angrily. "How could you stand by, God? How could you do nothing to save your people from these barbarians?" Devash yelled.

Devash noticed a rotund woman hovering over a body. The woman's gray hair was tied back in a scarf and she was sobbing. Walking over, Devash placed her hand on her shoulder. Before her laid a corpse of a well-dressed elder. His robe was daisy yellow and his beard went down to his chest. It wasn't obvious how the man had died but the stiffness of his posture suggested that he went to Sheol hours earlier. The woman's wiry hair poked out from her scarf as she sobbed.

Devash got down on her knees and with her arm around the woman's shoulder, pulled her close. With tears wetting Devash's dress, she just held the woman as she gazed at the body without really seeing it anymore. The woman quieted down after a few moments and just silently whimpered.

Devash stood up and then took in the scene. There appeared to be some twenty dead bodies on the ground or tossed over rocks. The sukkahs, the huts, were smashed. Bits of fruit and wood littered the ground. She could see that the altar, where all their sacrifices were offered, was broken into bits of burnt chunks of wood. Dead goats, lambs, and oxen with bulging eyes lay on their sides or even upside down. A few survivors walked around like she did, stunned and unsure of what to do.

Then some Israelites appeared on the main path. A young man arrived pulling a donkey. Glumly, he took out a bronze trowel and began to dig pits in the earth. Then another man arrived. This one had a cart full of shovels and he began to do likewise. Within an hour, men and women showed up still wearing their clothes from the night before. They searched the camp for loved ones. When a body was discovered, there were high pitched cries of anguish. Some people walked through and picked up anything that could be salvaged.

When the sun stood in the highest point of the sky, Devash spotted her mother. Tamar's hair was completely disheveled and her eyelids were swollen. Her festival dress from yesterday was thoroughly stained with dirt. However, when Tamar saw Devash, her face lit up.

"Devash, Devash!" She ran towards her. "You are alive! Thank God you are alive!" Tamar grabbed her stunned daughter and hugged her so tightly, Devash could barely breathe.

Releasing the teen, the older woman studied her, "Are you all right? Are you injured?"

Devash was happy to see her mother. "I'm not hurt but what about Shlomi, Savta, and Aba?" she sputtered.

She gripped Devash's arm. "Shlomi is fine and so is Savta. Your Aba though is injured. He has taken to bed. One of the spears punctured his thigh. He is resting."

Devash was troubled to hear this news. "Ima, I…"

Devash didn't get to finish her sentence. There was a howl in the distance. By the side of the camp, a woman screamed at the top of her lungs.

"They took my daughter! They took my daughter!"

It was Yael's mother.

Another woman came up to her and cried, "They took mine too."

The women wailed and Devash felt weak in the knees.

Looking at the women crying and the devastation surrounding them, Tamar said solemnly, "We must get back home. There's nothing to be done here."

Leading her daughter away, Tamar and Devash returned to their pillared house.

"Dee!" called Shlomi as soon as he saw her. He ran to the courtyard. His face had dirt stains on it. "You are here! You are home!"

Devash hugged her brother and then embraced Savta. Her grandmother's eyes were reddened. It looked like she didn't sleep at all that night.

With a weak smile, the old woman said, "So… happy… you are here! So… happy you are alive, my sweet honey one."

Devash saw her father lying by the wall. Her heart hurt with the sight. He laid on a thick layer of hay covered with a lamb's skin. Another furry blanket covered most of his body, with his right leg sticking out. It was wrapped in layers of white linen. Blood and puss seeped through the outer bandage. David's eyes were half closed, grimacing in pain, and his face was white.

"Aba! Aba!" cried Devash.

"Hmmm," he opened his eyes, "Devashi, you are unharmed?"

"Yes, Aba, yes but you..."

The wounded man tried a feeble smile. "I'll be all right. Help, help your mother."

And then he closed his eyes and fell asleep.

Devash stood frozen like a statute in front of her beloved father. Then, Tamar softly said, "Sit Devash, come and sit. Here let me bring you something to eat."

Stumbling toward the table, Devash sat and chewed the day old bread without tasting it. Even after a cup of water, she still felt tired and drained.

Tamar sat down next to her and her grandmother did as well.

Savta spoke as she slowly shook her head. "I've never seen a raid like this before in all my years." The old woman's eyes stared ahead without seeing. "We ran for our lives. Once we came to the cart…" Savta paused and looked at her granddaughter as her eyes welled up with tears. "We, we didn't see you there."

Tamar's face turned ruddy and she pursed her lips struggling to stifle her emotions. Somberly, she stated, "Your father was hit by an arrow. Your brother and I carried him to the cart. I looked for you. I called for you…"

Tamar stopped talking. She breathed fiercely like a bull before a charge.

Savta looked compassionately at her daughter and then to her granddaughter.

"We hoped you were with another family." The old woman took hold of Devash's hand. "I told them that you were likely with Yael and her father. That you were safe." Letting go of the girl's hand, Savta covered her face and silently shook.

Tamar, now able to speak, asked, "What…what…happened to you?"

Devash could barely think of what happened. It was all hazy.

"I…I…" she began tiredly. "I hid in the woods. I saw things. I…I…am all right, but Yael...." The girl buried her face into her hands. "They took her," she mumbled.

The rest of the day passed as a blur.

The next morning, Tamar sent Devash and her brother out with the goats.

"Make sure they eat plenty of grass." Tamar instructed. "They haven't properly grazed in days and their milk will completely dry out."

The children walked two hours to the south through the hills until they found an area with lots of leafy vegetation for their four goats. Devash and Shlomi sat under an oak tree, resting in the shade.

They both heard a distant buzzing. Looking up, Shlomi saw a large bee hive with many little flying insects swarming around it.

Shlomi stood up frightened and exclaimed, "We should get up and get away from here quick!"

Devash calmly motioned for him to sit again. "They are high above us, Shlomi. If we don't bother them, they won't bother us."

Unconvinced, he sat by her side and shifted uncomfortably.

"Aba is going to get better, right Dee?" asked the eleven year old boy. His eyes looked sad. His boyhood already passed him by.

Devash sighed and looked in the distance. "I hope so."

That morning Devash noticed that her father's leg had swollen to twice its size and became red as beets. The yellow leaves of Goldenrod weren't working. Devash listened intently as her mother and grandmother spoke of David's condition.

"Tamar, you know it doesn't look good." Savta put her hand on Tamar's shoulder. "If God doesn't will for his leg to improve, we'll have to remove it."

Tamar shook away the older woman's hand. "But he won't be able to plow the fields. How will he work?" She shook her head in denial. "He is proud of his independence. What kind of man would he be without his leg?"

Savta was quiet.

Tamar added, "Let's see what happens by tomorrow and we will decide then."

Devash looked at her younger brother and with a weary smile stated, "Aba is very strong. If anybody can recover from such a wound, it is him."

Shlomi smiled and nodded.

Three of the goats were grazing close to the youth but one had disappeared.

"Wait here, Shlomi," said Devash. "We can't afford to lose a goat."

Devash went around the hill, searching for the wandering animal.

Where could it have gone? she wondered.

After finding the lost goat, Devash heard a scream.

Alarmed, Devash ran back to the tree where she left her brother. Shlomi shrieked again.

Within moments, Devash was through the bushes. She saw a man in tattered clothing pushing her brother. His clothing was in shambles but he had a helmet with little horns at the temples. He must have been one of the Sea People soldiers. She thought. Why was he alone? Maybe he got separated from his fellow soldiers.

"You stupid Israelite boy!" The man hollered and stumbled. "I'm…I'm going to strip you, steal your clothes, your goats, and then kill you."

Shlomi was howling. "No…No… leave me alone!" he cried.

The man appeared drunk or deranged but even so, Devash knew he was bigger and stronger than she was. Looking up at the tree and then at the man, Devash thought for a couple of seconds.

Reaching down, she took hold of a couple of rocks beneath her. With her eyes on the attacker, she took aim and threw a rock above the man.

Suddenly noticing her, the man looked in her direction and grinned. "Missed me! Oh pretty girl, I certainly won't miss you when I come over there!"

"Curses!" Devash exclaimed under her breath as she took her second rock aimed it higher than the first one.

"You are a terrible thrower!" the man mocked.

The rock hit the bee hive right above him with thud. The hive began to sway back and forth and then it was free from the branch. Falling through the air, it exploded on the man's head. Hundreds of bees flew angrily from their ruptured nest.

"Run Shlomi! Run!" she yelled.

The bees swarmed the man's body. "Yaaaaah!" screamed the man as the bees attacked his face, arms, and back. He tried swatting them but that only enraged them more.

"Yaaaaaaaaah!" he shrieked.

Shlomi darted to Devash's side as she grabbed the goats. Both youth ran home as fast as they could with their animals.

They were out of breath when they came into the courtyard.

Savta was outside and the first to see them.

Panicked, she asked, "What happened? Is it Sisera? Are the Sea People attacking?"

"No…no…" Devash was wheezing from her run. Taking a deep breath, she said, "I think it was a lone soldier that separated from his unit. He was acting crazy."

They all went into the house. Savta ladled some water into cups for Devash and Shlomi.

Ima wanted to hear about what happened.

Shlomi told them both about how the man was going to steal the goats and hurt him. And then he described how Devash unleashed the fury of the bees on him.

Savta and Ima looked at Devash in wonder.

Nodding her head, Ima said, "That was some good thinking, Devash. You are a clever girl."

"Hmmmm," they all heard moaning from the wounded man on the straw. Devash ran over to her father.

"Aba, what's wrong?"

"Oh, my leg. It hurts but it's no matter." David's face was blanched and contorted in pain. "I..." He gasped. "I heard how you saved your brother." Raising his shaking hand to his daughter's face, he gently caressed her.

"You are not little anymore." David smiled weakly. "Devash is a little girl's name meaning honey. Times aren't sweet like they used to be." His eyes grew sad and then shined bright in pride. "It seems to me that we have a bee with some sting here."

Now Ima, Savta, Shlomi, and Devash gathered around Aba with some confusion.

"What are you talking about David?" asked Tamar as she held his hand.

The man's face twisted in pain. He stammered, "You are now Deborah. Be wise my daughter. Be str…str…ong."

"You are delusional, David," softly said Tamar.

"Aba?" his daughter asked confused.

David closed his eyes and said no more.

By morning, David breathed his last and was at rest with his ancestors.

CHAPTER 8
YAEL

The days were a blur for Yael as Sisera's caravan traveled north. She laid in his chariot like a sack of grain. Every bump rocked her battered body as she was taken further and further from her family, land, and friends. Sometimes she looked out and noticed how the land became greener. There were gently rolling hills lush with grass, flowering bushes, and more trees. She was a long way from semi-arid mountains down south. Some of the men's words were unfamiliar to Yael, their accent was foreign too, but more often than not they spoke the language of the land. They must have been in Canaan for many years already. Yael looked out numbly as the days passed.

Weeks later, they arrived by the banks of a long, unending river. Stone buildings spread out as far as she could see. There must be hundreds of people who lived here, thought Yael. The city was surrounded by mountains and lay in a verdant plain. A few of the town people ran up to the caravan and jubilantly greeted Sisera and his soldiers.

One man with a receding hairline over both temples came forward. He was dressed in a blue wool robe fastened at his right shoulder with a golden brooch.

"So, what have you brought back to us, our great commander Sisera?"

Sisera's face was tanned deeply from the sun and looked fierce with his horned helmet. He got down from his horse. He towered over the man.

"I have brought goats, sheep, and lamb." He answered gruffly gesturing behind him. "There are many bags of grain that will provide bread for our people throughout the cooler months."

The man with the golden brooch pursed his lips. "And what about other delights? I assume you brought maidens?"

Sisera nodded with a wink. By then a crowd of people gathered around them.

A woman wearing a colorful dress of lilac and gold earrings cast in the shape of a bull head pushed through the people.

"You are back! My son, so happy to see you." She went over to Sisera and kissed him on both cheeks affectionately. "Hmm," she scrunched up her nose. "It appears a bath will be in order as well."

"Yes, yes, mother," he answered dismissively.

Bags of wheat and barley were thrown from the chariots first. Then dirty animals were distributed amongst the people.

One man with short dark hair called out, "We'll feast tonight and celebrate Sisera's victory!" A cheer rose from the men.

Sisera's soldiers took the captives from the chariots. Wearing only a blanket to cover their nakedness, the twenty young women shook with fear.

"The fire-haired one is mine!" declared Sisera. "My men will give out the rest."

Yael was taken to the largest stone house in Haroseth-hagoiim. This town, only a day journey to the Great Mediterranean Sea, was just a little North of Jokneam. There were hills to the east covered in green shrubs and vegetation. Sisera's house was built out of lime stone and had two floors. One room on the top even had a balcony. Yael learned that this was his mother's room. Women servants took Yael by the hand and scrubbed her with rough rags. With her hair still damp, they dressed her in a long ivory tunic. Yael stared blankly ahead. She couldn't comprehend what was happening to her.

Off the main entrance was a room with two looms in it. Three women weaved woolen threads through yarn held taunt by round flat cylindrical weights. In another room, four heavy set women kneaded dough on a stone rectangular table. Sisera had a whole crew of women working for him.

That night, one hundred men, women, and children celebrated their victory over the Israelites in the village square. Over a large fire, a pig roasted on a long bronze pole. The aroma of sizzling meat wafted through the crowd. Wine was poured out from angled jugs. Yael had never seen pouring vessels like these. Their bent necks were in the shape of a horn and the jug was decorated with red inked diamonds and bold horizontal lines.

A woman wearing her hair in elaborate braids took a tambourine and shook it. To its beat she sang:

From Sardinia, we came.

Our people sailed the Great Sea

Conquering the people

Who swarmed like insects on the coasts.

Oh gods of water, bless us.

Oh gods of water, who gave us victory.

Make our men strong, our women fertile, and our children grow tall.

May our people grow and flourish in this land,

Our land, for ever and ever.

"Yaa!" the people cried in agreement. Men took deep gulps of wine and women passed out slices of pig. Sisera bit ravenously into the white juicy meat. Oil and juices seeped into his beard. He didn't even bother to wipe it.

One of his soldiers stood before the captivated town people. The man had just bathed and his wet hair clung to his neck. With one hand clutching his drink, he dramatically waved his right arm in sync with his words.

"We climbed over rocks and steep hills until we came across the Israelites. They had hundreds of soldiers waiting for us and then they charged!" Taking out his dagger with his right hand, he raised it to the sky. "We took our best weapons and fought with the might of the water god. We sliced and pierced! We cut off their heads and limbs!"

He dramatically swung his dagger to the right and left. "Those Israelite men of the hills fought like beasts but we were stronger. They never stood a chance. With our commander Sisera, we soundly defeated them all and forever more!" His voice rose in pride.

The people listening to him broke out in cheers.

Later, after many cups of wine, an Israelite girl, no older than eleven with arms tied together in front of her, was brought before the crowd on a raised platform. She looked so little as she trembled. Yael was standing by Sisera.

"Who wants this heathen girl?" announced a round headed man with a large nose by her side. "She is an insect of the desert."

Sisera looked on and chuckled. Yael was alarmed. This poor girl. Oh my God, she prayed to herself. Don't let this happen!

Looking at her captor, Yael pleaded, "Sir, please she is only a child. Don't let them do harm to her."

Sisera slapped Yael with his back hand across her face so strongly that she fell backwards. He then kicked her in the stomach as she laid in the dirt. “You shut your mouth! You foul animal of the hills.”

“More wine?” offered a fat woman to the onlookers with a chuckle. One of her huge breasts dangled out from her robe.

Yael heard Sisera’s voice in the distance. “This is what we did to the Israelites in the hill country!” He now stood over the quivering girl on the platform. Raising his sword, he stabbed her through the heart. The crowd roared. The girl’s body lay motionless.

Yael looked at Sisera and his men with hate and fear. She hated them for the travesty they did to that poor girl. She hated them for what they did to her father and her people. And she hated Sisera for what he was doing to her.

That night Sisera raped Yael again. She laid there imagining she was far away. She was instead a star in the sky above. A star far way in the darkness, a glimmer of light, where no one could reach her.

Days went by. Yael walked around the house detached. She felt nothing. The maids bathed her daily and dressed her. One morning when Sisera was out, Yael sat at the table nibbling on an olive. Sisera’s mother passed through the room. She wore a golden braided necklace with a crimson outer robe over her brilliant indigo tunic.

With a sneer, she said, “Oh, it looks like we still have a rat in the kitchen.”

Yael looked down, wishing she could disappear.

Sisera’s mother snorted, “I’m sure it will be killed one way or another.”

She left the eating area.

That evening, Yael told herself that she just had to survive, whatever it took. She had to live so she could see her family again. Her eyes welled up as she stared at the wooden ceiling. And then her eyes narrowed as she gritted her teeth. She had to survive so that she could be a witness for the cruelty of Sisera. If she could choose life, maybe someday she'll see the death of the commander of the Sea People.

After a week, to her relief, she noticed that Sisera didn't come to her at night. She prayed that he lost interest in her.

One morning, the maids dressed Yael and led her down to the eating hearth. Sisera's mother was dressed impeccably as always. Her outer robe was brilliant yellow and it was so long that it was folded over and cinched at her waist with a beautiful leather sash. She was wearing her golden bull head earrings again. Glowering with distain at Yael, she walked out to the olive trees where her son was relaxing.

Approaching Sisera, she asked, "How many days will we have that filthy Israelite girl in our home?"

Without looking at his mother, Sisera stared at the twisted tree branches. With a shrug, he replied, "Oh, I'm done with her. I'll give her away as a present or let her be the entertainment tonight at the feast."

Smiling with satisfaction, she went back into the house to supervise.

One of Sisera's men burst through the olive trees.

"Dear commander! King Jabin is on horseback. He just arrived and wants to meet with you," he said, out of breath.

"Send him here. I'll speak to him in my house."

Within an hour, fifteen men on horseback arrived. Seated on a black mare was a man wearing a burgundy turban on his head. His outer robe was scarlet and mauve with a golden sash around his waist. One of the men dismounted first and assisted the king down.

"I want Heber and Adan to accompany me inside." Jabin ordered.

The rest of his men stood guard outside Sisera's house.

Sisera, King Jabin and his two men, were seated at a table made of cedar wood. Adan's forehead was deeply lined with wrinkles and his gray beard reached his waist. Despite his apparent old age, he was sure of foot and mind. Jabin looked in his direction regularly to gauge his reaction. Heber, much younger, had the thinning hair of middle age but his face was handsome with gentle brown eyes.

Heber's family went back a generation in friendship with Jabin. Their fathers forged an alliance between the Kenites and Canaanites. It was more than a military arrangement because a friendship grew between their families over the years. Their sons spent much time in their youth together. Today, however, there wasn't much of an alliance anymore. Heber liked being on his own and moved away from his people, the Kenites, however his friendship persisted with Jabin.

Servants brought out ripe red grapes, thick slices of wheat bread, and olives on platters. From a large jug decorated with bold red arches and triangles, they poured fermented barley into the men's cups.

"Sisera!" exclaimed the king as he swallowed deeply. 'Well done! I understand that you single handedly subdued our enemies."

"Thank you, your majesty, and welcome to our town, Haroeseth hagoiim." Sisera smiled.

"You are my best commander, Sisera. I want you to know how much I appreciate what you have done." The king motioned for Adan and Heber to hand two baskets to Sisera. They were heavy and the men strained with their weight.

Setting the baskets on the table, Heber opened the first one. Inside were colorful emeralds, sapphires, amethyst, and lapis lazuli. Sisera's eyes widened in greed. Then Adan opened the second basket. It was filled with bars of gold and silver.

"This is for your victory and a down payment on keeping the peace," King Jabin stated authoritatively.

Sisera picked up one of the gold bars and admired it. Placing it back into the basket, he said, "I don't expect any more trouble from them. I put the dread of Sheol into them. The land is yours."

"Good, good," said the king. "Keep an eye on the roadways as well. I don't want them trading and getting their hands on weapons."

Reaching for a fist full of grapes, Jabin continued, "I expect a heavy tribute from them as well. At least a sack of grain or an animal from every family, every month. Can you enforce that Sisera?"

With a gulp, Sisera finished off his beer and wiped his mouth on his arm. "It's as easy as taking a girl's maidenhood," he said with a wicked smile.

Looking across the room, the king noticed a red-haired girl wearing a simple cream colored tunic. She was refilling the platers with food.

"Who is this?" he inquired.

"A captive Israelite girl that I fancied for a while. She is nothing to me. If you desire her, she is yours."

Heber, standing next to Jabin, kept staring at the red haired girl. The king noticed his friend's interest.

"Do you want the girl, Heber?" the king inquired.

Heber nodded his agreement.

"Ah, then consider her a gift of friendship for the sake of our fathers." Then, looking at Sisera, the king added, "May the Canaanites always be aligned with the Sherden, the greatest people to come across the sea."

"Amen," agreed Sisera.

Yael was led out of the house and on to the horse of Heber. She knew not to resist her fate. The only thing she could hope for was that Heber would be less cruel than Sisera. "Please God, protect me. Please make him kind and compassionate." She prayed as she rode away with Heber, King Jabin, and his entourage.

CHAPTER NINE
YEAR 1120
THREE YEARS AFTER SISERA'S RAID

A youth tilled the earth. His face was dripping in sweat as he lifted the plough. The ox strained to pull the metal through the dirt. The young man was trim with sinewy muscles on his legs and arms. His face, once full with youthful cheeks, now was tanned and lean.

"Shlomi!" called out a woman bent over with a cane. "Shlomi, here are some melon seeds from the last harvest. I forgot to give them to you."

The old woman had coarse gray hair waving in the breeze. She reached into her skirt and with trembling fingers handed the little white seeds to the youth.

"Thank you, Savta," replied Shlomi. He then began to scatter them into the newly ploughed dirt.

There was humidity in the air. It had just rained this morning. Shlomi and his family hoped that this growing season would be a successful one especially since they had to give half of their crops to the Canaanites. In the last few years, the rains barely came and the produce of the land wasn't enough to pay their toll.

Savta was forced to gather berries and weeds growing in the grasses. Despite her back pain, she always brought back something, even if it was only some daisies. Ima worked hard every day before the morning light and into the darkness after the sun set. Her hands were deeply calloused as she salvaged any piece of cloth, no matter how worn out, and fashioned it into a tunic, robe, or scarf. The past few years were difficult ones for the family and the entire people in the hill country of Ephraim.

They all tried to survive. Food was almost always scarce and Canaanite raiders came at any time and took anything they pleased. The family's livestock diminished to just one goat, two lambs, and one ox. Many Israelite men were lost in that terrible Sukkot raid three years ago, leaving boys to become men before their time. The youth took on the men's work of plowing and tilling the ground with inconsistent results. The women worked long days helping in the field and making meals out of very little.

"Devash! You are doing it all wrong!" complained the middle-aged woman. Abruptly grabbing the animal hide out of her daughter's hands, Tamar put it in her own lap. With a bronze needle, she quickly sewed the sides of the skin together.

"You will never survive a winter until you master this. How will you take care of your family, if you can't cook or sew properly?" With an angry glare, she sneered, "What would your father say if he could see you now?"

The young woman by her side was taller than her mother and grandmother. Her body was well built. Her thick brown hair was tied back and she wore a simple beige tunic that couldn't disguise her mature round breasts.

"Please stop calling me Devash!" the young woman stated resentfully. "Aba, on his death bed, changed my name to Deborah. This is who I am now."

With annoyance, Tamar looked at her, "All right, I'll call you Deborah, but you must try harder. You need to master these skills for your husband."

Deborah took a sharp intake of breath. "I am trying, Ima. Really, I am." Her green eyes pleaded with her mother. "I will learn all that you teach me but I have no desire for marriage."

"Oh you must," Tamar stated definitely. "What kind of life will you have if you don't marry and bear sons?"

Deborah turned and walked quickly out of the stone pillared house and into the courtyard.

The clouds were still overhead from the rains earlier. The sky was gray. Everything lacked hope; her family, her people, her, even the overcast sky.

An oak tree with a thick trunk stood out in the distance. As Deborah studied it, she recalled all the lessons her father gave her.

Oh Aba! We miss you, Deborah thought, as she searched the cloud formations above. I know you are at peace but life is so hard. A tear ran down her cheek. What are we going to do? What can I do?

Deborah grabbed her bow and arrows and went outside until she was in front of the oak tree. Half closing her left eye, aiming ahead, she pulled the taut string with her right hand. She was just ready to let the arrow fly when she saw a bird on one of the branches. Quietly now, Deborah moved the target to the bird's belly. In deep concentration, she let the arrow fly loose. Zap! The gray long necked bird went tumbling to the ground.

"Finally!" exclaimed Deborah as she ran to it. Lifting the bird by its legs, she inspected it. The arrow had perfectly pierced its belly. Running with the dead bird in one hand and her bow and arrow in the other, she arrived breathlessly back to her home.

"Ima! Look what I have," proudly declared Deborah.

Her mother looked up and wearily smiled in relief. "Yes, I will make soup out of the bird tonight." She took the fowl from Deborah. "I know you are good with the arrow but you still have a long way to go with preparing a meal. Come help me and learn."

The women were plucking the feathers when they heard commotion from the fields. Laying down the animal, they walked through the courtyard. There were two men on horseback looking at Shlomi. The women ran fast towards them. Shlomi lowered his plough and the men descended from their horses.

"What! I can't give you my ox!" he yelled. "Without it, I won't be able to till the earth and then we won't have crops to give you."

One of the men had a bushy beard that came down to his chest. "You haven't given us anything for over a moon cycle. It's time to make tribute to your king."

"Oh, your king's tribute is sheep dung!" Shlomi shouted as his body tensed.

"No! No!" shouted Tamar breathlessly. "Look," she said facing the men. "We just shot an Ibis. It is very meaty and its long neck will make excellent soup. Let us keep our ox and we promise to give you extra grain with the next harvest."

Tamar put her hand on Shlomi's shoulder. Pressing with her fingers, she gave him a glare.

"I'm willing to consider this," the bearded man said tentatively. "This time." He moved closer to Shlomi. "I do think this boy needs to learn how to honor one's elders."

Deborah immediately stepped between the man and Shlomi. "You…you are right. He's a foolish, foolish boy." With a pleading look, she continued, "Just go by the oak tree over there and I'll bring you our plump Ibis. We have already removed the feathers, so you can easily roast it."

With a nod of agreement from both men, Deborah ran back to the courtyard. Tamar gripped Shlomi's arm. Deborah came back quickly with bird in hand. After handing it over, the men rode away.

Later after the sun set, the family gathered around the cooking pot. Savta wilted some wild bitter greens into watery broth. It was hard not to imagine how satisfying the soup would've been with meat but no one uttered a word about it. Shlomi, Savta, Tamar, and Deborah instead sipped their soup quietly.

After a bowl of watery broth, Shlomi cried out, "Why did you stop me? I could've beaten them." His face flushed in anger. "They don't deserve anything."

Tamar put her bowl down and looked at her son. "They are indeed beasts but you must follow their orders. You must do as they say. Never, never provoke them," she said sternly.

"Someone must stand up to them!" exploded Shlomi. He sounded almost like man with his deepening voice but his face still was as hairless as a woman.

Deborah looked from her mother to her brother. "I agree that our condition is intolerable."

"There is no other way!" exclaimed the anguished Tamar. "Shlomi! You must promise me. You are never to do anything unwise. I...I…just can't lose you too!"

Savta wearily stepped close to her daughter and took her hand in her own.

Everyone sat glumly alone with their thoughts.

After a few minutes, Savta said, "These are hard years indeed but we must, we will survive. It is not wise to ask how former times were better than these." Looking at her family, the old woman continued, "We must look to today and then prepare for tomorrow. No matter, I believe, the crops will do better this summer. Things will get better."

The full moon of Nisan arrived. A hundred Israelites gathered for the Feast of Unleavened bread. It was hard to celebrate their freedom from Egypt when they were practically enslaved to the Canaanites. However, they brought some flat breads that hadn't risen and two lambs for the offering. The festivals these years were nothing like those of the past. Before, many traveled from the south and east of the Jordan River to sell, make a match, or just be part of the celebration. Now only those who lived in the hill country attended. There was little merry making, and song and dance was subdued.

Deborah easily found her friends Zack, Dan, and Shifra. Zack's skin had cleared up. Gone were the red pimples of his youth. Even his body began to fill out. His shoulders were no longer bony and his body looked strong. Dan was still strong and prickly hairs sprouted above his lips. Even Shifra had changed. Her round hips made her waist appear small. Her small breasts were perky, but her hair was still curly and unruly.

Deborah embraced Shifra tightly.

"It's good to see you Deborah. It's been many moons," Shifra said with her face pressed against her cheek.

"I'm sad to say that we have very little for the Passover sacrifice." Deborah stated sadly.

"Oh, you're not the only one," responded Dan. "It's almost impossible to grow enough food when we are feeding those cursed Canaanites!"

"It's not just the Canaanites," added Zack. "It's the Sea People as well. Their alliance has only deepened. They all have their food and now ours as well. May God wreak vengeance on them!" Zack spit on the ground.

"Remember how we were years ago?" Shifra wistfully smiled as she spoke. "We would chase each other around, play in the trees, and laugh."

Deborah nodded. "Things have indeed changed."

"Well, I am old enough to marry now," Dan said with a raised eye brow.

"What?" Zack exclaimed. "Have your parents found you a bride?"

"Yes," Dan pointed north. "From the Menasheh tribe, there's a girl with wide hips good for birthing sons. Her name is Kara. I'll marry her by the Feast of Weeks."

Unexpected yelling from a few cubits away interrupted all conversation.

One man with a beaked nose shook his fist. "You son of a donkey! You broke my one and only plough. You owe me a new one."

A young male with short curly hair stood opposite him. "You gave it to me. I am not responsible," he said defiantly.

"I only lent it to you to help you out," spat the older man.

"Well, maybe you utilized poor judgment. Sorry friend." The young man started to turn and walk away. The other raised his hand to hit him.

Deborah and her friends were now close by. Deborah feared a terrible fight was about to take place. She quickly uttered, "Stop! Stop both of you! The Canaanites and Sea People have taken everything from us. We only have one another."

Both men turned in confusion to look at the young woman.

Deborah looked at the younger man and swallowed the saliva in her mouth. "Whether it was lapsed judgment or not, you are responsible for the plough you broke. You must replace it and add one fifth of its value to make amends."

"I'm not going to listen to a girl," he snapped.

A small crowd had already gathered around them.

An old man with white hair said in a shaking voice, "The…the woman is right. It is the law of our people to be responsible for one another. You must replace what you have broken and add one fifth of its value in grain. By the Feast of weeks, you must comply or the rest of us here will not trade with you." The old man looked for affirmation from the Israelites before him.

They nodded in agreement.

"Amen, amen!" the young man sarcastically exclaimed as he turned away.

The crowd dispersed.

"Wow, Deborah!" Shifra turned to her friend. "I can't believe you said that. What if he turned and hit you instead?"

Deborah looked solemnly at Shifra. "I don't know. I just couldn't stand by. I had to act before they hurt one another."

The wild haired woman studied Deborah. "You've changed Deborah."

"None of us are as we were," Deborah replied.

The ram's horn sounded from the altar in a long melancholy hum.

"Time for the Passover offering." Dan led them to the central gathering area.

A middle aged man with big ears stood before the meager crowd of Israelites holding a handful of weeds.

"These are the bitter herbs," he declared waving them. "We are to remember the bitterness of slavery to Pharaoh."

Dan huffed and said in a low voice, "I think it represents the bitterness of life now under the Canaanites and Sea Peoples."

"Shhh!" silenced Shifra.

The man handed out the deep green leaves to those in attendance. One could only take a bite or two before grimacing. The flat unleavened bread was saturated in olive oil. The leader tore three breads into pieces, drops of oil clung to his fingers as he passed the moist flat bread out.

In between bites, Deborah felt a deep sadness within her. After swallowing a big lump of bread, she commented, "I miss Yael." Her chest hurt as she mouthed the name of her lost friend.

"She may still be alive," Zack offered as he ceased chewing the bitter herbs. "Sisera took over thirty women. Some say he brought them north. I believe that she can survive."

Shifra quietly added, "May God look after them and keep Yael safe."

A single lamb was offered and smoke rose from the altar on that first night of Passover.

CHAPTER TEN

The Feast of Weeks arrived fifty days after Passover. The yellow barley sheaves grew tall and spiny. Deborah and her mother Tamar cut the stalks and pulverized them with stones to extract the grain seedlings. Tonight, they were going to the flat summit to celebrate.

"Deborah, I want to talk to you." Tamar tucked a loose strand of gray hair into her scarf.

"Yes, Ima," the young woman replied as she hit the barley with a round stone.

"You are almost seventeen. It's time for you to marry. In Beth El, there's a man called Abidan. He has a son who survived Sisera's slaughter. His name is Lappidoth of Beit Abidan, the house of Abidan. It is a good family."

Deborah's body tensed. She knew this day would come even though she dreaded it. She wanted something different but what could that be?

As she thought to herself, her mother put a hand lovingly on her shoulder. "These are difficult times, daughter. Your father would want you to marry and have a family. You may find that it's better than you think."

Deborah looked at mother. Her Ima's eyes beseeched her. Deborah didn't want to disappoint her again. Maybe, it would be better than she thought. Maybe, she could be like the other girls.

"All right, Ima," the young woman said softly. "I'll meet him."

"Blessed be God!" Her mother's face lit up. "He will be at the Festival tomorrow."

The next morning, Ima woke earlier than usual. She took the finely ground barley flour and mixed it with olive oil and water and then shaped the dough into round mounds. Setting the dough on a clay pan, she placed it over the fire. The bread baked and swelled leaving a delicious aroma in the house. She reserved a small portion for her family's breakfast and the rest she wrapped up while it was still warm in a cloth for an offering to God. Sadly, there were no spare animals to sacrifice so the bread would have to suffice.

The sun rose above the horizon and the heavens transformed from ink blue darkness to azure. The family dressed and packed up the cart. Savta rode in the cart as it was drawn by their ox. Shlomi, Deborah, and Tamar walked on foot to the hill's summit.

Deborah spotted her friends shortly after their arrival. They all looked older. Shifra's cheekbones appeared more pronounced than before. Zack was taller.

"Where's Dan?" Deborah asked scanning the people around them.

"Oh, he's getting ready," Shifra answered. "In just a few hours, he is getting married to that girl from Manasseh." She gestured to the adjacent grassy hill to the east.

The shofar sounded.

"It's time for the offering. Let's go," Deborah said.

One of the old men of the hills known as Gath stood before the people at the altar. "We give thanks to God for the rain and for the harvest before us." He lifted two crusty loaves of bread before the people. With a smile, he tossed them into the flames. Black smoke wafted up from the fire. Taking hold of a goat, he slit its throat. Blood poured out into vessels under the altar. With bloody kidneys in his hands, he proclaimed, "May God bless us and guard us. May God's face shine upon us and may God protect us." Then he dropped the kidneys into the fire.

The sun was directly overhead in the sky.

A boy about ten ran through the crowd. "A wedding! A wedding! Over on the hill, come all!"

The people walked away from the altar towards the nearby hill.

Deborah's heart leaped in pride when she saw her friend. His combed-back hair glistened with traces of olive oil. His square chin accentuated his warm brown eyes. As he walked, his chest proudly swelled. The crisp white of his outer robe was belted at his waist with an ornate sash.

"Dan! What a handsome groom you are," Deborah exclaimed as she hugged him.

Right behind him was his bride, Kara.

Her hair was the color of wheat and she had wide curvy hips and large breasts. She smiled shyly.

Deborah smiled back. "I pray for blessing on both of you."

Dan took Kara's hand. "Thank you. It's now time for the wedding."

There was a rudimentary hut erected in the clearing with open sides and branches for a roof. Dan and Kara walked into it feeling the coolness of the shade.

Lemech, one of the leaders of the people, stood before them. "In this time of hardship, we still give thanks to you, God. Thank you for the Feast of Weeks and thank you for this marriage. We consecrate Kara to Dan as his wife."

Turning to the groom he said, "Dan you must promise to always provide food and clothing to her and to give her children."

Dan replied, "I agree."

Lemech continued, "Both Dan and Kara are married in the sight of their families, community, and God. Dan, Kara is now your woman, your wife."

The crowd broke into cheers.

Dan led his new wife towards a tent that was a few cubits away. Kara's cheeks flushed as she looked up at her groom. Dan pushed aside the animal skin flap and the couple disappeared within.

In the main gathering area, musicians took out the lyre and flute and played up-beat music. Men, women, and children danced as wine was shared from skinned pouches.

Deborah was just about to take a sip when an agitated Zack appeared at her side. "That son of a donkey!" he spit out.

"What's wrong, Zack?"

"You know, I only had a few coins. Well, that bastard over there," he pointed towards a man with a clean shaven face in the distance. "He promised to sell me an iron knife for three coins. I wanted to surprise my family. Our last good blade broke months ago. It turns out that he had painted the metal to make it look like iron. It's bronze!"

Zack's face reddened. "He tricked me. As soon as I realized it, I went over and demanded my money back but he said that no one had iron in the hills. He wouldn't give me my money back. I even went to Lemech about this but he said that since I'm young, I probably misunderstood him."

Zack looked menacingly towards his deceiver, "I'm thinking of 'accidentally' impaling his donkey with a spear."

Deborah placed her hand gently on his shoulder. "You are right. He took advantage of you." She could feel the tenseness of his muscles under her fingers. "However, if Lemech won't do anything about it, you don't have any options. Zack, you know the saying as well as I do, 'He who digs a pit will fall into it.' You are best to just let it be. Just never do business with him again."

"He's donkey dung. He's worse than dung," Zack spat out.

"Yes, he is. Let's tell anyone we know that they should think twice before trading with him. In the meantime, let's have a drink?" Deborah reached for her pouch and handed it to Zack.

"Deborah!" called out Tamar. She wore a buttery yellow outer robe over a milky white tunic. Her gray and brown hair rested in waves over her shoulders. With a smile not seen in years, she said, "Deborah, I have someone I want you to meet."

Deborah's heart started to race. This was it. Part of her kept hoping that her mother would change her mind, but she knew that wasn't going to happen.

Once Deborah was within reach, Tamar excitedly ran her fingers through Deborah's thick brown hair. Deborah stood motionless. Her mother declared, "You look beautiful! Come."

Tamar led Deborah by the hand through the crowds. They stopped by four people gathered around a plate of goat meat. One of them was an older man with a long beard flecked with brown and white hairs. Another was a middle-aged woman with her hair tied back firmly. There was a girl with pig tails younger than Deborah. And there was a young man. His sandy brown curly hair framed his round face. He was neither tall nor short, neither slender nor fat. His eyes, though, were kind and he smiled at the sight of Deborah.

"Abidan," Tamar said turning to the older man. 'I want to introduce you to my daughter, Deborah. She is bright and hard working."

"I'm happy to meet you, Deborah," said the man with the long beard as he bowed his head. "This is my family. My wife Dinah. My daughter Renat and this here," he pointed to the sandy brown haired man. "This is my son Lappidoth. We called him lightning because as a boy his hair was as bright as a bolt of lightning but as you can see it has darkened as he has grown up."

Abidan grinned as he lightly slapped his son on the back. Lappidoth stood silently as a goofy smile spread out on his face.

"So, do you have anything to say to your bride-to-be?" Abidan asked.

Deborah felt panic rise within her. Was it all completely arranged? She thought she was just going to meet him. It appeared that mother had promised her to him. What could she do? Deborah stared at the ground trying not to reveal how uncertain she was.

"I…I…" Lappidoth extended a hand in her direction. 'I…I'm happy to meet you. You are lovely."

Tamar nudged her daughter. Deborah looked up. He looked so hopeful. She felt bad about her reservation. Taking his hand in hers, she half-heartedly shook it.

His mother Dinah said, "Let's give them some time to get to know one another. Why don't we taste some of the rich festival bread?"

Tamar walked away with Dinah, Abidan and Renat leaving Deborah alone with Lappidoth.

"I'm sorry," he said. "Is this a surprise for you?"

Deborah looked at his gentle eyes. "No, yes, no, I mean… It's not your fault. I knew I was going to meet you. I didn't know that our marriage was already arranged."

Lappidoth took her hand. "Look, I know I'm not the most handsome man but I'm hard working. I've already ploughed an entire hill by Beth El. I'll grow lots of food. You will never go hungry. I promise."

Deborah thought ruefully to herself that she wasn't worried about hunger. If anything, she hungered for something else, but what? She could run away from this kind man. But to where? Her mother would be very upset. And what would become of her? Yael's fate ended badly. What if this man was the best she was going to have? Maybe it was him or nothing.

"Deborah? Did I say something wrong?" His expression was puzzled.

"No, no, I'm the one who is sorry." She looked up at him with weary eyes. "I think you are a wonderful man and I'm blessed to meet you, too."

Lappidoth smiled in relief and held her hand gently. "It's a beautiful day isn't it? There's not a cloud in the sky."

Deborah looked at the blue sky above and watched a bird fly higher and higher. "It's a good day. Tell me about yourself."

The young man described how his family had been tilling the same land for twenty years. They were successful farmers and always had plenty of produce to pay the Canaanite tax and some left over for trade. He hoped to give her a good home. Deborah just nodded.

"I hope we have many children, Deborah," he said happily. "So when shall we marry?"

CHAPTER 11

"Thwack!" Another arrow hit the bulky oak tree in the middle of its trunk. Deborah had been shooting arrows for over two hours. Her shoulder ached and her arm muscles twitched and yet she kept pulling back her bow and letting the arrow find its mark. The peeling bark of the tree was starting to blur before her exhausted eyes.

"Dee," a quiet voice said behind her. Shlomi was not little anymore. He was taller than Deborah and had a few dark wisps of hair above his lip. "You are an excellent shooter. I don't think I know anyone better than you. Maybe Esau, the hunter's blood runs through your veins." He smiled jokingly.

Deborah scowled in his direction and then raised her bow again.

"I, uhh, I need your help," he said. "I have this writing from Beit Abidan, the house of Abidan. As the only male, I'm supposed to agree to this but your reading is better than mine. Will you inspect it?" Shlomi held out a rolled piece of parchment.

Deborah knew what this was. It was the marriage agreement between the two families. Her mother was illiterate and didn't know Deborah could read better than her brother. She was glad that Shlomi was showing it to her.

Putting down her bow and arrows, Deborah sat down in the bristly grass and unfurled the scroll.

On the first day of the month of Elul, we give our son Lappidoth to be your daughter's husband. We will provide him with his own field and home within our family compound in the hills of Beth El. In exchange, your family will provide bedding, clothing for both husband and wife, and one goat.

May Deborah be the mother of myriad of thousands. May the sons of Lappidoth be blessed as the sons of Joseph.

Shlomi looked over at Deborah. "I understood most of it. How many animals were they asking for?"

Rolling up the parchment carefully, Deborah said quietly, "They are only asking for one goat. They know we don't have much. Lappidoth must really want to marry me."

Shlomi looked with confusion at his older sister. "Well, aren't you pleased, Dee?"

She could see his pained expression. They were so close and it was hard to hide things from him. However, she didn't want him to worry about her. She knew that this was a good match.

With a half-smile, Deborah said, "Oh it's going to be for the good. I know it."

The hot months of summer passed quickly.

Savta was walking energetically through their pillared home. "Deborah!" She called out cheerfully. "Tomorrow is the blessed day. I'm delighted that you will wear my wedding dress. I know that it's old but it has no holes and still looks pleasing." The old woman held out a tunic, the shade of a fig leaf, with a matching outer robe.

"Yes, Savta, whatever you want," Deborah said without looking up as she slid a twig under her nails to remove dirt. After she cleaned her finger nails, she was ready to rub olive oil into her hands and feet. Tomorrow, she would be a princess of Israel and she had to smell and look beautiful.

"Deborah…I… should talk to you about something." Her grandmother glanced at her with uncertainty.

Tamar had just walked in holding some freshly cleaned linen cloths. They were still damp in her arms. The middle aged woman glanced back and forth between Savta and her daughter Deborah.

Savta stated, "I was just about to talk to our bride-to-be about her wedding night."

With an affirmative nod of her head, Tamar set down the fabric and sat next to her daughter.

Deborah's hand was glistening in oil as her mother gently touched her arm.

Tamar began, "Deborah, ah…Lappidoth will…ah…'get to know you' on your wedding night."

Deborah's face turned beet red. "We don't have to talk about this. I know. I'm not a child."

Both older women looked intently in her direction. Savta uttered, "There are things…"

Deborah stood up. "Here, I'll go and pick some ripe melons." She started towards the door.

"Deborah," Savta continued. "First of all, you can't dirty yourself. Not till after you are married. We just want you to be prepared. Your wedding night will hurt."

Deborah stood motionless before them.

Tamar added softly, "It won't always be painful. Just initially."

The young woman let out her breath. "I understand. Please let's eat dinner."

Deborah went to bed early.

As she laid on top of her bedding straw, she wondered about her future. Maybe Lappidoth would be a good husband and lover. She hadn't been touched by a male for years, not since

Noah of the Salty Sea. As she pictured the tall boy with his mischievous eyes, she felt warmth flush her cheeks. If Lappidoth kissed her like Noah did, then, maybe marriage wouldn't be so bad. To know a man in this way could be good, she thought, as she imagined his hands cupping her breasts. I hope he finds me beautiful. Deborah then fell asleep.

In the morning, Savta gave Deborah warm goat milk steeped with cardamom and honey. Deborah inhaled its fragrance deeply and took a sip. It was warm and sweet. She nibbled on some ripe melon.

After breakfast, Deborah put on Savta's pale green tunic and robe. Tamar took small sections of her hair in the front and weaved them into two braids. Leaving the back of Deborah's lush dark hair to cascade down her back, she pinned the two braids to look like a crown on her head. Taking some ground black kohl, Tamar mixed it with a few drops of water and lined her daughter's eyes till they glowed like green coals of fire. Then she smudged some dried red clay on her lips and cheeks.

Stepping back surveying her, Tamar said, "You look so radiant, Deborah."

"Thank you, Ima." Deborah gulped.

Deborah veiled her face and got into the cart. About ten relatives stood outside. They were her aunts, uncles, and cousins from the larger family compound. They all were going to her wedding. This was time to celebrate Beit David and Beit Abidan uniting in marriage and hopefully more trades as well.

It was only a few hours before they arrived at Beth El.

Wild brown grass and layers of white and burnt orange rocks dotted the hills. A shepherd passed by with five sheep baaing. On a gentle sloping hill, they approached Abidan's home and they could see a hundred people gathered there. Beth El was a popular village. It is said that Jacob dreamed of a ladder reaching up to the heavens. God promised him that this land and all of Canaan would belong to him and his descendants. At least, Beth El still belonged to the Israelites.

Deborah nervously fingered her veil as her eyes searched the crowd. Then she saw him. Lappidoth was wearing a brilliant silver robe that rippled in the breeze. His beard was neatly trimmed. When he saw her, he grinned.

Two boys came dancing towards her cart as they played flutes. Deborah stepped down and saw the guests part into two rows. Walking through them, with her mother and grandmother by her side, she approached Lappidoth.

One woman said to another, "Look at her! She is as beautiful as a queen. Her eyes look like the Great Sea."

Others murmured, "Blessings to man and woman, groom and bride."

Lappidoth took Deborah's hand in his own. His hand felt clammy in hers. Yet his gentle brown eyes looked at her happily. Now they stood hand in hand before his grandfather, the elder of Beth El. His face was heavily wrinkled and he leaned on a cane.

The music stopped and he spoke, "*Baruch Habaim*! Blessed are you who have come to the wedding between the house of David and house of Abidan. Through this union, we strengthen the people of Ephraim. May Deborah, daughter of David, and Lappidoth, son of Abidan, have a fruitful marriage. May Deborah have many sons and may Lappidoth be blessed with ample crops. We pray for health for this couple, safety from danger, and many children. Deborah, you now belong to Lappidoth. Lappidoth, we give you Deborah as wife."

Their families shouted joyfully, "Praise to God!"

The grandfather added, “It’s our custom to have a celebration meal before the couple retires to their tent. Thank you, Adonai, for the bounty of our harvest. We thank you, God, for the food we are about to eat.” The people answered, “Amen.”

Goats and lambs were slaughtered and roasted for the meal. Women walked through the celebration carrying baskets full of ripe orange persimmons, soft apricots, and dates. Deborah took a bite of apricot. Its sweetness filled her mouth. Maybe it was going to be all right. She looked at her husband who was laughing with his cousin. He’s a good man from a good family. Maybe, I will be content with him. Deborah smiled for the first time in days and drank heartily from some sweetened wine passed to her.

Hours passed by. She felt tired as guests began to leave. Lappidoth took Deborah’s hand and led her to a tent.

Once inside, they looked at one another awkwardly.

“Ah, I, ah…” Lappidoth stuttered. He removed his head covering, his hair was tousled. He looked at her both shyly and hungrily at the same time. “I… I’m glad we are married.”

Nervously, Deborah answered, “Yes, yes, me too.” This felt so odd. She didn’t know what to do. Was she supposed to take off all her clothes at once? She and Lappidoth were strangers. They exchanged a few sentences with each other and now they were husband and wife. Just go with what will follow, she told herself. After every night, there is always a morning.

Lappidoth gently ran his fingers over her face and then kissed her. His lips felt like a fish puckering. They were wet with saliva. She tried to kiss him back.

His hands wrapped around her waist bringing her closer to him. His kisses grew more intense. Deborah wanted to wipe the drool from her face but didn’t want to offend her husband.

Lappidoth then untied her robe and removed it. Clumsily, he pulled up her green tunic and tossed it on the floor. His breathing grew ragged as he urgently fondled her breasts. Deborah didn't know what she was supposed to feel. She just knew that this was her duty as his wife. Lappidoth quickly disrobed. His yerech stood erect as a small spear head, pink and pulsing. He laid her down on the lamb skin and started to penetrate her.

"Ow!" she yelped.

"I'm sorry." He pulled back uncertain. "I...I don't want to hurt you." His breath reeked of garlic.

"Just give me a moment," she said grimacing. "All right, go ahead."

"Are you sure?" he asked, hoping she meant it.

"Yes, just, just finish." She braced herself as he plunged into her. It seared. It felt like he was tearing her. Biting her lip, she endured more thrusts. Just as she was praying for it to be over, Lappidoth cried out, "Oh God!", and then he collapsed on her quivering. She could feel the weight of him on her.

Then Lappidoth kissed her cheeks, neck, and then one more time on her lips. He stared at her in awe and smiled. Then he moved onto his side, wrapped his arm around her, and fell asleep immediately.

Deborah laid there, feeling pain still in her nether regions, and her husband's warm arm around her waist.

CHAPTER 12

There were ten wooden stalls on both sides of the dirt road that ran through in the center of Beth El. On one table, lay purple pomegranates arrayed in neat rows. Another stall featured tiny firm cucumbers. The booth on the end had live pigeons in wicker cages beating their wings against the sides. Throughout the market place, one could find olives brined in salty water, pottery bowls with bold horizontal red lines, acacia leaves, and flowing tunics in shades of pale yellow, sandy brown, and white.

Deborah was wearing a long skirt that folded at her ankles and reached back to her waist. Cinching the material in place, was a leather belt that also held a pouch with a handful of bronze coins. They jingled as she walked. Deborah was one of twenty people walking through the Beth El marketplace that morning.

Deborah was looking for some olive oil. Ever since she ran out, the dry bread stuck in Lappidoth's throat and he had to drink a large cup of tea with every bite. Standing behind a table made of knotted oak wood, an old woman with no teeth smiled as she displayed jars of oil.

Surveying the young woman before her with long brown hair tied back, she inquired, "Hmmm, I don't recognize you. Are you Lappidoth's wife?"

"Yes, yes, I am." Deborah tried not to stare at the woman. Her mouth reminded her of the empty caves in the Judean hills. "This is my first time at the market. I want to make a good dinner for my husband. I'm not proficient at working the hearth." Deborah confessed.

"Oh, the love of youth," grinned the old woman. Her mouth was a gaping dark hole.

"Cooking is not so important. Just to have children." The old woman's eyes scrutinized Deborah's thin frame. "You need more fat but you should be able to bear sons."

Holding up a small clay jar, Deborah could hear the liquid swishing inside. Quietly, she said, "Yes, I hope to have many children but not immediately. I hope to get used to my life here first."

The old woman pursued her lips as she stood silently for a few seconds. "Well, I may have something of interest to you." She picked up small bowl with golden yellow gum. It sparkled in the sun. "This is sap from the Acacia tree. You put it, well," the old woman cackled, "you put it inside you and it will spare you a pregnancy until you are ready."

"Really?" Deborah eyes brightened. "That would be wonderful. How much?"

"I'll tell you what," the woman said. "You buy the largest jar of oil and I will give this to you for free. I know what it's like to have a child when you don't want one. Both you and the child will suffer."

Deborah handed over five bronze coins and placed the full jar in her basket. The acacia gum, she hid in the folds of her skirt. "Thank you. What is your name by the way?"

"I'm Para," the old women replied as she put away her payment. "I'm one of the widows of Beth El. It's good to see a nice young woman join our village."

"Para, I thank you from the bottom of my heart." Deborah nodded her head and walked away.

When Deborah arrived to her home, she put the jar by the cooking hearth. This dwelling was similar to the one she grew up in. It had stone pillars supporting a second story loft. On the first floor, goats, sheep, lambs, and an ox slept in a long rectangular room separated by a wooden fence. The smell of grass and feces greeted her. In the middle of the room, was a circle of rocks surrounding burnt remnants of wood. To the far right, behind a wooden partition, were containers full of dried barley, lentils, and wheat.

Deborah stood over a small wooden table close to the cooking hearth. She mixed ground barley with the newly purchased oil, water, and dripped brown date honey into it. After a fire was lit and the flames radiating heat, she poured the mixture into a bronze round pan and set it on the smoking wood.

As the bread cooked, Deborah took hold of deep green leeks, rinsed them in water till the dirt floated to the surface. Chopping the leeks with chunks of squash, Deborah poured olive oil over the vegetables in the clay bowl.

“Oh no, I forgot to sew Lappidoth’s robe,” she exclaimed.

Climbing the rope ladder to their loft, she seized his robe and started to repair a large rip in the material.

“Shalom!” Lappidoth cheerfully called out from the doorway. He was sweaty and dirty from the field but he grinned widely when he saw Deborah above. “What’s that smell?” He wrinkled his nose. “Is something burning?”

“Oh, no!” Deborah practically jumped down from the loft and ran to the fire. The cake was smoking. With a thick cloth in her hand, she removed the pan from the heat. The acrid smell was everywhere now.

“I forgot about the cake. I’m sorry.”

“It’s all right,” Lappidoth consoled. “I’ll eat it anyway.”

Sitting down at the wooden table, Lappidoth took a spoon in his hand and chipped away at the burnt crust. Hesitantly, he took a bite.

Swallowing the hard lump, he declared, “It’s not so bad. I’m sure it will only get better as I eat more of it.”

“Don’t! I have some bread from yesterday left. We can eat it with the squash and leeks.” Deborah offered.

The two of them ate the old bread with vegetables saturated in olive oil.

“How was your time in the field?” Deborah inquired.

Lappidoth wiped his mouth on his sleeve. “It was fairly good. I was able to trim back some of the barley sheaves and I can see that we’ll have plenty to store for winter. Also my ox was working hard. There was this rock that wouldn’t budge. We persevered though. The ground seems rich. I can see a layer of thick dark soil with insects just beneath the surface. ”

Even though Deborah looked at her husband, she stopped listening to his words. His face was round and his hair messy from work. She could smell the sweat of his body. No matter how much she tried, she couldn’t get used to it. He was now laughing as he described this worm in the soil. He was uninteresting. She knew that she had to stop thinking like that but it was hard to believe that she was married only a month now. Her life back with her mother, Savta, and Shlomi seemed so far away. She missed shooting arrows into the trees, reading with Shlomi, and even talking with her mother and grandmother.

She was trying to be a good wife to Lappidoth. He was a good man, a nice man. She went to the market every other day and tried to sew and prepare meals for him. She knew she wasn’t good at this. She just needed to try harder. All the women seemed to be happy taking care of their husbands and staying close to home. What’s wrong with me, she thought, as Lappidoth took a chunk of bread and mopped up the oil pooling under the vegetables.

After washing down his bread with watered down wine, her husband smiled playfully towards Deborah.

Oh no, is he giving me that look? She thought to herself. Tonight, she would do her duty as his wife. She kept telling herself that it would get better. Yes, it didn't hurt any more but she just didn't enjoy it. His breath was almost always sour. Even the pouch sacks of his yerech looked and smelled like unbaked dough. Its yeasty scent repulsed her.

She stopped kissing there after only once trying it. Instead, she would lay down and let him enter her and flail until he finished. Fortunately, he had not succeeded in impregnating her. Not willing to trust that her luck would last, she decided to start using the acacia gum tonight. It'll give me more time, she thought, more time to love him and my life.

The days passed.

On the full moon of the fall month of Cheshvan, Lappidoth's father came to the door out of breath.

"Son, daughter!" Abidan was nearly bald and his head had dark brown blotches from years in the sun. "One of the Canaanite soldiers came through town today."

Lappidoth's eyes widened.

"He said we have to… double our contribution." Abidan said out of breath. "King Jabin demands it. And if we don't…he will take two children from every Israelite settlement as slaves."

Deborah couldn't believe what she was hearing. "He would do this? It's too much. It's not acceptable!"

Her father-in-law just shook his head. "What choice do we have? We don't want another war. We will have to give him the grain he desires and make do with less."

Lappidoth shook his head in resignation. "At least we had a good fall harvest. We can pay him what he asks."

In the market, the next day, everyone was talking about the Canaanites. "They are donkeys! They are turds!" exclaimed one woman as she bought a woolen shawl.

Her vendor, an old man, added, "They even demand of us in the market to give them thirty percent of our wares. Thirty percent! We won't have enough for ourselves."

Deborah was wearing a tangerine orange scarf tied around her head. She looked at the people around her. She knew that they couldn't take much more of Jabin's cruelty. The day would come when they would rebel against him just like her people did to Pharaoh.

Then two women at a fruit stall broke into argument.

A mature woman with high cheekbones started to yell, "You promised me that you would bring melons to market today. We have almost nothing to sell!"

A stout woman with rolls of fat under her chin looked defiant.

"I just wasn't able to do it. I was busy. Sorry. I'm sure you'll be able to sell what you have."

Deborah looked at the two vendors. They argued around a table with a basket of dates, ten tomatoes, and two ram's skins.

The older woman wailed, "You are so lazy and unreliable. If I knew you weren't going to take care of the melons, I would've picked them myself. I wouldn't have you here if you weren't married to my brother."

"Oh, it looks like you can do business here by yourself." The double chinned woman huffed and walked away.

"Tsk!" the high cheek boned woman said noticing Deborah. "I'm sorry you had to see that."

Deborah adjusted her orange scarf. “I understand. I have always agreed with the saying, ‘Better not to vow at all than to vow and not fulfill.’ I’d be happy to purchase your rams skins. I’m not very good at treating animal hide.”

“Thank you. I know, I have always lived by my word. I wish my brother never married that lazy woman but what can I do?” The woman shrugged her shoulders. “By the way, I’m Binah.” As she smiled, her face softened.

“I’m Deborah. I may be able to help you further. My husband and I have an excess of melons. Our harvest was good. Tomorrow, I can bring you our fruits and we can split the proceeds.”

Binah looked at Deborah in surprise. “You realize that it’s not always safe, especially for a woman, to be in the market. Would your husband agree for you to do this?”

“Oh, you don’t have to worry about that. He’s out first thing in the morning every day and doesn’t get home till sunset. And I can look out for myself.”

Binah puckered her lips thoughtfully. “All right, come tomorrow and we’ll see your fruit.”

“Halleluya! See you tomorrow.” Deborah smiled as she exchanged two bronze coins for the ram skins.

The following week went by quickly. Deborah was excited to go the market every day. She took Lappidoth’s melons and sold them easily. At the end of the week, she proudly showed her husband her earnings.

“What?” he exclaimed. “You’ve been selling at the stalls?” He put down his wine cup.

“Yes, yes,” Deborah quickly spoke. “We had all those extra fruit. I was able to sell them and purchase clothing for you, fresh bread, and one pigeon.”

"I...I don't know." Lappidoth said slowly. His forehead scrunched up in confusion. "I thought you were going to learn to make bread yourself and weave clothing from the loom."

Deborah placed her hand on Lappidoth's soiled arm. "Being there is invigorating. Some days the stalls are overflowing with ripe melons and olives. You can see beautiful dyed wool tunics flapping the wind. And often there's freshly baked bread." Deborah eyes opened wide. "What I love the most, though, are the many different types of people coming through with fascinating stories of their homes and challenges. Every day is different."

Caressing his arm, she consoled, "Of course, I'm just selling a few hours in the morning. We can purchase whatever we need with the money I earn."

"But isn't it dangerous?" Lappidoth moved his arm away. "I hear sometimes Canaanites go through and take whatever they want. Sometimes they don't want just a melon but..."

"Look," Deborah said sternly. "I'll bring my bow and arrow. Have faith that I can take care of myself."

Both husband and wife continued to drink their wine in silence as Deborah thought wistfully about the market.

CHAPTER 13

The wind rustled through the almond and oak trees. It was getting darker earlier and earlier and the rains began to fall. Deborah had been married eight months by now. Her mother-in-law finally stopped asking if she was pregnant when Deborah retorted in the presence of Lappidoth, "Sarah and Hannah also didn't get pregnant for a long time. It is up to God." Of course, she clandestinely kept inserting the acacia gum.

During these winter months, the cool drops of water filled the cisterns and saturated the soil. Deborah was at the market every day now whether the sun was out, behind clouds, or even in rain. She sold side by side with Binah any extra produce Lappidoth grew. It was satisfying to contribute to their household needs but even more importantly, she felt needed here.

Today, Deborah was selling onions with Binah at their table.

"Four onions for one coin," Deborah explained to an older man leaning on his walking stick. "But for you, Shelah, five onions."

Shelah shopped at the market at least twice a week. Every time, he sweetly inquired how her husband was doing and the quality of their soil. After initially asking whether she was with child, he fortunately stopped when he saw how flustered she became. His last word was that God will see to her joy.

With relief, Deborah enjoyed learning about his family. Shelah was one of the first settlers in Beth El. As a young man, he plowed three fields in one day and he could even lift an ox with no assistance. His strength was legendary. For years, he made the land fertile and helped build up the settlement of Beth El. Other families came here when they realized the land was farmable. In time, he became the proud father of three sons and two daughters. All of them were married with children of their own. Shelah's back was so hunched over, he had to look up at anyone he was talking to. "Actually," he said with a wavering voice. "I'm not here to buy, at least, not vegetables."

Shelah leaned in close to Deborah so only she could hear.

"I, er… I fell again this morning." Shelah closed his eyes and grimaced. "I was laying on the floor. My ten year old granddaughter cried out, 'Saba!' Then she struggled to help me stand." The old man looked fiercely at Deborah. "I can't stand feeling helpless. I'm old. I've lived past my time. I don't know why God has kept me alive."

Deborah's eyes teared up. "I'm sorry. It sounds like a terrible morning."

Shelah continued, "It's not just today. It's been like this for too long. I love my children and my grandchildren but I know I'm a burden to them. I can't work anymore. The only thing I'm good for is coming to market. Even on days when I come, I walk slowly and can't carry much of anything back. I don't want to eat food that my grandchildren could be eating. I don't want to wear clothing that my daughter-in-law can put to good use." His wrinkled hand firmly grabbed Deborah's arm. "I want to die. Please sell me a root or something that will end my suffering."

Deborah took a deep breath and exhaled slowly. She looked at the old man. His thin frame bent over and his eyes looked cloudy.

"Come," she beckoned to a stool close to their stall, "sit."

Deborah sat down facing him and took his hand in her own. She felt his protruding veins on the tops of his hands and the roughness of his skin.

"You have done much over the years. God gave you strength and you put this blessing to good use. You ploughed, sowed, and harvested. You built up Beth El. I realize it is difficult to no longer have the energy and might as in the days of your youth."

The old man's eyes welled up.

"Everything we have," Deborah continued, "is on loan from God. It is given to us but only for a while and it can be taken away at any point. You have been fortunate to have your strength for so many years, however it is not the only thing that you have." Shelah looked at her confused. "I know you treasure your family and feel that you have nothing to offer but that is not true."

Deborah squeezed his hand.

"You have years of experience and wisdom. You are the living history of our village. You have ideas, advice, encouragement, and love to give not just to your family but to our people as well. God isn't ready for you just yet. Try, as hard as it is, to look at what you can do as opposed to what you can't. You are here for a reason. I know it."

Tears were streaming down the old man's face. They both sat in silence for many minutes. After a while, he stood up and said, "Thank you," as he dabbed his face with his sleeve and limped away.

Deborah came home late that day. Too late to put together a meal or do the chores. She frantically rushed to milk the goat but accidentally spilled the contents on the floor. "Curses!" she exclaimed as she seized an onion and sliced it quickly. The sun was setting and she was nowhere near ready with dinner.

"Deborah!" shouted Lappidoth as he came through the door. "I've brought two of my cousins to join us for our evening meal."

"Oh!" Deborah said as she tucked some loose strands behind her ear in a feeble attempt to appear put together. She looked at the two young men with dirt stained tunics with her husband. "Well, who would like some wine?" she offered.

"Sure!" Lappidoth said as he kissed her cheek.

One of his cousins was Ramah who was twenty five years old with a long pointy nose and the other one, known as Erech, was only fourteen with closely cropped yellow hair. They were helping in the field today with the promise of gaining ten percent of the harvest.

They sat down at the wooden oak table. Deborah went to the side room and brought out a burnished red jug full of wine. As she poured the liquid into their cups, she offered, "You may not need honey with this batch. The grapes were especially sweet before fermenting." Deborah attempted to sound cheerful as she looked gloomily at the empty cooking hearth.

"I can't believe how you scared away that bird, Lappidoth!" Ramah declared.

Lappidoth laughed as he removed his outer robe and tossed it on the floor. A musty odor emanated from his arm pits. "Yes, it swooped in," he said as he raised his right hand high and dropped it quickly to the table. "I took my staff." Lappidoth pretended to raise an imaginary rod. "And I hit it! It went flying!"
"It was so dazed," quipped the light haired youth. It flew away like it was drunk."

"Wife, bring our meal," Lappidoth shouted joyfully. "We are famished."

"Sure, sure," she responded nervously. "But first, more wine!" she poured another round. The men drank heartedly. "Just a moment." And she ran into the side room.

What am I going to do? What am I going to do? Deborah frantically looked around her. She spotted some three day old bread. Its crust was so hard, she had to use all her strength to cut it up. Taking a brown onion, she sliced it and arranged it around the bread. We need something else, she thought. Damned! I sold all the fresh fruit and vegetables today. I completely forgot about dinner. What remained?

Deborah uncorked one of the clay storage jars and took out a handful of dried, rock hard apricots. Quickly, she placed them in between the raw onion slices.

Deborah carried the platter to the hungry men around the table. "Here's the evening meal," she said sheepishly and withdrew to the side room.

Lappidoth looked at the hard brown bread and scowled. He didn't know what to do or even say to his guests.

His older cousin, Ramah, noticed Lappidoth shifting uncomfortably. He took a chunk of bread and placed it in his mouth. It was so dry and hard, his teeth crunched with every bite. After a painful swallow, he grabbed his cup of wine and quickly drained its contents. Ramah feebly smiled, "Dinner it is," and reached for an apricot.

The younger man Erech took a strand of raw onion. He didn't want to be impolite. Lappidoth sat there seething quietly. After ten minutes, both cousins got up from the table and with thanks left hurriedly.

The platter laid there full as Lappidoth stared at it. After a few moments, he stood up and called out, "Deborah, I need to speak with you."

"Yes," Deborah walked over to the table.

"This is awful! I've never felt so humiliated!" Lappidoth exploded.

“I’m sorry.” Deborah looked at the dirt floor. ” I just wasn’t able to make dinner.”

“Was it because you were at the market today?” Lappidoth bellowed.

Deborah stood silently.

“I say, no more market. You need to be a proper wife.”

Deborah looked at him in surprise and then squeezed her fist in anger.

“Proper wife? I’ve been making some money to help us. I just got home late today.”

Clenching his jaw, he spit out, “It’s not just tonight but its many nights. You don’t get home early enough to make dinner, you aren’t taking care of our clothing, nor tending the garden.” Lappidoth stood up quickly and then looked away and spoke almost in a whisper, “Oh and you haven’t given me a son yet.”

“I’m sorry,” Deborah said in a calm voice. “I need to work at the market but I’ll try harder. Tomorrow, I make you the best dinner ever.” She smiled towards him.

Lappidoth looked wearily at his wife. “I wish you didn’t go to market at all.” He then sat down in resignation and tried to chew the stale bread.

The next day, Deborah was especially eager to go back to the market. It was becoming more and more of a refuge. She liked talking to the people, knowing what was happening in their town and surrounding hills, and helping others.

Binah was a great partner. She always brought good products to sell such as tanned ram skins, fresh produce such as lemons and oranges in the cooler months, ripe black figs in the spring, and the sweetest apricots in the hot months of summer. Deborah took pride, when she could, in contributing olives, grapes, barley, and melons from Lappidoth's field. She decided that she would purchase some breads from another stall a few tables down. Tonight, she would make things right for her husband.

A woman approached Binah and Deborah. She had leathery skin even though she didn't appear old. Perhaps she spent her days in the fields, Deborah thought. She held a rolled up piece of parchment in her hand.

"Shalom," she looked nervously at the women in front of her. "My name is Luda. I was moving my sheep to greener fields the other day when two men dressed in plated armor vests approached me. I was so scared. I begged them not to harm me."

A few curious men and women surrounded her. Deborah listened intently as the woman continued.

"I was afraid to even look at their faces." The shepherdess shifted from one foot to the other. "One of them dismounted from his horse. I could see that he had a long sword tied to his belt. He thrust this paper into my hands." She held out her fist holding the parchment. "The soldier told me to pass this on. I don't know what it says or who to give it to."

Deborah looked puzzled at the outstretched paper. Noticing the onlookers, she said, "Let me take a look at it. I can read." She untied the string, unrolled the document, and read out loud.

"People of the hills

You have not paid your debt to King Jabin.

Your produce and grain are woefully inadequate.

Remedy this immediately or face the consequence."

Deborah's hand began to tremble.

Binah exclaimed, “I hope this doesn’t mean they will raid our town. I thought we were paying them. How could it not be enough?”

A loud shriek erupted in the distance. What was that? People looked at one another in confusion. More screams ripped through the air at the far end of the market. Deborah hurried to the front of her stall and scanned the main dirt road. She spotted three men on horseback wearing helmets with horns. One of them raised an iron tipped spear. Cocking his arm back, the soldier released the weapon. It shot through the air and harpooned an old man. He fell face forward into the dirt. A woman with a faded yellow scarf on her head ran to the fallen man. She collapsed on her knees and cradled his head as she sobbed. Luda immediately turned around and ran in the opposite direction. Binah stood by Deborah in shock.

A second soldier dismounted from his horse and walked over to one of the stalls that sold live pigeons. He punched the man behind the table directly in the face. He shrieked and fell backwards. Then the soldier grabbed all six pigeons and stuffed them chirping into a large sack.

The third soldier descended from his horse and went to the next stall.

“You haven’t paid King Jabin anything for many weeks,” he said menacingly.

There was only an old woman and her twelve year old granddaughter shaking before him.

The grandmother spoke, “I…I…I’m sorry. Please, please…we ran out of grain. As you can see, I’ve been selling scarfs. That’s all I have.”

The soldier sneered and then stared at the girl. “I know how you can pay us.” And he grabbed the girl and pulled her around the table as she screamed.

The old woman hollered, "Please, please leave her alone. Leave her alone. Take me instead. Take me instead!" Her body trembled violently.

The soldier pushed the twelve year old girl onto the table. The grandmother tried to pull him away but he forcefully shoved her back.

Two vendors closest to the attackers, hid deeper into their stalls, trying not to draw focus on themselves. Others such as Binah stood transfixed in shock. One woman muttered, "Dear God, please save us!"

Deborah grabbed her bow and arrow from inside their stall. She now stood in the middle of the dirt road. Her heart was beating out of her chest. She was scared. She was angry. "I'm not going to let this happen. I'm not going to let this happen." She muttered to herself. The soldier was lifting up his robe and approaching the crying girl.

Deborah narrowed her eyes in the direction of the soldier. She pulled the string of her bow back. Her hand was shaking. She never took aim at another person. Birds and squirrels, she killed without thinking, but this was different. The arrow was lined up perfectly but she couldn't release it. Instead she stood, as if hypnotized, staring without seeing. "Ehhhhh!" The girl shrieked in panic with the soldier above her.

Suddenly, the man froze, half standing, half leaning over the girl. His face immobilized. The pointy tip of an arrow protruded from his chest. He then collapsed to the ground. The grandmother grabbed the terrified girl and all looked towards the young woman standing the middle of the dirt road.

The soldier who had just speared the elderly man looked in disbelief at his fallen comrade. He then glared towards the woman fiercely clutching a bow. Her dark hair was waving over her shoulders. Her slim figure stood erect as her eyes met his.

"How dare you!" the soldier yelled. "Your debt is so great, you will never be able to repay." He started to run towards her with his spear raised. Deborah without a second thought, reached for another arrow. She aimed it with cool precision and let it fly. It hit the man directly in the torso and he fell backwards hitting the ground with a thud. Deborah didn't think or feel anything. She stood there looking at the fallen soldier, and time stood still.

A rustle broke her out of her reverie. The last combatant stared at her from the distance and looked in disbelief at his fallen comrades. He turned and ran away, quickly mounted his horse, and galloped fast out of the market at Beth El.

Binah looked at Deborah, astounded. Vendors and shoppers came out and stood around her. They didn't know what to say.

Binah spoke tentatively, "Deborah, the men, they will be back. They will be looking specifically for you."

Deborah looked at her in confusion.

A woman in a blue linen dress approached Deborah. Shaking a finger, she angrily declared, "You have made things worse for us. King Jabin will seek revenge for this. You never should've done this."

"No," the grandmother walked uneasily towards them. "She saved my granddaughter," her voice rose, "and she likely saved some of you today as well. We owe this amazing woman our gratitude." She hugged Deborah who stood still in a state of shock.

A man who sold barley cakes two stalls down spoke, "We owe thanks to Deborah however Binah is right, they will return looking for her." He glanced towards Deborah and to the crowd of people around them. "I suggest we say that she's an outsider and had just come to our community days ago. Let's say that we chased her out as a trouble maker and that she will never ever be welcome here again."

There was a hum of agreement.

"What do you mean?" Deborah said dejectedly.

"It is only what we will say," the old man consoled. "But you can't come to market anymore. It is too public. This is where they will search for you. At least for a while."

Shelah, the man whom Deborah had just spoken to yesterday, added, "Why don't you seek refuge in the palm trees between Beth El and Ramah during the day. No one goes into that area. It will give you safety for a while."

"I...I..." Deborah stuttered, "All right, I'll avoid the market from now on." She looked pleadingly at her townspeople. "I'm sorry."

The grandmother embraced her again. This time hugging her so tightly she could barely breathe.

Deborah returned home that evening. When she saw her husband, she told him she was ill and went immediately to bed.

CHAPTER 14

In the morning, Deborah chewed her figs slowly. Her teeth pierced the thin black flesh and sunk into the red seeded pulp. Its sweetness filled her mouth.

Last night, she went to bed early without revealing anything to her husband. She knew, though, it wouldn't be long before he heard what happened in the market. Lappidoth had already left for the fields. Deborah sat at the table with the last ripe fig between her fingers. She knew that she couldn't go back to the market today or perhaps ever again. What could she do?

Looking up from her breakfast, she saw the two sheep and three goats grazing on straw in the long room to the left. On the opposite side of the house were clay jars of dried barley, lentils, and apricots. Next to them were two containers of olive oil and four vessels full of fermented grape juice. Deborah glanced towards the back and sighed as she saw one sheep skin coat and two tunics in need of repair.

Deborah had to make a decision, at least for today. Would she stay home and take care of the sewing, cooking, and animals? That would be right thing to do. Walking half-heartedly to her loom and the torn clothing, she wearily sat down. Time went by so slowly. When the sun was at the midpoint in the sky, she finished with the sheep skin. It wasn't a good job. Her stitching was crooked. Deborah threw down the coat in disgust. "God! What am I supposed to do?" she cried angrily.

Gathering a pouch of water and a handful of dried apricots, she walked outside. The sun was shining brightly. Deborah walked through the courtyard, past the stony wall, and down the hill. Prickly grasses grew high in between the squat bushes. Carefully avoiding thorny weeds, Deborah walked briskly east until she left Beth El.

As her pace picked up, so too did her spirits. Gently sloping hills surrounded her as she continued her journey. In an hour, she arrived half way to Ramah. There was a little oasis with several big date palm trees. One towered higher than any one she had ever seen. Its branches sported many pointy leaves and dates grew ripe in clusters towards the top.

Surrounding her were five smaller palm trees. Their roots reached into a small basin where water naturally gathered. Deborah collapsed under the big palm tree and looked at the shallow water just several cubits from her feet. White and burnt orange limestone rocks glistened through the water. It was peaceful here and the trees obscured her presence to the world around. Deborah sat and reflected.

After two hours, Deborah walked west, back over hills, to return to her home in Beth El. As soon as she arrived in the courtyard, she was surprised to see Lappidoth's father, Abidan, standing next to her husband.

"Peace to you," she offered hesitantly to both of them.

Lappidoth just stared at her with wide eyes. His simple tunic was saturated from sweat. Her father in law, though, was cleanly dressed with a long outer robe tied at his shoulders with a bronze clasp.

"Deborah, we need to speak," Abidan stated. "Come inside."

Deborah's heart beat fast. She walked through the doorway with her head down. She knew she was in trouble.

The three of them sat on stools around the black hearth.

"Word is spreading fast about the incident at the market yesterday," Abidan began. He pulled up his outer robe so its hem wouldn't touch the dirt floor.

Deborah stared at the ground with her hands clenched in fists on her lap. Lappidoth sat as still as a boulder.

"We heard of the attack. We heard of the soldier's ruthlessness. We also heard…" the older man stroked his salt and pepper beard and then stared intently at her. "We heard about you. It was hard to believe. Did you actually kill two of the soldiers?"

Deborah didn't know what to say and was mute for many seconds.

"I was thinking," she began softly and then fell silent as she saw Lappidoth glaring at her furiously.

Deborah sharply took a breath and sat up straight.

"They were hurting, they were… killing our people." Deborah declared. "Someone had to do something. I…I just couldn't watch." She looked directly into her father in law's eyes. "I couldn't watch and do nothing. I can't..."

"You shouldn't have been there in the first place!" spitted out Lappidoth as though he just woke up from a trance. "You are my wife. You are supposed to be here at home."

The older man looked from husband to wife and then he slowly stood up. "I believe you two can discuss this." He glanced once more towards Deborah, shook his head in disapproval, and left. A cold silence filled the room.

"Lappidoth, you must understand," Deborah murmured.

"Oh, I understand." He ran his dirty hands shakily through his chestnut hair. "You prefer the busyness of the stalls, the action…" His eyes reddened, "rather than building a home with me."

"I don't think it's as simple as that," Deborah said meekly.

Lappidoth leaned towards her. "Well, you have put yourself and this household in danger. You realize that don't you?" He shook his head and looked away from her. "Of course, our town people will lie and say they don't know who you are. You are a stranger who passed through town only a week ago and left immediately after the attacks. They'll say that you fled to the coast. They will lie to protect you."

He clenched his jaw. "I…I don't even know why they care for you so much. What do you even do in the market? I thought you only sold some fruit and vegetables, but father says that you are the counsel of the people." His bloodshot eyes met hers. "Who are you Deborah? I don't know who you are."

Deborah squirmed on her stool. "I'm sorry, Lappidoth. I didn't mean to upset you. I really didn't."

Lappidoth grimaced. "I don't understand. Why won't you stay at home?"

"I don't know." Deborah reached out to touch his arm. "I'm sorry. I'm sorry. I'll try harder."

"It's not the way it should be." Lappidoth got up suddenly. "It's not..." He angrily ascended the rope ladder to the sleeping loft above.

Deborah tossed on her straw mattress throughout the night that never seemed to end. As light started to peak through the rafters, she studied the knotty wood ceiling above her. The oak wood was discolored and protruded in odd places. She knew that she was odd and peculiar as well. Her marriage was a mess and she had unwittingly provoked conflict with the Canaanites. Bits of straw poked her back through the blanket.

She shifted uncomfortably. What should she do? She could pretend that it all never happened. She could stay at home, become a good wife, and bear sons for Lappidoth. She could learn to love him and cook and sew. Anything was possible. She nodded to herself. Just forget it happened. She just needed to forget everything.

"Deborah!" called out her husband below.

She sat up and could see down below an old woman and a girl. Deborah scrambled to put on a beige tunic and climbed down the ladder.

"Here," said the old woman as she extended a woven basket towards Deborah. "This is for you. Thank you for saving my little girl." She looked lovingly at her granddaughter.

Lappidoth stood in surprise as Deborah accepted the gift. Deborah could smell warm honey bread. There were two baked loaves on top. Nestled between them was a purple cloth. Setting the basket down, Deborah reach into it and unfolded the material. She gasped. Inside was a gold cord fastened to a small green luminous rock. "It's beautiful!" Deborah exclaimed.

The old woman took it from her hands and put it around Deborah's neck. "I've had this for many years. My grandmother brought it from Egypt and saved it. I want you to have it. Deborah, you saved something more precious to me than jewels. Keep it. Wear it. Know that we are grateful."

Lappidoth silently watched the exchange with his mouth hung open. After the guests left. Deborah stood before the basket of sweet breads wearing the little jeweled necklace.

"What was that?" Lappidoth dumbly uttered.

Before Deborah could respond, there was another knock at the door.

Lappidoth opened the wooden door in a daze.

A scrawny, young man stood there, nervously looking over his shoulder.

"May I enter?" he whispered.

He wasn't even wearing sandals and his hair was curly and unruly.

"I'm sorry to disturb you. I am Oded," he said to Lappidoth as he dashed into the house.

As soon as Oded saw Deborah he smiled.

"I…I was hoping," he stepped closer to Deborah. She could smell the pungent odor of his body. "That you could teach me how to work the bow and arrow. You are a skilled shooter. I was hoping with just a little advice and I…"

"What is all of this?" Lappidoth shrieked as he stepped in between the man and his wife. His face was as red as pomegranate. "Is our home to be your market, Deborah?"

Deborah placed her hand on his shoulders calmly. "I am sorry, Lappidoth."

Stepping to the side of her irate husband, she said, "My husband is right. Why don't you meet me later when the sun is at the midpoint in the sky at the big palm tree between Beth El and Ramah? I can help you there." Even as the words passed her lips, she couldn't believe she said that and her cheeks reddened. Oh curses! She was going to be the good wife and now she just offered to teach someone how to shoot an arrow.

"Thank you, Deborah! Thank you!" the young man excitedly replied as he exited.

Lappidoth looked at her and muttered, "I never wanted this."

He quickly left for the fields.

When Deborah arrived at the palm tree, she saw Oded already there. With a quick word of greeting, she immediately got to work showing the skinny young man how to bend the wooden bow and affix the leather string. As she demonstrated her technique, she remembered how patient her father was with her. Her Aba showed her how to craft arrows from the straightest sticks or reeds and to affix bird feathers.

With an image of her loving father in her mind, Deborah demonstrated the proper stance by positioning her left shoulder towards the target and then grabbing the bow in her left hand. She rested the arrow on the wooden notch and pulled back the string with three fingers. With her right elbow raised, her eyes locked on her target, she released the arrow. Oded looked in awe as the arrow hit the tree ahead directly in the middle of its trunk.

"In a few weeks, you will be able to easily reach your target," Deborah told him, as he pulled back the bow.

His face was glistening in sweat and his black curls stuck to his forehead as his eyes focused in determination. "I want to be ready," Oded said as he pulled the string back. "I want to be ready the next time Sisera or King Jabin sends men to terrorize our people." He released the string and the arrow soared pass the palm tree.

After two hours of instruction, Oded left and Deborah sat under her tree. Poor Lapiddoth! she thought. He was never going to be happy with her. It was hard to imagine him sending her away with a bill of divorce no matter how much she irritated him. It just wasn't commonly done. But how could they live? Maybe, maybe, there could be a compromise? Maybe there was a way to give to Lappidoth the life he wanted while she could live her own.

That night, Deborah arrived home before the sun set. She started a pot of boiling water with onions, parsnips, and dried lentils. After an hour of simmering, she tossed in a couple of handfuls of fennel leaves and then sprinkled in sea salt. After one more hour, she took one of the loaves of sweet bread and sliced it thickly.

It was dark outside now, the only light came from the fire and a few bowls of oil with thick wicks in them.

The door opened. A very tired Lappidoth entered.

He was filthy from head to foot and his eyes were half closed from exhaustion. However, as he stepped into the house, he inhaled deeply and faintly smiled.

"Deborah? Did you cook dinner?" he asked surprised.

"Yes, yes, sit down." She beckoned him to the table.

She handed him a bowl of water to rinse his hands. Clouds of dirt rose to the surface.

"Here," she passed him a cup of sweetened wine as he gazed with appreciation at the table. He reached for a slice of sweet bread as Deborah filled his bowl with the lentil and vegetable stew. Lappidoth gulped down his meal. Deborah refilled his soup bowl twice. As her husband ate, Deborah sat silently sipping her wine and nibbling a small crust of bread.

Lappidoth belched. "This is a good evening meal."

"We have something to discuss, Lappidoth. I've been thinking." She put down her bread. "We can't help who we are and what we want. Fate though brought us together. We are married even though we are so very different."

Lappidoth gazed at her intently.

Deborah paused for a moment. "You can't change any more than I can. I've been thinking about Sarah, our matriarch."

"What does Sarah have to do with this?" inquired Lappidoth

"Well," Deborah said tentatively. "She and Abraham had a problem. They were without child and were unhappy. We are unhappy but perhaps Sarah's solution would work for us?"

"Sarah's solution?" Lappidoth was really confused.

"I know this is unusual but not really when you think of Sarah and Abraham. Sarah gave Abraham her handmaid Hagar to father a child."

Lappidoth broke out in laughter. "What are you talking about? Did you drink too much wine? You don't have a handmaid, unless you are hiding her in one of the storage jars." He continued to chuckle.

Deborah said with a straight face, "I would like to suggest that you take a second wife."

Lappidoth stopped laughing and looked in shock at her. "You are serious? All right, you know we don't have much to offer another wife. I'm not a wealthy man and especially during this time of subjugation, we have even less to offer."

Deborah shook her head. "I was thinking of a woman who would feel lucky to live in our house, cook, and take care of your needs. In the fields, we sometimes see a young woman picking the fruit at the corners of your field. Have you noticed her? She seems to have a pleasing face."

Lappidoth sat in great confusion. He couldn't believe what he was hearing. "You mean Mara? Mara is an orphan. Her parents were killed in Sisera's raid and she is a beggar."

"Yes, yes, I know," said Deborah. "She has nothing. No dowry or anything to offer a household and yet, look at her, Lappidoth. She strikes me as someone who will work hard and be grateful."

"I don't know what to think," Lappidoth uttered.

"I understand. I have an idea. Why don't I invite her to dinner and you can get a closer look at her."

Lappidoth drained his cup of wine and reached for the jug to pour another glass. "I never would've thought that you of all people would suggest such an arrangement, Deborah."

"I just want you to be satisfied, Lappidoth. Let's see what tomorrow will bring."

CHAPTER 15

The next morning, Deborah woke up before the sun rose. Today was the fifteenth day of Shevat, the day the trees are judged by God. If there is enough rain, then the trees' roots will soak up the water and in a month or two they will put forth leaves and buds. It was chilly this morning. Deborah wrapped herself in a sheep skin coat that draped over her shoulders and walked the perimeter of Lappidoth's fields. She saw one of the workers. He was stretching and getting ready for the day's work.

"Excuse me," Deborah said as she approached him. "Do you know the orphan Mara?" she inquired.

The worker's forehead was deeply lined in wrinkles. "You mean the woman who regularly picks at the corners of our fields?" He arched his back. "Yes, I do."

"Do you know where she slumbers? I need to find her."

"I am not certain," he said thoughtfully as he straightened up. "She always comes from that direction." He said pointing at the hills to their north.

"Yes, thank you." Deborah began to walk to the north.

As she approached the grassy hills, she noticed a small cave opening. She quietly approached it. Anything could be in the cave. It could be a person. It could be a lion. Deborah walked to the entrance and peered in. It was dark and hard to see anything. Deborah took a step inside and her eyes began to adjust. She made out the figure of a small woman sleeping in the corner on top of straw.

"Mara," Deborah said softly.

The girl stirred. She turned over and looked fearfully at Deborah. Suddenly standing up, she cried out, "I don't do anything. I vow to God above. I t…t…take from the corners of the fields, nothing else, just, just as the law teaches." Her lip quivered. "I don't take anything else." Her tunic hung like a large sack on her petite frame. Mara's eyes were wide in fear.

"No, no, I know you haven't done anything wrong." Deborah consoled the girl. "I'm here for a different reason. I know this sounds odd but I wanted to invite you to our home today. You can bathe and I would be delighted to offer you a change of clothes." Deborah took a step towards the frightened woman. "I was hoping you could join us for dinner."

"Why?" Mara gripped her tunic in bunches. "Why w…would you want me?"

"I just want to spend time with you. That's all. Just today. Please say yes," Deborah implored.

The girl stared at Deborah. Seconds ticked by.

Mara grabbed a torn lamb skin coat and threw it around her shoulders. Then she said, "I'll come."

Mara and Deborah walked back to Deborah's pillared home on the hill. Now that Deborah was close to her, she got a full whiff of her foul aroma. Mara smelled bad like a rotting melon. First, I'll give her some breakfast and then a bath, Deborah thought to herself. As Deborah passed through the fields, there were puzzled stares by workers and members of her husband's family. She disregarded them and led Mara inside her home.

"Here, have some sweet bread with me," Deborah implored. "I haven't had breakfast yet either." She handed the orphan girl some tea and bread and sat with her at the table. At first, Mara tentatively took a little bite of bread but then quickly stuffed the moist bread into her mouth and swallowed hard. With just two gulps, the tea cup was empty.

After she finished eating, Deborah brought out a wide basin of water. "It's important for you to clean yourself. Let me show you how." Deborah took some cloth and dipped it into the liquid and then wiped her own face with it. Mara watched her and then cautiously did the same. As the orphan woman wiped down one side of her face, the remaining side was clearly three shades darker. Once the cloth was immersed in water, brown grime colored it. She was much dirtier than Deborah had realized.

"Keep scrubbing." Deborah instructed. "After your face, you must do the rest of your body. Remove your tunic."

Mara with her face still moist shook her head no at Deborah. Her body was now straight as a pillar.

"It's all right," Deborah consoled. "Keep your tunic on, just try to clean your arms."

Wearily, Mara took the wet cloth and ran it up and down her thin arms. Streaks of skin peeked out from the dirt.

Deborah brought over another jar of water and piece of cloth. Handing them to Mara, she said, "Good. Now see if you can get your legs and feet."

As Mara cleaned her legs, Deborah went to the back room and took out a faded blue cloth with an aperture for a woman's head. "I thought you could wear this if you want." She held it out in front of her. "You can keep it as well."

Mara smiled for a second and then her smiled disappeared. Taking a step back from Deborah, she suspiciously said, "Are you trying to trick me? What do you want?"

Deborah set the tunic down on the table. "You are right to be skeptical, Mara, so I'll be honest with you. The truth is I'm looking for help for my husband. I'm not able to take care of him and the home." Deborah felt embarrassed at this confession but there was no going back now. "I want to see if you can please him. If so, you can live with us."

Mara stood frozen in place with her eyes fixed on Deborah.

Taking a step towards the orphan woman, Deborah pleaded, "You will have shelter over your head, clothes for your body, and plenty of food."

Mara didn't move and her face was expressionless.

Seconds felt like minutes until Mara erupted, "But I'm an orphan. No one wants me. I'm cursed by God."

"I know," Deborah said. "I know what you are but I don't think you are cursed." Deborah reached for her hand. "Rather, I...I… think you may be a blessing. You remember the story of Hagar." Deborah spoke quickly. "She was only Sarah's servant but she ended up being loved by father Abraham, and the mother of a great people."

Mara's face relaxed as she allowed Deborah to hold her hand.

"Here, let me help clean you up. I have a sense that you are pretty."

Mara allowed Deborah to lift up her tunic. She was thin but her breasts were firm and her nipples stood out like almonds. Deborah took the rag and ran it between the young woman's legs. A pungent odor greeted her nose but Deborah continued to clean Mara. After a few passes, Deborah went through two pots of water. Mara gave in to the cleaning. Then Deborah took lavender scented olive oil and rubbed Mara's body with it.

"You smell better already." Deborah said as she inhaled deeply.

She sat the young woman in a chair and leaned her head backward into another pot of water. Deborah scrubbed her scalp. As she did this, she thought of her mother. She remembered the loving care with which Tamar washed her hair when she was little. Deborah felt lucky that she had a family who cared for her. Tenderly, she squeezed the water from Mara's hair and then carefully brushed it out.

The sun was past noon by now. Deborah reached for some crimson blush and black kohl eye liner and carefully applied the colors to Mara's face. There! She was unrecognizable. Mara had lush black hair. Her eyes were honey brown and her lips were full. While no one would sing of her beauty, she was agreeable to look at. Deborah thought she could please a man, hopefully, Lappidoth.

The two women set out to prepare the evening meal. Deborah showed Mara how to knead bread. After barley flour was mixed with water, Deborah said excitedly, "We should have a celebration dinner tonight."

Motioning for Mara to join her, Deborah grabbed hold of one of their pigeons and went outside. It chirped loudly. With a quick twist of her hand, she severed its spirit from its body. The bird laid limp in her hand. With a rusty bronze knife, she cut off its head and set it aside. The head could be used for soup. Its feather could provide softness to pillows, its bones for stock, and its innards could be roasted and eaten.

Deborah cut through the muscle and set aside the innards to be rinsed and salted. Mara carefully removed the feathers and wrapped them in a cloth.

The afternoon went by quickly.

Lappidoth came through the door weary from his day but his eyes lit up when he saw the feast on the table. There was roasted pigeon meat, fresh barley bread, cucumbers steeped in vinegar, and fresh purple figs. He blinked his eyes twice in disbelief. "Deborah?" was all he could say. He was smiling at Deborah and then he noticed a strange young woman.

"Is this one of the town's people?" he inquired pointing at Mara.

Deborah beamed. "I knew you wouldn't recognize her."

Lappidoth puzzled over the young woman in the light blue tunic before him. The black liner showed off her honey brown eyes and her hair cascaded over her shoulders.

"No! Lappidoth exclaimed. "No, this can't be! Are you…are you Mara?"

The orphan girl looked down sheepishly and said, "Yes, my lord."

"I can't believe it. You…you look pleasing."

"Thank you master," Mara said while still looking at the ground.

The three of them sat down for dinner. Mara stood up whenever Lappidoth required more wine and eagerly ran to the side room to fetch more for him. In between bites, Lappidoth met Deborah's eyes and smiled. When the meal was finished, the three of them sat at the table together.

"So what do we do now?" Deborah asked.

Lappidoth looked at Mara who shyly smiled in his direction.

"Well, this is foreign to me," Lappidoth said as he shifted uncomfortably in his chair. "Mara, do you know why Deborah invited you here?"

Mara looked down at the table. "I, uhh, she, uhh…"

Deborah interrupted. "I told her we needed her help. That I'm looking for someone to take care of all my husband's needs." Mara flushed a deep rose and kept staring at the table.

Lappidoth looked from Mara to Deborah and spoke slowly. "I've been thinking about this today. I'm willing to try it but I need to tell you something." Turning towards the orphan woman, "Mara, I can't marry you. I think you know that. My family will not accept you."

Mara nodded as she stared at the table. Lappidoth continued, "However, you can be here as a helper of sorts, more than a helper. I…I mean you can be Deborah's maid." Lappidoth licked his lips. "Do you want this?"

Mara now looked up and met Lappidoth's gaze. With a nod, she said, "Yes, I want to help."

Lappidoth smiled shyly.

Days went by as the women worked together in the household. Deborah taught Mara how to tend to the fire, clean her body, and prepare a meal.

Within weeks, Lappidoth and Mara were conversing. She seemed genuinely interested in his work tilling the soil. Lappidoth warmly smiled as she laughed for the first time.

And then one night, he asked her to join him for sleep.

On the other side of the loft, Deborah saw Mara climbed onto the straw bed with her husband. She thought she should've felt jealous but it was only relief. It didn't take long before Deborah heard Lappidoth moaning. The wooden rafters began to shake. She had no idea if this was Mara's first time or not. If it was, there was no sign of it. Deborah fell asleep to the gentle rocking.

In the morning, Lappidoth was beaming. Mara had put up some hot water and asked Deborah how to prepare tea. After setting up a breakfast of cut up melon, bread, and tea, they all sat down together.

As Lappidoth sipped his hot liquid, Deborah said, "I'll be going to the palm tree today."

Lappidoth said cheerfully, "See you at nightfall."

CHAPTER 16

The sun warmed the cool morning air as it rose higher in the sky. Deborah worked with three young men this morning. One youth had wind swept hair that stuck up in the back as if he had just woken up. His name was Yonah. He had two other friends, Shmuel and Ner, who also wanted to learn how to shoot. Shmuel was short with full cheeks while Ner was lanky. Even though they didn't admit it, they knew they didn't have the strength to wield a heavy sword. They wanted to learn archery. The bow and arrow is ideal in many ways. Like the sling, it could reach one's opponent from a distance and speed was more important than strength.

However, Deborah could see that both Shmuel and Ner were uncoordinated. Deborah slowly broke down the technique and put Yonah to oversee their practice. After they shot all their arrows, she sent them to retrieve them. After an hour, Deborah and her trainees collected pliable wooden branches to make additional bows.

As they searched the nearby hills, a twenty something year old man arrived at the oasis. He had a dark black beard that was shaved close to his face. His gray outer robe was fastened at the shoulder in a circular bronze clasp and across his back was a long wooden staff with a metal blade attached to it.

"Shalom Deborah!" he greeted.

"Peace unto you. Do I know you?" She studied his face.

"I am Yarom. I am from Manasseh. I hear that you are training our people to rise up against King Jabin. I offer my services to you."

Deborah was taken aback. "While I'm teaching a few people how to use a bow and arrow, I'm not starting a revolt."

"No, not yet," he said with a steady gaze. "But I am proficient with a battle ax. I could help train more men. Maybe in time, we may be able to offer resistance to King Jabin and his blood thirsty Sea People."

This was more than Deborah anticipated. "I am not sure this is the wise course," she hedged. "I don't want to see more bloodshed. Our people have suffered so much already."

"Our people have indeed suffered." Yarom's lip curled upward revealing his teeth. "They have been murdered, raped, and kidnapped."

Deborah stood motionless studying the man before her. He looked like he knew how to fight.

"Certainly," Deborah conceded. "If men come wanting to be trained, I'll send them to you. Let's be deliberate about when and how to fight back. We want to make sure if we fight, that we win." Deborah was really trying to stall him. She didn't want war. She didn't want her people to suffer more than they already have. As bad as things were, they could always be worse.

Through the palm trees, Deborah saw an older woman approaching. Her silver hair reached all the way down her back.

"Deborah," she looked at her and then at Yoram. "I want to talk with you privately."

Yoram nodded as he walked away. The woman sat down next to Deborah.

"I am Aviva." She looked ahead. "I heard from my friend Shelah that you are knowledgeable. I, ah, I…" She became quiet.

Deborah patiently waited. She learned some time ago that there is a time for words and a time for silence. People just needed time to think before they could talk.

A flock of white birds flew overhead. There must have been fifty of them flying in formation towards the west. They all had a common purpose and would undoubtedly get to the sea by evening.

"I don't know how to say this." Aviva began. "Ever since my husband died..." She became silent as she struggled to suppress her sorrow.

She erupted, "I can't bear being alone. I mean, I have my son and grandchildren but I am very lonely." Aviva hid her face in her veined hands.

"Loss is always painful," Deborah began. "But losing a partner in particular poses one of the greatest challenges. If we are blessed with love and companionship, then death brings solitude." Aviva still sat with her hands covering her face. "We no longer have our husband to share our bed, talk to in the morning, decide issues of family and even share meals."

Aviva's shoulders began to quiver. Deborah placed her hand on her shoulder.

She continued, "We mistakenly think that how we feel today is how we will always feel, but that is not true. Who can predict what God has in store for us?"

Aviva dropped her hands and looked at Deborah.

"Perhaps, God will give you love again. Maybe God has a great purpose for you that will fill the void left by your husband. Sometimes even in darkness, we must have faith that light is still possible. Try to live, Aviva."

Her fingers griped her shoulder. "If not for yourself, live for your family. Try to keep busy. Go to the market. Help others when you can. Try not to isolate yourself. Have faith that the pain you feel today will lessen in time."

The old woman took a deep breath.

"I will try," she said as she attempted to stand.

Deborah took her hand and helped her up.

"Thank you, Deborah. Thank you for listening."

Deborah arrived home before the sun had set. To her surprise, she saw Lappidoth and her father-in-law Abidan waiting outside for her. Was she in trouble again? She thought everything was arranged. She walked through the stone fence. Mara was peeking out of the window of her pillared house. Her heart began to beat faster.

"Deborah," called out her father-in-law.

Lappidoth stood by his side. His face looked at her with concern.

"We just got a message from your family in the hills." Abidan began. "Your grandmother, she passed last night in her sleep."

Deborah looked at Abidan and then at Lappidoth. What do they mean my grandmother? I just saw her a couple of months ago at the Sukkot festival. She looked as vibrant as ever. How could this be?

Deborah searched the faces of Abidan and Lappidoth hoping for a smile to indicate that this was a joke. Their faces however were somber and serious.

"Savta is dead?" Deborah said weakly.

Lappidoth reached for her hand. "I'm sorry, Deborah. I know how much you cared for her. We can give you a donkey and you can leave at first light tomorrow."

"Yes, yes," Deborah replied. The sky had an orange glow as the sun began to set beyond the horizon.

At dinner that night, Mara prepared some porridge. Lappidoth's sister had come by earlier and taught her how to make it. At first, his family didn't know how to act around Mara but once they realized how happy Lappidoth was, they tried to help her in any way possible.

Mara poured Deborah and Lappidoth some wine as they sat at the table.

"My mistress," Mara spoke.

"You can call me Deborah. It's all right Mara."

Mara came closer to Deborah still holding the wine jug.

"Would you like me to travel with you tomorrow?"

Deborah shook her head. "No, stay with Lappidoth. This is where you belong. I'll be fine." Deborah's stomach was tied in knots. She could only swallow one spoonful of porridge.

Draining her wine cup with one gulp, she said, "I'm going to sleep. I'm exhausted." Deborah then climbed the rope ladder to the loft above.

She could hear Lappidoth and Mara quietly talk as she laid on her straw bed. Oh Savta, I wish I could see you one more time. Tears filled her eyes as she pressed her hand over her heart. I wish I could talk with you, Savta. Turning on her side, Deborah struggled to fall asleep.

Morning came and Deborah labored to open her eyes. With a heavy sigh, she descended the ladder. Mara had already filled a water skin made from a goat's bladder to the brim and wrapped slices of bread and salty cheese in a cloth. Deborah grabbed the provisions and reluctantly walked out the door.

Deborah walked numbly for hours leading her donkey by a rope. High weeds scratched her legs. The sun seared her face. Little bugs buzzed by. With just a few sips of tepid water, she walked on and on. The sun began to descend on the horizon and Deborah found a gully surrounded by long grasses. The donkey greedily chewed the greens and she sat down in the dirt. Her body felt tired. With a few nibbles of salty cheese, Deborah laid down looking at the darkening sky above her.

Oh, Savta! She could feel the old woman's wrinkled hands running through her hair. She could hear her robust laugh and see the kind eyes. She missed her so much. The last time she was home was one year ago. So much happened since then. Deborah's lip quivered as she heard the howl of wild dog in the distance.

The next morning, Deborah woke up ravenous. She ate almost all her bread and cheese. Deciding she needed to pick up her pace, she rode on the donkey for the rest of the day. She traversed east through grassy hills, thick forests of oak trees, and over rocky terrain. One more night she slept under the stars and then the next day she could see the familiar hill in the distance.

Its slope was verdant from the winter rains however few vegetables were growing from the tiered ridge. The plants looked wild and unkempt. Some of the stones had shifted and the terraces appeared slanted. Beit David, the family compound, had certainly seen better days. Deborah ascended the hill and stood by the stone fence. The rough boulders jutted from the wall and just over it she could see her home.

Walking the same path, she could see the limestone pillars supporting the second floor. The exterior walls were caked in dried clay. Deborah didn't want to go inside. Her stomach hurt as she stared at the house.

Then the wooden door creaked open revealing an older woman with black and gray hair spilling out haphazardly over her shoulders. The apron around her waist was stained with mud, as were her hands.

"Ima!" Deborah cried. The last time she saw her mother disheveled like this was at Sisera's raid years ago.

Tamar opened her arms and Deborah hugged her. They both tightly held one another for many minutes.

"How did it happened?" Deborah finally asked.

Tamar looked at the ground sadly. "Savta said she was having pains in her chest and asked to lay down. In the morning, she didn't get up. God took her soul as she slept." Tamar's eyes glistened.

"Have you buried her already?" Deborah asked. She already knew the answer to this question. Deborah remembered how it was only hours after her dear Aba passed that they placed him in the ancestor cave. It was always considered disrespectful of the dead to allow their body to decompose. This is why they always buried within hours of passing.

"I want to go visit the cave," Deborah said before Tamar could even answer the first question.

Tamar led Deborah out of the house. They walked down the hill to the west and over rocks. In the next hill, there was a cave carved out. Rocks were piled at the entrance. Deborah moved two of the larger ones hurriedly and went inside.

A putrid odor filled her nose. She knew the smell of death. Deborah's eyes adjusted to the dimness and then saw her grandmother's body lying on stony platform. "Oh Savta," Deborah fell to her knees before her grandmother. "Sleep…sleep well with our ancestors, my grandmother."

Deborah stood up heavily and to her left saw the skeletal remains of her father on another platform just a few cubits away. With her chest constricting, she whispered, "Goodbye Aba, once again."

How long Deborah stood there, she didn't know.

When she left the cave, fresh air filled her nose. Taking a deep breath, Deborah moved the boulders back into place, and rejoined her mother.

Their walk back home was quiet.

When they arrived to the house, night was starting to fall.

"Ima, where is Shlomi?" Deborah asked feeling the emptiness of the house.

The two women sat down at the wooden table.

"He left this morning to spend time with his future in-laws."

"His in laws?" Deborah turned to face her mother.

"Yes, Shlomi will be getting married during the Feast of Unleavened bread in two months."

Shlomi getting married? Deborah knew he was old enough. It was hard to imagine him as a husband and a father though. Wasn't it just yesterday they were chasing each other down the hills and peering into the cistern?

"Who is he marrying?"

Tamar smiled. There were traces of grime on her face. "Yaakova, the girl from Micah's family, in northern Ephraim."

Deborah thought for a moment. Yaakova? Wasn't that the slender girl who rarely said anything? Well, she did seem sweet. Deborah furrowed her brow. I guess she was pretty.

"Will they be living here, Ima?"

"Yes, as a wedding gift, I'm giving them this home within a year. I'm going to live with your aunt Milcah just two houses away. I will be close enough to be a savta when they need one." Tamar's sadness dissipated for a moment as she smiled.

Deborah took her hand into her own. "Ima, let's wash up and I'll help you with dinner,"

The young woman simmered a pot of water with barley, chunks of garlic, and dandelion leaves. Tamar sprinkled in oregano leaves and salt before ladling the soup into bowls.

Deborah took a sip. The warm savory liquid was comforting.

"Are you going to be all right, Ima?" Deborah asked with concern.

"In time, I will adjust." Tamar put down her spoon. "It gives me comfort to know that you are married and that Shlomi will be shortly. When my time arrives to go to Sheol, I will go in peace."

Taking her mother's hand. Deborah said, "I pray not for a long time, Ima. I love you."

"I love you too, Devash, I mean Deborah." Tamar said quietly.

CHAPTER 17

The last of the winter months went by quickly. The rains came and saturated the soil. Lappidoth was enthusiastic about the crops this year. He woke up before the sun breached the horizon. As he climbed down the rope ladder, he saw that Mara had already boiled water for his mint tea. With a smile, she quickly sliced the coarse barley bread, spread a thick layer of goat cheese on it, and then added a few salty bright green olives on his plate. Lappidoth yawned happily and sat down at the wooden table. Mara's hair was tied back with a crimson string.

"Thank you, Mara," Lappidoth looked up at her gratefully as he took a bite of the chewy bread.

Deborah descended the ladder. "Good morning of light, Deborah." Mara looked towards her. "May I bring you some bread and tea?"

"That would be nice." Deborah was only wearing her night tunic and sat down opposite her husband.

Lappidoth's face was rounder and his chin flowed seamlessly into his neck. His cheeks were ruddy and his hair framed his boyish face.

"So how is our settlement of Beth El?" Lappidoth glanced towards Deborah as he sipped his tea.

"I'll find out more today but even though our people anticipate good crops, they are worried about King Jabin and his ever increasing tolls." Deborah took a slice of bread and sunk her teeth into it. The salty cheese was creamy and the bread was thick with seeds. After swallowing, she continued, "We still get reports of more raids by the Canaanites. I believe things are getting worse."

Mara looked from Lappidoth to Deborah and back again. "Would either of you like any more tea?"

Mara had been living with Deborah and Lappidoth for three months. She now knew how to keep a home. Deborah had taught her some basics such as sewing cloths and making a simple gruel of grain, water, salt, and oil but it was Lappidoth's sister who really broke down the tasks and worked with her.

Mara was now confident in her ability to cook stews and even bake bread. She could fix any clothing in need of repair and knew how to wash clothes. Furthermore, Mara looked healthy. It took time for her to put on weight initially but now her hips had rounder, softer curves. She smiled much of the time. She really seemed to take a liking to Lappidoth. Looking after him gave her purpose and she began to make herself truly at home.

Deborah was happy for both of them and grateful that Lappidoth no longer pressured her to be a wife of the home. They were still married but no longer shared a bed. It felt like they were friends. This was a nice development.

Thank God for Mara, Deborah thought to herself as she finished her tea.

Lappidoth, swallowing the last olive, said, "I hope there's better news today, Deborah."

"Me too," she replied, "and I hope the earth gives way easily to your plow."

Two weeks went by and it was time to celebrate the Feast of Unleavened bread. Mara learned how to bake a flat bread. The trick was baking it quickly after adding water and punching little holes in the dough. A delicious earthy aroma filled the home. As soon as it cooled, Lappidoth attached a lamb to the back of the cart and placed bundles of bitter greens into the wooden structure. Mara, Deborah, and Lappidoth joined his extended family as they caravanned to the gathering site in the hills.

During the many hours of travel, Deborah found herself thinking about the past. It was hard to believe that she was twenty four. Ten years ago, that terrible Sukkot raid devastated her family and changed life for the Israelites in the hill country. Compounding her loss, she thought of her Savta's kind smile. Wincing, Deborah tried to suppress the grief. This was no time for sadness, she thought. In just a few days, her brother would marry. This was a blessing for him and her family. Ruefully, Deborah pondered, everything changes. You can't go back. The past is in the past.

After four hours of walking through the green hills lush with new growth, they arrived at the plateau. A hundred Israelites were already there. Deborah spotted her mother. Tamar was wearing a cream colored robe and her gray and brown hair was tightly pulled back into single braid. Deborah could see the deep wrinkles lining her face.

"Ima! Shalom!" Deborah called out.

Tamar hugged her daughter. Behind her was a tall man with dark black hair.

"Shlomi?" Deborah looked at her brother. "You look like a man."

He hugged Deborah and lifted her feet off the ground. "Yes and tomorrow, I'll be a husband."

As he set her back on the earth, she said gasping, "You will be a superb husband and father. Blessing for you and Yaakova, and of course for Ima as well."

"Deborah! Deborah!" waved a woman with long dark curly hair.

"Shifra!" Deborah ran towards her and embraced her.

"I haven't seen you at any of the festivals for two years." Deborah lovingly touched Shifra's curls. "How is your family?"

Shifra smiled and pointed to her right where an older woman held a sleeping infant.

"Noooo…" Deborah smiled. "You are an Ima! You look the same Shifra. Really. How is your husband, Asher?"

"He's good. He has learned to forge metal and makes arrow heads and swords. He complains that it is always hard to find tin."

"Yes and then you need copper too." Deborah nodded in agreement. "One can't make bronze without both copper and tin, at least that's what the blacksmith in Beth El told me."

"Have you heard of a new metal?" Shifra asked "I think it is called iron."

Deborah pursed her lips knowingly. "Yes, I've heard of it. I believe the Sea People use weapons made of it and the Canaanites possess it as well. It appears to make a strong and sharp blade. We don't know how they create it though. I wish we did."

A ram's horn sounded throughout the camp.

"Must be time for the Passover offering," Deborah commented.

Shifra walked to her mother-in-law and picked up her sleeping baby. She and Deborah walked closer to the altar.

A male with a thick chest walked forward leading a lamb with a rope tied around its neck.

"Is that Dan?" Deborah asked.

They both studied the male.

"Yes, yes, it is!" announced Shifra.

They eagerly hailed him.

Dan caught their eyes and smiled broadly towards them as he delivered the lamb to the priest.

In these years, the sacrifices were very few. The lamb was just one of the three offerings to be made this Passover.

Dan joined his old friends.

"Deborah!" he put his arm around her shoulders and squeezed. "How are you? How is your family?" He scrutinized her figure. "You don't appear to have any children."

"No, no, Dan," Deborah chuckled. "Life can be unpredictable but it is good."

A spry man with short pin-straight hair turned quickly in their direction.

"Is that you, Deborah?" he inquired.

"Yes, do I know you?" Deborah looked him up and down.

"Not yet. But I have heard of your instruction by the palm oasis," he said fervently. "I want to join your training group. War is coming. I want to be part of it."

Shifra and Dan looked from the man to Deborah in confusion.

"What are you doing Deborah?" Dan asked as his eyes narrowed.

Deborah's face became very red and she looked at the ground momentarily.

Collecting herself, she swiftly raised her eyes straight at the stranger before her.

"After the seven days of Passover, we will resume. What is your name?"

The man replied, "I'm Shin and we should've struck the Canaanites long ago."

Deborah didn't even look at her friends whose mouths hung open. Lowering her voice, she said, "Shin, let's not speak of this here. I'll look forward to seeing you after Passover."

After the man left, Shifra finally spoke.

"Are you leading a revolt, Deborah?" Shifra just couldn't believe what she was asking.

"No, yes, no, I…." Deborah was flustered. What was she undertaking? She really didn't take time to think about it. She knew people came to her for counsel but they were also coming to master shooting arrows, sling shots, and wielding swords. What was she doing by the palm trees?

Dan was now looking intently at Deborah.

"I'm doing what must be done." Deborah spoke quickly, "We all know that King Jabin has Sisera and the best army in the land but we must defend ourselves."

Shifra studied her perplexed. "What does your husband think of this?"

"Oh, well, we have found a way for peace in our home." Deborah said this very quickly and looked towards the people in front of the altar.

From the crowd of colorful robes, cheers erupted as the priest sprinkled the blood seven times over the altar. The lamb was roasting on the fire as women walked through the people holding jugs of wine.

Dan asked a woman wearing a light green head scarf to refill his pouch and then drank deeply from it. He then passed it to Deborah and then to Shifra.

Two women wearing flowing sunflower dresses danced through the crowds chiming finger cymbals. One man held a reed pipe and blew a joyous melody. An older woman with her silvery hair flowing over her shoulders held a flat drum in her left hand and beat it with her right. The Israelites started to dance, laugh, and celebrate their freedom from Egypt.

Deborah drank a lot of wine. She didn't even keep track. She was happy to see Shifra and Dan. She was happy that her brother was getting married tomorrow. She was happy just to forget for a while Jabin and the People of the Sea.

Close by, there was a male wearing a snowy shepherd's robe. His auburn colored hair was long and tied back with rope. Standing a cubit higher than Deborah, she had to raise her head look into his brown eyes. His eyes gleamed as he smiled back towards her.

Deborah felt a warm flush to her face. Was it the wine? Was it the festival? Was it just too many years since she had romance? She didn't know. She swayed her head knowing that her thick hair moved sensuously over her shoulders. It felt good to flirt. Shyly, she met his gaze.

The man took a step towards Deborah. "So, who is this beautiful woman before me?"

"Oh, just a woman from the hills."

"I'm Yira and I'm from Machir. I haven't been to one of these festivals before."

His voice was deep and silky. Deborah felt pulled towards him.

Shifra already went back to her family and Dan had left some time ago. Deborah was standing alone with Yira and was entranced by his smile.

"Are you often at the festivals?" Yira asked. His eyes looked a liquid brown.

With a smile, she said, "Yes, for as many years as I can remember my family and I celebrate Sukkot, Passover, and Shavuot." Looking at him puzzled, she inquired, "How is it that you have avoided the holidays? Didn't you feel obligated?"

It was certainly unusual for anyone to avoid these gatherings, Deborah thought. This was how the people celebrated, shared their lives, and found some solace and joy.

Yira stared ahead. The trees cast shadows as the moon's light shined through the branches. "Oh, I've always been one to keep my own company but tonight I would like nothing more than a walk through the trees with you." Yira's eyes gleamed. "Would you like a respite from the crowds?"

Deborah was unsure of how to respond but then she tentatively said, "Yes. Yes I would."

Branches crackled under their feet as they walked to the perimeter of the summit where many trees created a canopy under the stars.

Yira looked over at her and said, "It is now I regret not coming sooner to these celebrations. If I knew a woman like you was here, I would've come long ago."

Deborah didn't know how to react. Oh to be courted felt good but she also knew that it was wrong.

As she deliberated quietly, Yira inquired, "Tell me," his voice deepened. "Are you married?"

Deborah turned her gaze forward abruptly and she walked faster between the ancient oak trees. Yira took longer strides to stay side by side with her. She didn't know how to answer this. It was a simple question really, but it was complicated.

"Yes, I am," Deborah admitted while fixating on a big, gnarled roots of at tree ahead. "It's not…" What could she possibly say? Oh, that they share the same home like brother and sister.

"It's not what you hoped for. No matter." Yira gingerly took her hand.

He doesn't care was the first thought that flickered through Deborah's mind. Most men would avoid a taken woman. What is it about him that is different? She almost pulled her hand away but kept it there. His fingers felt warm and Deborah felt the hairs on her arm stand straight.

She knew that she shouldn't be alone with a man who was not her husband. However, it felt so good to feel a man's hands around her own. Maybe there's no harm, she reasoned. He is unknown and everyone is occupied with the festivities. Lappidoth has his needs taken care of, certainly he wouldn't begrudge me this. Or would he? I'll just enjoy what I can for as long as I am able. Deborah gripped Yira's hand more firmly as they walked together.

"Look up at the heavens." Yira pointed. "You can see a big bear. He's coming out of hibernation."

Lifting her head upwards, Deborah felt the chill of the night breeze but it was refreshing. "Yes, I see it," she smiled.

"A bear always needs to come out of his isolation, especially in the presence of a delightful woman."

Yira turned towards her. Deborah could smell the wine on his breath and see the white of his teeth. Her heart began to beat faster. What was she doing here? She didn't even know this man. Around them rustled the leaves in the wind. Deborah felt her body moving closer to him as though of its own mind. Yira leaned towards her and...

She stepped back. Actually stumbled. Deborah could barely breathe and her voice came out high pitched, "I...We...need to go back. My friends will be looking for me."

“All right, Deborah,” Yira consoled as he mischievously smiled towards her. “Perhaps, we’ll see each other again. There’s always another festival.”

Still trying to catch her breath, Deborah mumbled, “Yes, always another festival.”

They walked back to the clearing. Dropping his hand, Deborah continued slowly ahead on her own.

CHAPTER 18

The wood on the altar was reduced to smoking embers. The Israelites were in the last stages of the evening celebration when Deborah snuck in behind Shifra. The dark haired woman turned around.

With half closed eyes, she said, “Odd, I didn’t see you there before.” Shifra looked in the direction of Yira slinking away.

“Well, it’s easy to miss many things in the dark,” Deborah quickly replied.

Shifra just shook her head silently.

“Tomorrow afternoon, my brother is to be married.” Deborah broke the awkwardness.

“Hard to believe he’s a man already,” her friend said joyfully. “Blessings Deborah, to you and your family.”

“Thank you Shifra. I’ll see you tomorrow.” Deborah waved goodbye.

That night, Deborah laid down in a big tent made of sheep skin with Mara and Lappidoth. She slept deeply.

The day went by quickly. The sun was only a couple of hours away from setting. A pleasant cool breeze blew across the hill’s summit. Fifty people gathered around the young couple. Shlomi stood tall and proud wearing his father’s royal blue robe. David had worn this during his wedding many years ago. Tamar had cleaned and repaired it carefully for the ceremony. When Shlomi first put on the robe, Tamar’s eyes grew misty.

“You are just as handsome as your father,” she announced and then struggled to contain herself. “He would be so proud of you, Shlomi. You are a good son and you will keep the memory of your father going to the next generation." Tears ran down Tamar's face as she hugged her son.

Yaakova, Shlomi's bride, wore a light purple dress that reached well beyond her feet. It was doubled over and cinched at her waist with a purple braided cord. Her eyes were lined in black kohl and lips in deep crimson clay. Deborah thought she looked pretty but Shlomi was completely transformed. He was beaming. He seemed happy as he looked down at his bride. With tenderness, he reached for her hand and led her before one of the elders of their community.

There weren't many weddings these days. Too many young men and women lost their lives in Sisera's raids. Those in attendance were the survivors and they were determined to celebrate and be happy at least for a few hours.

The elder with a long coarse beard and deep wrinkles on his forehead said, "Since the time of Abraham and Sarah, our people remember God's covenant. We are the keepers of the commandments and maintain the traditions of our people. We pray to you, Adonai, that you will give Shalom, the son of David, and Yaakova, the daughter of Micah, health and peace from our enemies. May they have years of marriage and may Yaakova be the mother of thousands. May the blessings of Abraham be upon you. May your descendants be as numerous as the stars in heaven and may they seize the gates of our foes. We pray that this union is blessed with children. You are now husband and wife as witnessed by our community."

A cup of wine was passed between Shlomi and Yaakova. They each took a long sip.

One man gleefully cried, "Time for the wedding tent! Time to consummate the marriage!"

Shlomi smiled shyly at the crowd as Yaakova looked down, blushing. They were led to a tent decorated with pomegranates on the outside. As the flap opened, they saw a thick layer of straw on the ground and a soft linen cloth covering it. One of the Israelites handed Shlomi a pouch of wine. "This is for courage and for pleasure," he said laughing.

Shlomi gratefully took a long gulp of the honeyed liquid and handed it to his bride as they escaped into the enclosure.

The rest of the attendees backed away from the tent. Wine was passed out along with some flat bread sweetened with date honey.

Deborah was standing next to her mother as she took a bite of the bread.

"He looks happy, Ima," Deborah said with a smile.

Tamar nodded her head. "Both of my children are married. Now I only lack grandchildren. I hope you will be pregnant first, Deborah," she said as she took Deborah's hand into her own.

Deborah didn't know what to say so she just nodded and squeezed her mother's hand.

Two hours later, a young man ran up to the summit. He was filthy and clearly exhausted. His hair was matted to his face and there was a little trickle of blood coming out of his ear.

Deborah was standing next to Shifra when the man collapsed by a group of Israelites.

"Get him some water quick!" one of them cried out.

Shifra ladled some water into a cup and brought it over to the man. He was propped up by two other Israelites and Shifra brought the cup to his lips. He gulped it with his eyes closed. After a few swallows, he opened his eyes and grabbed the cup and drank it dry. Shifra ran to refill it. Deborah stood next to some men as they looked in alarm at the man before them.

"I am Loter of the tribe of Machir. It took me two days to come here." He coughed. Shifra handed him another cup of water that he drank quickly.

"The Sea Peoples! They, they…" Loter sat up with his eyes wide. "Sisera came through my town of…" He hoarsely coughed. "He said…he said we weren't paying enough tribute to Jabin. He…he…" Loter was breathing heavily now and his face became red.

After catching his breath, he continued, "Sisera came through and demanded a goat or lamb from every family. But many did not have it. He refused to accept a pigeon instead. He said that we must pay in blood and fire."

The men gathered around Loter and stared at him intently. Deborah's heart began to race. It was getting worse. Sisera was demanding more and more for King Jabin. They were never satisfied.

Loter continued, "Sisera's soldiers ran through the streets..." His voice gave out. One of the men placed a hand on his shoulder and shouted out. "Wine, bring this poor man some wine!"

A nearby woman gave her wine pouch to Loter. He was shaking so violently, he could barely drink it. After a few moments, he calmed down. He took a long, long gulp of the fermented grape juice and resuming speaking. "Sisera murdered men, women, and children alike. He had no mercy. His men asked, "Where is your animal for the king? If someone said they didn't have one, they said, 'We will sacrifice you for his majesty then."

Loter's breathing quickened. "They stabbed men through the hearts, sliced off children's heads, and raped our women!

My wife, my wife…They took her from my house." His eyes closed as his body tensed. "She screamed! A soldier hit me in the head and I don't remember what happened afterwards. I only know that when I awoke there were so many dead bodies. My neighbors! My friends were laying in the dirt with their blood soaking the earth. And my wife, my wife… I didn't find her body. I looked. I looked!" His voice yelped in a high pitch.

Deborah stood there grinding her teeth silently.

"My wife! Where is my wife? I don't know!" Loter cried out as his body convulsed again. "I came here to warn you. To tell you. Someone had to know. Someone."

Many of the men looked at Loter and frowned. One of them named Haggai stared angrily at the ground and then he raised his eyes tentatively to Deborah.

"I hear that you are training our people to fight. Is it true?" Haggai burst out. The other men looked in amazement at Haggai and then at the woman standing by their side.

Deborah felt panicked. What should she say? She tried to keep this all secret. How would they respond? She already knew she was an outcast. She swallowed hard and said nothing.

Haggai asked again, "Times are dire. Tell me, are you the Deborah who is at the palm tree between Beth El and Ramah?"

Deborah looked at Haggai. He was probably around eighteen and his face was already sprouting hairs from his chin. The other men around them continued to stare at her uncertainly. Even Shifra stood frozen unsure of what would happen next.

The seconds went by slowly.

"I am Deborah." She spoke just over a whisper. "I am the one by the palm tree."

"Thank God, it's true!" Haggai exclaimed. "I hear other men say you are wise and an excellent teacher of shooting arrows. I also hear there are others who work with you teaching our people to wield a dagger or sword. I want to come and learn."

One of the men standing by, known as Calir, said incredulously, "What is this sheep dung! Are you saying this woman is helping to fight Jabin?" He pointed derisively at Deborah.

The rest were confused. They didn't know what to believe.

Deborah was at first afraid but now she was just angry. She stood up straight, stared at him directly and said, "Listen here, my dear man. You can choose to cower in your fields or under the robe of your Ima or you can do something about this."

All the men stared at Deborah. Even Loter looked up to hear her words.

"Sisera is getting bolder by every moon cycle. We cannot hide from him or wish him away." Deborah's body tensed and her voice rose. "We have to fight. The next generation will celebrate our victory over King Jabin and Sisera. There is training under way. You decide, if you will join the fight."

Deborah's heart was beating so fast, she thought it would leave her body. She couldn't believe what she just said. The words came out. Now what?

Shifra looked at Deborah and then back to Calir in shock. Deborah stood and willed herself to look Calir directly in the eyes as his face shifted from indignation to confusion.

Haggai smiled, "I will train with Deborah and her men. I will fight the bastard Canaanites. We will destroy Sisera!"

The other men around them nodded their agreement. Calir, recovering himself said, "I will come and see what you do." His eyes narrowed. "If you are like all the other women, then I will spit on you like any other whore who led me astray. We will see."

Deborah looked at the men around her, felt strength in their agreement and said, “Yes, there are many things for us to see and understand. There is a long road ahead.”

CHAPTER 19

The days were long at the palm trees between Ramah and Beth El. Rocky hills surrounded the small valley where streams of water from the mountains nourished the trees. Every day more Israelite men appeared. Word was spreading that a rebellion was at hand. Today there were two hundred people! Deborah assessed every new recruit and put him in a group suitable to his level of experience and ability. For those who had no experience in battle, they were sent to Yoram from Menasheh. Yoram always kept his black beard closely shaved and looked well-kept compared to those who let their facial hair grow at will.

Yoram stood facing ten men of different ages.

"You! Haggai, raise your arm over your shoulder. The movement should be seamless. Don't waste extra energy pulling back."

Slender Haggai raised his arm trying to imitate Yoram's instructions.

"There, there! Now slice cleanly through the air. Don't drop your shoulder!"

Haggai lowered the blade. "But I'm tired. My arms hurt! I'm exhausted."

Yoram stepped close and leaned close to Haggai's face. "It doesn't matter if you are tired. It doesn't matter if your back feels like it's on fire. Death waits for no one." Yoram's eyes reduced to slits. "You will be killed all the same."

Yoram then looked at all the men in his group. "All of you must see your body as your tool. You are more than your body. Even if it's aching, even if you have been stabbed, you are more than flesh. Pain is irrelevant. A warrior must rise above the pain. He must persevere no matter what."

The men stood silently taking in Yoram's words.

"Now, Haggai, begin again!" Yoram bellowed.

Deborah trained the women and any males without the strength to wield a sword or battle ax. Today, she was working with thirty people. Dividing them into smaller groups, Deborah walked them through the basics of stringing a bow, feathering an arrow, and how to hold the bow. Deborah leaned over a girl with a long wavy hair called Leah. Even though she claimed to be seventeen, Deborah guessed she was a few years younger.

"Here," Deborah coached. "Close one eye as you look at the tree before you. Now open it. Can you see the difference? With one eye, you can narrow your focus."

Leah followed her instruction. Deborah looked at her and remembered her father so patiently teaching her many years ago. Aba, Deborah thought to herself, thank you for believing in me and giving me the tools to help our people.

Deborah turned back to the girl and said, "Now shoot."

Some distance away, Deborah heard males voice rise in excitement.

As she approached, she saw three newcomers. One of them was large with small beady eyes and thick red lips. She recognized him immediately.

"Calir!" Deborah swallowed hard. "Welcome."

Calir walked towards her forcefully. With just a cubit between him and Deborah, he scowled and surveyed the people training over the valley.

"So, this is your army?" Calir stated derisively.

"For now it is. What can you do?" Deborah inquired.

Calir snorted. "What can I do? What can't I do?" He took out his sword and stepped back and sliced powerfully through the air. "I've decided to see what is happening here. I'm here to be of service." His tone of voice mocked Deborah.

"Okay, go over to Sira's group over there." Deborah pointed to a group of twenty men working with swords behind the palm trees.

Calir walked with his head held high accompanied by his friends.

The day passed quickly. The sun began to set with brilliant red and orange streaks in the darkening sky.

Deborah took a long angular ram's horn and sounded it.

When all looked up, she said, "Let's meet tomorrow when the sun is breaking over the horizon. That way, we will have a full day."

That night, Deborah was exhausted. Lappidoth and Mara looked worried as she slowly ate her red lentil stew. They never saw her so tired. Deborah didn't share much of what she was doing but they heard the rumors. Many spoke of the young female judge by the palm trees and the increasing numbers of people training. These nights, Deborah came home, ate and just went to sleep. As soon as Deborah finished her bowl, she climbed the rope ladder, and collapsed on her bedding straw.

The next morning the sun shined bright. Deborah opened her eyes and then sat up in alarm. What time was it? Did she oversleep? She pulled on her outer robe and descended the ladder quickly. Mara was bent over the cooking fire and stood up to greet her.

"Deborah, I'm glad you are awake. You seemed so tired last night, I didn't want to wake you." Mara looked at her in compassion.

Deborah shook her head. "I wish you had. It's been some time since the sun rose. I've got to get going quickly."

"Here," Mara extended her hand. "Here is a cloth containing apricots and bread. I have a pouch of water for you as well."

Grabbing the provisions, Deborah looked towards Mara. She was putting on weight around her middle. Her pregnancy was progressing, Deborah thought. "Thank you Mara. Thank you for this. I appreciate it." And Deborah was off.

One hour later, Deborah arrived at the rocky plateau. Before her were hundreds of men arguing and yelling. Calir, wearing a flowing taupe robe, stood on a rock above them. What is going on? Deborah wondered.

"We cannot wait any longer!" Calir bellowed. Spittle flew from his lips. "Sisera has a small group raiding Shechem just a half day journey from here. We must teach him a lesson. Never to trouble our people again!"

Deborah stood aghast. "No! No!" she yelled from below. "We aren't ready. The training isn't complete. The timing is all wrong."

Calir jeered towards her, then surveyed the crowd. "What does this woman know?" Calir's loud voice boomed over the people. "Who is ready to strike terror into the heart of all the Canaanites? Who is ready to avenge our people? Who is ready to join me now?"

One heavy set man called out. "I'm with Calir. I'm tired of waiting. I will fight now!" There were some muted cheers around him.

Yoram, who was standing at the back of the people facing Calir, called out, "Calir is mistaken. Deborah is right. We need more time to prepare. It will be disastrous to fight Sisera now." His voice strained. "Let's get back to training." Then he walked away from the crowd with many following after him.

Calir raised his sword over his head and roared. “Those who are with me, let’s go. Let’s fight! We fight for vengeance! We fight for glory!” About fifty people raised their daggers, swords, and spears into the air and cheered.

Calir leapt off the rock confidently and his small army followed him to the north.

Deborah’s back tensed up. Shooting pains of tension went up her neck so that even turning her head hurt. Haggai came to her side and looked at her. Timidly he asked, “Do you want us to stop them, Deborah?”

Deborah shook her head. She wasn’t going to lose any of her people in an internal skirmish. “There’s nothing to be done.”

Haggai blurted out, “I hope they bring back Calir’s head in a basket to you.”

“I don’t,” Deborah said wearily. “May God look over them and bring them back safely.”

The remaining one hundred and fifty people went back into their groups to train.

It was midafternoon when a couple arrived on the backs of donkeys. The woman’s hair was billowing out under her head scarf in dark tiny curls.

“Shifra!” Deborah exclaimed.

Shifra and Asher descended from their animals.

“I’m glad to see you here,” Deborah said in astonishment.

Asher was light haired with defined cheekbones. He spoke first. “Deborah, I want to offer my services to you and our people.”

Deborah’s eyes widened in surprise.

Shifra added, "I told him of what you are doing. I assume you will need weapons. Asher is the best metal worker in Ephraim. He can make arrow heads, blades, anything as long as he has the metal."

Asher nodded and said, "King Jabin has gone too far. We can't live like caged beasts awaiting a slaughter." His voice was earnest as he extended his hand towards Deborah.

As she grasped it, she could feel the many callouses and the thickness of his skin. This was a man who had clearly worked with his hands for years.

Deborah's eyes teared up a little. "Thank you, Shifra. Thank you, Asher. I really needed some good news today."

"I'm going back home. Make use of my husband." Shifra hugged Deborah.

"Yes, yes," Deborah said gratefully. "All right Asher, I'm sending you over across the creek. There is a stone fire hearth and men there. Just tell them what you need and we'll assist you."

The next two days were a whirl of activity.

Yoram graduated his first class of beginners and Deborah scrutinized the newest arrivals. Asher sent men to procure copper and tin, so he could fashion more bronze weapons. "Get anything you can," he instructed them. "I can take old utensils, jewelry, or pots. I know tin is rare but I don't need a lot of it. With a hot enough fire, we can forge the weapons we will need."

On the third day, as Deborah was organizing more Israelites, she saw in the distance a group of men moving slowly toward them. She strained her eyes peering into the distance. They were certainly Israelites by their robes. There were animals with them. They were moving very slowly. Deborah let out a long breath. She recognized the man in the lead. The tall man walking with a limp. It was Calir. But where were the others? She wondered as she counted only nine men with him.

Deborah took the ram's horn, placed it to her lips, and sounded it twice. Training stopped immediately and all looked at the rag tag group approaching.

"Get some water!" Deborah cried. "We'll need some linen cloths too!"

Several of her men ran towards Calir and his group to assist them.

Calir finally arrived. His clothes were torn and bloody. His cheek was sliced and blood oozed from the wound. His men were in worse shape. One of them was missing his hand and the remainder of his arm was tethered to his shoulder by a rope. Another man wore a gauze soaked in blood on top of his head.

Deborah's men and women quickly tended to the wounded. They washed their wounds, bandaged them with clean cloths, and dripped water into their mouths. Everyone worked silently and quickly. Deborah examined Calir and what was left of his army.

Calir, after being tended to, glared up at Deborah, and then dejectedly lowered his head.

"We charged Sisera with all our might. We thought we could surprise them but we were outnumbered." Calir mumbled as he stared at the ground.

When he looked up, his eyes were pinpoints of blackness. "Sisera was laughing as he and his men attacked us with their iron swords." Calir snarled revealing his yellowed teeth. "We didn't last an hour. After my animals were slaughtered and many of my men, I blew the horn to retreat. Sisera didn't even chase us. He just yelled, 'Come back when you are ready for another lesson!'"

Calir's shoulders drooped and he stared at the dirt once again.

Deborah was so angry at Calir's actions. The needless loss of life. She wanted to strangle him for his arrogance or at least to scream at his stupidity. However, she knew that admonishments couldn't change what occurred. Deborah turned and silently walked away.

Early the next morning as all were working, Deborah pulled Yoram aside.

"We need to think ahead," Deborah stated. "We need to go beyond today and the next few weeks. Yesterday was a terrible day for the Israelites."

Yoram nodded his head sadly. "Well, the only good from Calir's 'expedition' is that Sisera will truly believe that we are no threat. This should give us time."

"Exactly," Deborah agreed. "We must use our time well though. We will need more fighters and more leadership. You and I can only do so much. We need someone with battle experience who can get the best out of our people."

Yoram turned his head to the north and stood pensively.

"Well, now that you mention it…There is a great warrior from the tribe of Naphtali. I believe he is one of the sons of Abinoam," Yoram suggested. "His name is Barak and he strikes like lighting. I hear he has cunning and great ability to command an army."

Deborah looked at Yoram hopefully. "We could use a man like him. When can you bring him to me?"

Yoram looked earnestly towards Deborah. "I can leave immediately but you should know that he's a bit of a bull. I mean, if his reputation is correct, you may want to keep the female cows away."

"We'll deal with that later. See what you can do," Deborah said curtly.

CHAPTER 20

Tomorrow was the Feast of Weeks. It was hard to believe that Passover was only two months ago. The days and weeks passed very slowly. The barley and wheat stalks were high and the initial harvest was already under way. Lappidoth came home every night after the sun set, covered in dirt and exhausted. Smiling, he collapsed into a chair at the table.

"We are going to be all right. There is plenty of grain to go around. Thank God."

Mara pushed a full to the brim cup of wine in his hand. Lappidoth raised it to his lips, smelled the aroma of fermented grapes, and drank deeply.

Deborah had only come home minutes before him. She just sat with her head resting on one hand staring at the wall.

"Can I get something for you, Deborah?" Mara inquired. She was now very rotund. The midwives thought Mara was seven moon cycles pregnant.

"Oh Mara, I should be the one asking you in your state." Deborah looked at Mara kindly.

"No, no, I'd rather move around. I like being useful." Mara smiled warmly at Lappidoth who just grinned back at her.

The people of Beth El had by now accepted Mara. Lappidoth had explained that just as Abraham took in Hagar, he had brought Mara into his home. All knew that a man could have more than one wife. Jacob, the father of the twelve tribes, was married to Leah and Rachel and took Bilah and Zilpah into his bed as well.

Today, though, it just wasn't common in the hill country. In order to have more than one woman, one still had to provide for her food and clothing. During this time of hardship, there were few resources to spare. Lappidoth, though, was a good farmer, the people reasoned, and had enough for his household.

Lappidoth finished his cup of wine and let out a low belch. Mara quickly refilled his vessel and gave another one to Deborah.

"Would you like a basin to clean your hands and face, Lappidoth?" asked Mara.

"Yes, yes, I suppose, I certainly need it," laughed Lappidoth. He took a piece of cloth and dipped it into the cool water before wiping his face on it.

With his face glistening with beads of water, he said to Deborah, "You seem even more tired than me."

Deborah took a sip of wine and replied, "It's better for you not to know."

Lappidoth's chest quivered with another burp. "Maybe it's better that way. I hear the rumors of our revolt growing every day. Hopefully with this spring harvest, we won't need it. I expect we will have plenty to pay King Jabin and keep our family fed." As Lappidoth spoke his hand reached out to Mara and he caressed her expanded stomach. She stepped back, with her face now crimson, and fetched the bread and vegetable stew for their evening meal.

The next day, they traveled to the hill summit for the Shavuot festival. Deborah estimated that there were only a hundred people this year. They were all wearing their best and most colorful clothing. A sea of yellows, blues, greens, and reds filled the plateau. Almost everyone brought two loaves of thick barley bread for the offering. However, very few had a lamb or goat to spare. Deborah walked through the thin crowds of people to see if any friends or family were there.

Shifra appeared before her. "Deborah! So happy to see you!" She greeted her childhood friend.

Feeling a hard bump pressing into her, Deborah said, "I see you are with child again. May your child be born at the right time and healthy."

"Thank you, Deborah. How are you? Asher tells me you have all been working hard."

Deborah nodded her head. "He's right. We have new men and women every day but very few weapons. I'm glad Asher is helping us with swords. He is an asset. Thank you for sparing him on some days to help."

Shifra smiled, "Anything for our people. Anything for a dear, dear friend." She kissed Deborah and went to rejoin her family.

"Dee!" called out a young man with plush dark facial hair. Deborah stared at him for a few moments.

"Shlomi? Is that you? You look like Aba with that beard." Deborah ran over to him to hug her not so little brother.

"Well, maybe it's married life or just time passing." He grinned. "How is the husband? I hear he coaxes seedlings from the earth as easily as a mother bird feeds her young."

Deborah nodded her head. "Yes, Lappidoth has always been good with the soil."

A bald man with bushy hair coming out of his ears suddenly appeared in front of them. "Are you Deborah? Are you the one leading our fight against the king?" he asked breathlessly.

"Ahhh," Deborah started.

Shlomi's smile disappeared.

“What is this, Deborah?” Shlomi looked sternly at his sister. “What’s this man saying? It can’t be true.” Shlomi’s face was full of concern.

Deborah’s eyes shifted back in forth between her brother and the man before her. How could she even explain this to her brother? It’s not that she wanted this responsibility. It came to her. How? She just couldn’t even think clearly at the moment. All at once, Deborah felt exhausted.

A shofar sounded by the altar.

“Oh, it must be time for the offering of the first fruits,” Deborah announced in relief. She walked quickly away from both men.

She stood among the people facing the altar. The priest in front was very old. He was dressed in stained purple and crimson robes. The breast piece over his chest dragged his shoulders down. With a shaking hand, he took hold of one of the lambs. Two younger men ran to his side to restrain the restless animal.

Deborah said out loud quietly, “Before too long, we will need a new priest.”

“I think we needed a new one a solar year ago,” a familiar voice said immediately to her right.

Looking over, Deborah gasped at the reddish-brown, long haired man at her side. His soft brown eyes twinkled as he smiled towards her.

“Yira?” Deborah looked at him in puzzlement.

“Oh, I’d hoped to encounter you here today. It’s been a couple of moons since we last saw one another.” Yira’s eyes met Deborah’s.

Deborah’s heart began to beat a little faster at the sound of his deep, seductive voice. She didn’t imagine seeing him again.

Suddenly she was overwhelmed with a desire to touch him and feel his lips on hers.

"Can I interest you in some wine that has been sitting in this pouch perhaps for a couple of days?" He laughed holding up a leather container. "There's nothing like wine that has come close to fermenting into vinegar. Kings and queens will exclaim the wonders of this particular batch. It has the aroma of ripe grapes but the finish is like the bite of a serpent."

Deborah laughed. "All right, I'll take a sip if you will just stop talking about it." Yira handed her the wine and she took a big gulp. The bitterness made her mouth water. Grimacing, she said, "Well, I have to say you are right about its bite."

The priest sprinkled the lamb's blood seven times thus concluding the ceremony. Two people turned around to face Deborah. "I thought that was you behind us," a young woman stated.

Her companion added, "Tell me how are the preparations going? Will we be at war soon?"

Deborah looked at Yira who was carefully studying the exchange in front of him. She replied to the couple, "There is much work to be done in the weeks and months ahead. I don't take war lightly and neither should you."

The woman laughed. "Well, my cup is feeling a bit empty, now that you mention it. Maybe another cup of wine and the head of King Jabin is what I need right now."

The man by her side put his arm around her shoulders and started to turn her away. He called out to Deborah over his shoulder. "You heard her. Next festival, we expect the king's head on a platter." Deborah covered her eyes with her hand and took a deep sigh.

After a few moments of silence, Yira said, "You look like you need a respite. Would you like to walk?"

Deborah gratefully looked at Yira. He was as good looking as she remembered him. She thought of him during some of the long nights of the last couple of months. She imagined his well-built chest pressing against her own and his hair brushing her face. What would it be like to wake up the next morning with him? Even as she told herself to banish such thoughts, they still lingered on even late at night. Oh, to have the embrace of man she desired. It was not possible, but here she was.

She took his hand and let him lead her into the forest of oak trees.

Once they were alone, Yira bent his head and slowly grazed her lips. Heat radiated and coursed throughout her body. She returned his kiss and as it deepened, it was delicious.

Oh, but the thoughts. It was wrong. She was married. She shouldn't be here.

Another long, lingering kiss. Deborah fought the urge to press her body into his, to hold him tightly to her. She put her hand on his chest and pushed gently.

"What is this princess?" Yira asked surprised.

"I…I…cannot do this." Deborah said in between breaths.

"What?" Yira reached his arm to her waist and started to pull her close to him again.

"No!" Deborah said decisively. Taking a step back, Yira's hand dropped.

"I must return. I am sorry."

Yira nodded his head, "No, it is I my dear princess, who is sorry."

They walked silently back to the gathering site.

When they arrived, a number of the Israelites turned and silently stared at her. It felt very uncomfortable, she thought, was something wrong?

Deborah ran her fingers through her hair tugging at the snarls. Yira strutted confidently as though he were a vulture who had just nabbed lunch.

"Er, Yira, I'm going to find my family." Deborah said awkwardly.

"Yes, my beauty. Go in peace."

As Deborah walked away from him, more and more people just continued to stare at her.

She quickly found Lappidoth and Mara by their tent. They were the only ones who were not acting strange around her. "Are you thirsty, Deborah?" Mara asked. "I have some fresh goat's milk." Deborah took a cup of milk from her. Lappidoth smiled and hummed as he stretched his arms.

Sipping her milk, Deborah tentatively turned her head and was surprised that others didn't stop staring at her. She noticed that their conversations stopped as she approached. Finally, she spotted Shifra. Her friend waved in her direction.

"Shifra, something odd is happening here." Deborah whispered in her ear. "Do you know why everyone is acting so peculiar around me?"

Shifra let out a long breath and nodded her head. "Why don't we go over to the ridge?"

Deborah allowed herself to be led away from the people. They walked over the grassy plain and just over the side of the hill. The sun was shining brightly now in the late spring sky.

When the two women were alone, Shifra began, "You know what this is about Deborah."

Deborah frowned. "Was there an attack? Did somebody die? What happened?"

Shifra's teeth grinded together. "Deborah, what kind of reaction did you expect going with that man?"

"What do you mean?" Deborah's heart started to beat faster.

"I mean, here you are a married woman, leading our people, and you spend an evening with the greatest adulterer in the community."

"Ah," Deborah stumbled. "I really don't know him. Is that his reputation?"

"You stupid donkey!" Shifra now looked angry. "It's not his reputation, it's yours! Here the people are looking up to you. They could stone you for this. What are they supposed to think of you now? Are you a lustful goat that can't control yourself?"

Deborah collapsed on a white boulder. She thought she was going to pass out.

"Shifra," she said pleadingly. "You don't understand. My marriage with Lappidoth isn't... I gave him Mara to make him happy. And I did not lay with Yira."

"This has nothing to do with Lappidoth and his concubine. This is about you. Whether you laid with Yira or not, people believe it could've happened. Even if you weren't married, this would be terrible behavior, but it's even worse now that you are. You can't do this, Deborah. You have to think of your people, your responsibilities."

"I, ah, I..." Deborah had no idea what to say. "The weight of this, confronting Jabin, I only wanted to alleviate the burden, for a little while."

"Then go climb a mountain, Deborah! I mean it. Find other ways to relieve the strain." Shifra stated angrily.

"This isn't reasonable," Deborah began again. "Am I supposed to be celibate the rest of my life? Will there be no love or companion for me?" Deborah was now looking intently at her friend.

Shifra's face softened. "Deborah, I don't know what to tell you. You can act the harlot but you can't be a leader of our people. You have to choose."

"I don't want to choose between being a human being, being a woman, or helping our people. There is no man who would have to deny himself like this." Deborah looked despondently out to the sky. There were white clouds rimmed with gray against the blue sky.

They both sat silently for minutes.

Shifra placed her hand on Deborah's shoulder. "I...I know it's not fair, but Deborah, I think our people really need you. Maybe, this is your sacrifice. Maybe, this is your offering to help our people at this moment of time. I believe that you are a judge for this era and that you can bring peace to our people once again."

Deborah lowered her head and said no more.

CHAPTER 21
YAEL

Heber put on a thick wool robe over his tunic. The sky was overcast and a wind blew from the west. There was a dampness to the air.

"Yael! I'm leaving," he called back into the tent.

After some rustling, a red haired woman peeked her head out of the folds of goat skin. Yael's cheeks were full and her eyes sparkled, "Good fortune, I hope you catch some fish today."

Heber smiled warmly towards Yael. "The sea should be filled with fish on a day like today." He looked up hopeful at the clouds above, got up on his donkey, and rode eastward towards the Kinneret Sea.

The day was overcast but Yael didn't mind. It would make her work outdoors more pleasant. She stepped out of the tent and inhaled the sweet moist air. The Red Bud trees were finally blooming. Their vibrant pink flowers over took the branches and looked so beautiful against the gray sky. Yael remembered the hope they offered her years ago during those first weeks in the Galilee after Jabin had given her to Heber.

Yael recalled that the journey to the banks of the Kinneret Sea was solemn. Heber barely spoke to her but then again he didn't touch her either. She was grateful for that. Yael prayed silently those weeks as they traveled through the huge lush mountains. King Jabin and his entourage ignored her. Only when they stopped to eat, did they throw some crusts of bread to her like she was animal. As she sat in the dirt, eating pieces of stale bread, Yael muttered to herself, "I must survive. I must survive if only for my people. If only to witness and condemn. If only to avenge."

When the group arrived at the crossroads between Kedesh by the Kinneret Sea and the road to Hazor, Heber bid his farewell.

Bowing from his waist, Heber said, "To the greatest king in the land, the greatest king in the Mediterranean, I say thank you."

King Jabin was sitting on his black mare and looked at his servant. "You have proven to be the most loyal of friends, Heber, even more than all the Kenites. In memory of my father to your father, from me to you, I bid you farewell." Jabin regally waved his arm and signaled his entourage to turn towards Hazor.

Heber stood by two donkeys and his dazed slave Yael. She watched the king, his men, and animals disappear in the distance. She felt fear. What was going to happen to her? How would she get through today? Her heart beat faster. She felt light headed.

Heber glanced in her direction and handed her his leather pouch. "Here, you look pale. Drink," he said.

Yael took the water with a shaky hand and drank deeply while keeping her eye on her captor. Heber's hair was thinning and a few strands were tucked behind his ear. His eyes were gentle like his voice.

"We travel this way." Heber pointed to the east. "My village is just on the outskirts of Kedesh. I don't like being around many people."

When they arrived, Yael noticed the towering mountains to the north. One even had a white cap on its summit. It appeared covered in mineral salt. Could that be snow, she wondered. The valley before them was lush with green vegetation. Heber explained that the inland sea was just a two hours walk away. Yael saw some rudimentary stone structures spaced far away from one another. Heber led her to a rustic dwelling with a big animal tent in front of it.

"This is our home." He pointed to the structure that didn't look like it could even fit three horses much less humans and animals. "My house is small as you can see, this is why I have a tent as well."

Yael gulped as she surveyed the tent, stone house, and verdant hills around them.

Heber showed her the cooking pit in the center of the only room in the house and the storage jars filled with almonds, olives, and wheat along the wall. "When it's not too cold, I like to sleep in the tent, but it's up to your choosing."

Yael was confused by his tone. Was he trying to be considerate? It was likely a trick to let her guard down. "What would you like me to do?" she stuttered.

"Help with the fire. I'll gather some wild greens," he offered.

That night, they had stew with bitter greens, wheat berries, and various herbs that Yael never tasted before. By evening, Heber stretched his arms over his head and yawned.

"Like I said, sleep where you wish." And then he went into the outdoor tent, laid on a fuzzy sheep skin, and went to sleep.

Yael was puzzled. Wasn't she going to be raped? Maybe not tonight. All right, it's a respite. She found in the stone dwelling a lamb skin, laid it on the floor, and closed her eyes.

When she awoke, Heber was standing in the door way studying her. "Are you hungry? I have some eggs." Heber started the fire and took out a pan. He knew how to cook. Yael wondered how long he lived by himself.

"You will notice that there are about twenty of us who live in this village. It's called Elon-bezaanannim. My brother's family is over there." Heber gestured beyond the walls to his right. The family of Boaz lives beyond them. And the others, I barely talk to. As I said before, I like being on my own."

Yael sat quietly listening to him as he finished cooking the eggs. "Can I assist you?" she offered.

"Yes, over there in the red painted jar by the wall," he pointed. "I have some dried plums. Those would be good."

Yael quickly found the jar. It was filled to the rim with the dark purplish fruit. Heber put the eggs in a pottery dish and handed one of them to Yael.

"I was married once," he spoke as he chewed on his eggs. "Sera died some years ago in childbirth. The baby died as well," Heber said softly. "Maybe it's because I'm old but I don't want to die without any children. I never saw anyone with hair like yours. You are the most beautiful woman, I've ever seen." He looked up at her admiringly and wiped his mouth on his sleeve. "I begged King Jabin to give you to me."

Yael swallowed hard. She steeled herself to prepare for what would happen. Looking down she trembled.

A gentle, warm hand covered hers. She looked up in surprise. Heber had reached over the table to hold her hand. "It's all right, little one. I have waited many years for children. I can wait until you desire it too. I know you have been through much."

Yael looked up at him in disbelief. How is this possible? But Heber just held her hand and she felt calm. With a nod, Heber finished eating, told her that he was going to check on his orchard and fields, and left.

Yael was stunned. She stared at the unadorned walls of her enclosure for a few moments and then cleaned up for the remaining hours. When Heber came back, he was holding a basket full of deep purple mulberries, barley, and few oranges. Yael had never seen such odd looking berries.

"Here, try one," Heber offered as he noticed her puzzled expression. Biting into the bumpy fruit, Yael tasted sweetness like honey. She smiled and then helped him with the evening meal. Once again after dinner, Heber told her to sleep where she wanted and he went into the tent.

The following weeks, the same thing happened. Heber would go out for the day to procure food or tend to his fields, Yael increasingly helped out on the home front, and at night they slept separately. She was relieved. On the third week, when Heber left, Yael stood outside and looked to the towering mountain in the distance.

"Oh, God of my fathers, thank you for having mercy on me. Thank you for giving me a kind man to be with. I will never see my family again but at least I will not suffer anymore."

Yael grew accustomed to Heber. She appreciated the kindness in eyes and the smile he greeted her with.

It was thirty days since she arrived at his home. After dinner, Heber yawned as he always did after their evening meal. Yael walked over to him and placed her hand on his shoulder. It was strong from years of hard work. He looked up at her in surprise.

Yael quietly spoke as her hand began to caress the back of his neck, "I would like..." She fell quiet. Heber moved his hand on top of hers and held it still.

A few seconds passed, Yael spoke again, "I would be willing, I mean, I will sleep with you in the tent tonight."

Heber stood up and faced her. His eyes grew a little misty as he leaned in to kiss her lips. They were warm and sweet. Yael found herself responding to him. Heber took her by the hand and led her into his tent.

Once inside, Heber ran his fingers through her wavy red hair. She shivered as she closed her eyes. “You are so beautiful, Yael.” He kissed her gently. As he trailed his fingers over her shoulder, his eyes met hers. He seemed to look for permission. Yael took his hands and placed them on her breasts.

The next morning, Yael woke up on her side with Heber’s arm around her waist. He kissed her back warmly. “I have to get going early,” he whispered. “It’s time to catch fish.”

Yael turned around to him. “Fish? Isn’t that only from the Great Sea?” she asked.

“Yes, no, we have plenty of fish in the Kinneret Sea. I’ll bring some home tonight and we’ll have a glorious fish stew!” Heber exclaimed smiling.

The days and months went by. Yael could see her belly start to protrude. She stopped having her cycle. When Heber came home one day from the fields, she shyly pointed to her waist. “Are you sick?” Heber looked worried.

“No, no, I think, I’m with child,” Yael said slowly.

Heber held his hands up high and said, “Hallelujah! Hallelujah!” And he fell on his knees and kissed her stomach.

It was hard to believe that was years ago. Yael pulled her burgundy robe over her shoulders. The air was crisp today. A ginger haired boy was darting between the towering Cedar and Oak trees.

Something was moving in the distance. Yael squinted her eyes to see better. There were five men on horses even further away.

“Merar!” she called. “Merar!”

The boy stopped his playing and looked up.

“Come back!” she summoned.

As the boy came to her side, the men on horses came closer and closer. Yael recognized the red turban and long dark beard of King Jabin. He changed little except for the gray streaks in his beard. She gulped pulling her son closer to her.

The horses approached. King Jabin nodded his head toward Yael. "Israelite slave of Heber," he said scornfully.

She gripped her son's hand tightly in her own.

"Where is my friend Heber?" he barked.

"Heber…Heber…," stuttered Yael. "He's gone to the sea today. He'll be back at sunset. He's at the sea."

Jabin looked at the sky and could see the sun three quarters of the way through the expanse. "That's only in a few hours. We'll wait. Bring us wine, woman," he commanded.

Yael urgently pushed her son into the stone structure and followed behind him. She filled cups of Heber's best wine and raced outside to serve them.

Jabin and his men sat on flat stones and laughed as they kept calling out for more drink.

Yael had never been more relieved to see Heber coming home sitting astride his donkey.

He had two baskets full of shiny fish on both sides of his animal. As soon as he saw the guests, he immediately leapt from the donkey.

With a panicked look towards Yael, he collapsed on his knees. "Your majesty!" he exclaimed bowing his head. "What an honor to have you here."

"Thank you, Heber," Jabin replied. "It's good to see you, old friend. We have much business to talk about."

"Yes, your majesty. Allow me to unload our fish and my wife will prepare dinner for you and your men."

"Excellent idea-ea, Heber. Excellent id…." Jabin drunkenly stuttered.

Yael roasted the fish whole over the fire stuffing them first with garlic and thyme. She carefully kept her son indoors. "Don't let them see you again," she warned.

"But why, Ima? We never have visitors," he whined.

"These are dangerous men. Stay indoors!" she barked.

Yael brought out the fish, freshly baked wheat bread from the morning, and goat cheese. Jabin and his entourage ate greedily while Heber nervously moved his food around his plate eating nothing.

Once the king finished his meal, he said, "Heber, I need your help and the help of the Kenites." The king slapped his hand on Heber's back. "It's those damn Israelites. They are growing restless. I'm going to need as many men as possible to defeat them once and for all. A messenger from Sisera conveyed that the battle may even end up close to here."

Heber looked with surprise at the king, who had some fish sticking out between his teeth.

"I need to raise up an army and I want you fighting and your Kenite people as well."

Heber shook his head in alarm. "But your majesty, yes of course, I'll do anything for you but, as you are aware, I've pursued a quiet life and haven't had contact with the other Kenites in many years."

"No concern!" the king bellowed, "Go to them anyway. Tell them their king commands it. If they don't, then they'll suffer the same fate as the bastard Israelites. Sisera will command them. Tell them, Heber! Tell them."

Lowering his head, Heber said, "Yes, your majesty. I will do as you wish."

With a loud laugh, Jabin said, “You are indeed the most loyal of friends.”

Yael looked on shivering in the doorway of her home.

CHAPTER 22

There was a frenzy of activity by the palm trees between Beth El and Ramah. The nighttime breeze was slowly warming as the dark sky turned to light gray. Deborah called for everyone to arrive before the sun rose. It was going to be a hot day and she wanted most of the training to conclude before the sun scorched the hills. Yoram had finished preparing two groups of men. These newly minted soldiers were in charge of teaching the basics to any new man or woman who arrived.

Deborah had been meeting with men and women at the oasis for just about a year now. Haggai, Ner, Shmuel, and Yonah could wield a dagger with purpose, brandish a sword with good technique, and even shoot most arrows straight. Deborah looked out with pride over the five hundred people who overcame their own fears to join her.

However, she knew they weren't ready yet. She needed many more good men and women. They also needed to train longer to overcome any hesitation that can come in the heat of a battle. Sisera commanded thousands and had hundreds of chariots and iron weapons. The Israelites had to be ready and only strike when they stood a good chance of victory. As Deborah surveyed the people, she knew that she would only have one chance.

"Deborah! Deborah!" exclaimed Haggai as he ran to her side. "Look out there!" he pointed to the north. A small group of men were approaching the palm trees. Deborah squinted her eyes. There were only four men. One on a horse and the other three on donkeys. Their weapons weren't drawn.

"Let's see what they want," Deborah said cautiously.

Within minutes, the men arrived at Deborah's camp. Her fellow Israelites circled the newcomers in curiosity. The man sitting astride his horse had curly jet black hair. He wore a waist leather skirt and his wide muscular chest looked bronze in the sun.

"Barak! You've come!" exclaimed Yoram joyfully. "Welcome! We are so glad you are here!"

Barak scrutinized the closely shaven man and then cast his gaze on the crowd around him. The three men with him descended from their donkeys and stood silently.

Pursing his lips, Barak athletically leapt off his horse. He was shorter than his companions. With a glance towards Yoram, he said, "Yes, I received your message. I see you already have a small army here, but where is the woman leader you wrote of?"

Deborah stepped through the people. Her hair was braided down her back and her sleeveless tunic revealed strong arms. "I am Deborah and these are my people. I have heard you are a good military commander, Barak. I welcome you here, as well."

Barak looked at her in surprise and then grinned. "So the mother of Israel is a beautiful woman." He got down on one knee, took her hand, and kissed the back of it.

No one acted like this with Deborah. Many people shifted uncomfortably, unsure of how Deborah would respond.

She stood there glaring at him as his warm lips grazed her hand. Feeling her face flush with indignation, she pulled her hand sharply from his and said, "You must be thirsty and hungry."

Looking at a slender man to her right, she called, "Ner! Please take Barak and his men to the shade of the palm trees and give them some nourishment." She turned abruptly and walked away as Barak stared at her until she disappeared.

Sometime later, after Deborah finished with target practice, she knew she would have to talk with her new guests. With a deep sigh, she walked slowly towards the palm trees as their spindly leaves waved in the sizzling breeze.

Barak was reclining under the palm branches, with his back supported by the tree's trunk. Even relaxed, his arms looked powerful. His comrades were sitting by his side.

"Shalom, Barak, I wanted to make sure you have eaten and drunk to your satisfaction," Deborah stated.

Barak smiled and slowly stood up. He was barely taller than Deborah but his shoulders were wider than any man she had met. Running a hand through his coarse dark hair, he said, "You are most gracious. The water was sweet and cool, the cheese delectable, and the bread was satisfying." He paused as his eyes met hers.

"Let me introduce you to my friends." He raised his hand, motioning for his men to stand as well.

"This is Elon from the tribe of Zebulun. We have known each other for twelve solar years. We have staged a few little incidents on King Jabin. With only nine men, we chased his soldiers liked scared girls out of six settlements." Barak mischievously winked at his companion.

Deborah looked with curiosity at Elon who looked as sturdy as a tree with his thick muscular legs and round, dense waist.

Barak pointed to his second friend. "This is Helon from my own tribe of Naphtali. Helon and I grew up together at my father, Abinoam's house." Helon smiled towards Deborah.

"And my good friend, Maon, also of my tribe. Maon is the best fighter I have ever known. I trust him anytime, anywhere." Barak playfully slapped his back.

Deborah looked over the three men. Maon was much thinner than Elon but Deborah could see the lithe strength of his arms. She imagined that he would be quick in battle. While

Elon looked fierce and Maon capable, Helon smiled at Deborah with a placid smile.

Considering the men before her, Deborah responded, “I’m pleased to meet all of you. These are hard times for our people and we need all the help we can muster.”

With a quick nod to their leader, she said, “Barak, I would like to see you work with our more experienced men and women. Yoram has trained them as far as he can. We need to raise the level of expertise, if we will ever have any hope of defeating Sisera.”

Barak studied Deborah intently.

After a few moments, he said, “Give me your best and I’ll see what they can do.”

The sun was shining in full force in the sky above. The men and women rested in the shade of the trees and drank water to hydrate.

When the worst of the heat passed, they all went back to work. Some joined Asher in making arrow heads and daggers, the new recruits worked with Ner and Shmuel under Yoram’s guidance, and those ready to take their skills to the next level went to train with Barak and his friends.

Deborah watched from the distance as Barak worked with the thirty men. He had them line up in a straight line holding a sword as he scrutinized their posture.

“You might think your arm is the most important weapon,” he said. “But this is not true,” Barak pointed to his head. “It is your mind. It is your thoughts. It’s how you see yourself, your men, and your perception of the enemy.” He fell quiet and looked at his men standing straight. “Today, we will work on your body but know that the mind is the best weapon any warrior can wield.”

Barak showed the men how to move efficiently, wasting as little energy as possible. "No unnecessary movements," he warned. "You will be tired during a battle and hungry and thirsty. You must conserve and make every thrust count."

The day came to an end. Barak set up a tent at the oasis to sleep through the night while most of the others went home to their families.

Deborah reluctantly went home that night. She knew that soon it would be better if all her soldiers camped together. This would save precious time in training but also build up stronger relationships with one another. When Deborah stepped through the doorway, she saw a very pregnant Mara standing over a pottery jar.

"Mara, let me help you," Deborah said.

Mara rubbed her lower back in some discomfort.

"Just sit. I'll get whatever you need." Deborah motioned to a chair.

"Thank you, but I like doing for myself." Mara said with a slightly pained expression. "It feels worse just sitting."

Surveying how far her belly extended, Deborah said, "You look ready to give birth any moment, Mara. I'm happy for you, Lappidoth, and… for me too."

With a wide grin, Mara's cheeks puffed up. "The midwife said she thinks it will be in a couple of weeks."

After dinner with Lappidoth and Mara, Deborah collapsed on her bedding in the loft and fell asleep immediately.

It felt like it was only minutes later, when Deborah was jarred awake. She was sweating. Was it another nightmare? She sat up. Lappidoth was snoring loudly on the other side of the loft with Mara peacefully slumbering beside him. Then she heard loud knocks on the door down below. Her heart started to beat fast. Deborah scrambled down the rope ladder and raced to the doorway. There was her father in law, Abidan. He was out of breath and wearing his nighttime tunic.

"D…Deborah!" he said with ragged breath. "King Jabin sent a group to raid Beth El. There must be fifty men. They are looking for you. You must get away while you can!"

"What? But Sisera is up north. This can't be," Deborah said dubiously.

"It's not Sisera. They claim to be sent by the king. They are going house to house. Go! We'll tell them you ran away to the sea. Go!"

Deborah saw the panicked look to his eyes and turned around to quickly dress. She grabbed a loaf of bread and a pouch of water and ran to her donkey out front. The sky was charcoal gray. Just a sliver moon shined dimly in the distance. Deborah could barely make out any stars above. Deborah made her way through the darkness to the path that led to Ramah.

Hours later that morning, hundreds of Israelites descended at the oasis.

Ner, in great upset, exclaimed, "King Jabin has overtaken Beth El! He has men stationed practically by every home. The soldiers have beaten some of the men."

Deborah looked at Ner in great worry. "Is Jabin in Beth El?"

"No," Ner shook his head. "He sent an emissary. One of the lesser known captains called Zonar."

Yonah, with disorderly hair added, "They are terrorizing our people. What if they don't leave?"

There were hundreds of upset men and women surrounding Deborah under the palm trees and hundreds more already training in their groups. Barak and his companions had just joined the conversation.

Elon erupted, “This perhaps is our time to attack. Reports state the Canaanites only have fifty men in Beth El. We could easily overtake them.” A number of the Israelites cheered at Elon’s suggestion.

Deborah listened quietly.

Haggai yelled out, “Let’s take revenge. Let’s wreak vengeance on King Jabin!”

More cheers erupted.

Barak called out, “No.” His face was the shade of copper and his eyes were black as night. “Now is not the time for direct confrontation.” Everyone quieted down.

“But that doesn’t mean we do nothing,” Deborah added. The men turned towards her. Speaking deliberately, she continued, “We will stage small raids from within Beth El. Small attacks and then retreat. We’ll….”

“Are you saying retreat? We aren’t cowards!” yelled Calir from the Israelites.

“No! No one is a coward but we must be strategic, so we can ultimately win,” Deborah stated defiantly.

Barak looked thoughtfully at Deborah.

After a few seconds, he spoke. “I believe our leader may indeed be right. Let’s go for a smaller victory with smaller losses. This could be a way of sending a message to King Jabin not to trouble us.”

Yoram moved to the front. “Let’s give Barak and Deborah a few moments to work out our plan. We’ll discuss our course of action in a few hours. Everyone go back to your training. It will certainly be needed now more than ever.”

At the end of the day, Deborah and Barak stood before the Israelites.

Deborah spoke first, “We have continued reports of Jabin’s men harassing our people in town. We are going to send two groups with no more than five people to go into Beth El at sunset to attack a few soldiers at a time. When the moon is visible, they will retreat back here.”

Calir commented, “This doesn’t seem to be a brave way to attack.”

“Yes, yes it is,” Barak added. “This was how we inflicted damage to Jabin’s forces up North. If we do it right, we should be able to expel his soldiers.”

“Remember,” Deborah said, “The population of Beth El is our people. They will help us so we can help them.”

CHAPTER 23
SAVING BETH EL

The sun started to descend behind the horizon. A faint orange glow lingered in the evening sky. Deborah was with Yoram, Haggai, Ner, and Shmuel. They stealthily moved from behind trees and homes. Wearing taupe robes and head coverings, they blended with the neutral stones around them. Cautiously, avoiding the Canaanite men, they finally, arrived out of breath at Binah's stone house close to the market-place. The nervous woman quickly let them in before they were seen.

As the wooden door hurriedly closed behind them, Binah gripped one of the oak wooden pillars. Surveying her guests, her heart slowed down.

With relief, she exclaimed, "Deborah! Deborah, it's you!" Binah took two steps towards her old friend. "Look at you," she said stepping back and scrutinizing the fine lines radiating from the corners of her eyes and raised cheekbones. "You seem older."

Deborah embraced her friend and spoke in a hushed tone. "We'll only be here until dark. You won't see us again afterwards." Deborah motioned to the men to sit down as she anxiously looked out the window.

In the meantime, Barak took Maon, Helon, Elon, & Yonah with him to Shelah's house on the other side of town. He, too, watched the sky change.

The darkness of evening began to envelop the town as most of the people went to their homes. A man with a wide forehead stood erect in front of his men in the courtyard. With a sword at his side, he said, "These Israelites have robbed our king of his tribute. We are here to teach them to respect their rulers." Zonar coughed and spit a glob of yellow phlegm on the ground.

"Yes, our Lord!" cried out the men with him.

"Some of us should stay in the square, the rest of you find whatever you desire," Zonar proclaimed.

One young soldier stood with his comrades. "Let's grab a jug of wine from that old man's house. I think his name is Shel or Shelah. I hear it's the best in the town," he said with a grin. "Who wants to take what is ours?"

A few men went with the young soldier in the direction of Shelah's house.

Twenty other men dispersed while the remaining thirty Canaanites gathered in the market square tossing chunks of wood on the fire.

A goat was braying as it was dragged towards the fire pit. Shadows moved behind the men. One of the soldiers took a knife to the animal's throat as it whined. Just as the blade touched its hide, the man suddenly jerked upright, eyes bulging, and gasped. A tip of an arrow poked out between his ribs. A woman with brunette hair waving over her shoulders stood twenty cubits away with a raised bow. The dying man looked with pleading eyes to his comrades around the fire. Their faces were frozen in shock as he collapsed.

The bushes rustled behind them with Israelites dashing out. Zonar stood up hurriedly and yelled, "Men! Quick! We are under…" A bronze blade went through his neck and blood gushed over his tunic.

The two remaining Canaanites reached for their daggers and swords, however, Yoram, Haggai, Ner, and Shmuel quickly overpowered them.

Within minutes, Zonar's men, who had remained in the courtyard, lay dead around the crackling fire as the goat bleated and scampered off.

The people of Beth El, in the meantime, tentatively peered out from behind windows in their homes.

Deep throated screams and muffled yells exploded from homes and walkways.

Three soldiers were surprised by Barak. They turned and charged him. Within seconds, he stabbed them to death. Maon, Helon, Elon, and Yonah had separated and stealthily, they picked off the remaining soldiers one and two at a time until they could find no more Canaanites.

An earie quiet descended over the town. Deborah saw Barak in the distance and fervently waved her arm. It felt so heavy. Was it possible that they succeeded? She surveyed the dead soldiers.

Barak approached her as he peered into the darkness, searching for any survivors. The only ones moving in the night were the Israelites.

"Hallelujah," exclaimed Ner. "We have defeated the Canaanites!"

Deborah wiped her sweaty forehead on her arm. She drew a long breath as she stood tensely.

The town's people cautiously came out of their homes. Shelah hobbled to Deborah. He leaned on his staff and said exultantly, "You saved our town, Deborah. Thank you."

"It isn't over, old friend," she said warily. "Today, we started a war."

"It is a war that we will win," Barak interrupted. His muscular chest heaved as his breathing evened out. "But that will be for tomorrow. I think our people have earned a reason to celebrate tonight."

The people of Beth El declared the following day a festival. A holiday celebrating a victory over King Jabin and the vanquishing of his commander, Zonar. They brought out lambs, goats, and sheep to be roasted. Deborah's people at the oasis were invited to join the celebration. The sun moved west along the sky as vegetables were sliced, fires lit, and wine poured.

The air was fragrant with the smell of sweet bread baking and meat roasting. Two of the townsmen began to play their flutes and timbrels as hundreds of people descended joyfully into the market square.

A round faced man walked over to Deborah.

"Lappidoth! Shalom," Deborah said as soon as she saw him.

A big smile spread on Lappidoth's face. "It's a great day, Deborah! Our town is safe and we have a daughter."

"A daughter?" Deborah looked at him confused. "Mara! Mara gave birth?"

"Just this morning. She is resting." Lappidoth beamed. "Mara wants to call her D'vori, named after you, of course."

Deborah hugged him tightly. "This is truly wonderful news, Lappidoth. I look forward to meeting her tonight."

"I think I'll have some wine." Lappidoth licked his lips. "Many, many things to celebrate tonight."

An entire lamb roasted on a metal spigot over the flames. The aroma of smoked meat was tantalizing. Deborah sat back and slowly drank her wine as she surveyed the people in front of her. A young man and woman flirted with each other on the other side of the fire. Some held up their wine goblets singing:

"To King Jabin's permanent defeat!

May Sisera be engulfed in flames!

To Deborah, the mother of Israel!

To Barak, the fiercest warrior of all

To Life!"

They took hearty gulps of wine as music filled the air. Deborah saw Barak sitting next to the wine jugs. His arms were defined, his chest powerful, and his dark curly hair accentuated his face. No doubt about it, Barak was a handsome man. Deborah stared at him. Suddenly, Barak looked up and caught her stare. A big grin expanded across his face. Deborah looked away quickly.

Olives brined in salt were passed out on platters along with cucumbers and wild greens. Platters of roasted meat and fresh bread to soak up the juices came next. The people ate, danced, sang, and some fell asleep even while holding their wine cups. Later, Deborah saw Barak cozying up with a giggling young woman. His arm was around her shoulders as she nestled closer to him. Moments later, they vanished.

Deborah guzzled three more cups of wine and stumbled to her home she shared with Mara and Lappidoth.

CHAPTER 24
KING JABIN

King Jabin resided in his administrative building in Hazor. This city was built around Lake Hulel, north of the Kinneret Sea. Charred limestone formed the walls of his palace. Two sets of six stone pillars separated the main meeting room from the two smaller rooms on the side. In the big central space was a large ornate wooden chair with carvings of two bull heads on the shoulders.

As Jabin sat back on the throne, the amber wood creaked. It was one of the few things that survived Joshua's attack from years ago. Joshua's Israelites traveled north and easily conquered settlements. Townsmen fled in terror when they learned that the warriors who devastated Jerricho were en route to their homes. Those remaining were barely able to fight back. It was a dark time, indeed.

Before Joshua, back in his father's generation, thought Jabin, Hazor was the greatest city of all. It spanned acres and acres! Jabin closed his eyes and smiled. There were over twenty thousand residents spread out over the higher and lower plains of the city. Slaves built homes, buildings, and even shrines dedicated to the gods of Baal and El. Jabin remembered fondly, as a boy, the caravans of traders that visited his father bringing tin for the metal workers to transform into bronze. The riches then! There were golden bowls brimming with sapphires, amethyst, and lapis lazuli.

"Jori, my son," his father King Jabin said to him when he was eight years old. "Someday you will be king over the entire land." His father took his hand and waved it in the air. "The land to the east, west, north and south will be yours to command. Learn well, my son."

Jori looked up to his father. He looked impressive with his indigo robes as he sat on the newly made chair with carved bulls. The wood was polished so smoothly that it gleamed when the sun shined through the window.

That was years ago, before the Israelite attack, before Joshua murdered his father.

King Jabin's forehead furrowed as he gripped the nicked arm rails. His knuckles whitened and small splinters of wood pierced his finger. As a few beads of blood dripped onto the floor, Jabin's mind raced.

As though victory wasn't enough, the Israelites set the city on fire. Smoke billowed out of the shrines, homes, and palace. Jori was ferreted away from the city by Adan, the king's most trusted advisor. He remembered the terror of the flight and how his feet ached from newly formed blisters. Adan growled, "Hurry!" and the boy ran even though it felt like scraps of metal lodged into his tender feet. After hours, he and Adan stood on a hill and he could still smell the acrid smoke. Jori felt nauseous, as his feet throbbed.

Days after the attack, Jori and Adan returned to the destroyed city of Hazor. As soon as they saw the burnt remains, the advisor fell on his knees with his face contorted in emotion. The boy stood petrified in place.

Adan then noticed some survivors hobbling towards them. Getting up quickly, he glared at the boy. "Stand up straight!" hissed Adan. Jori looked at him confused. "I said greet your people."

Jori only reached the height of Adan's chest but he felt even smaller.

Three men approached them. One had a bloody rag wrapped around his head. The second man limped on one leg and used a stick to lift up a mangled leg. The third's face was swollen with purplish and blue bruises.

"Tell the survivors, you are sorry," Adan counseled, "but the day will come to avenge them. Tell them you will rebuild. Tell them that the gods Baal and El were angry but they will now fight on our side."

The men staggered toward the shaking new king.

"Your majesty, we are sorry. They defeated us," the man wearing the bloody rag said sullenly.

Trying to hold back tears, Jori just stood there transfixed. Adan jostled his shoulder abruptly.

Jori stuttered, "I…we…" and he coughed. Adan stepped forward with a low raspy voice. "What our young king means is that we will avenge our people. The bastard Israelites will pay!" His face was beet red in rage, and Jori stood ram rod straight with eyes wide open.

That was only twenty years ago. And so much had happened. When Jori turned thirteen, he took his father's name, Jabin. He wanted the Jabin name to be resurrected to honor his father and redress his people. And then he began to rebuild. It was slow at first because the destruction was great. Jabin and his fellow Canaanites scavenged anything that could be salvaged from the wreck. The new king Jabin rebuilt many personal homes, two of the shrines, and even the palace. When he found the throne, he saw only one leg of it remained attached, the seam was split open, and the bulls splintered. Jabin restrained his emotions as he ordered its repair. Wood was glued and its pieces were put back together. Jabin decided he would rule from the cracked throne and when he was successful he would build a new one.

Even as a twenty year old king, Jabin knew that he needed more soldiers. Adan, now with gray thinning hair, had an idea one day.

"Your majesty, there are Sea Peoples known as the Sherden who have crossed the Great Sea," said Adan. "They are building settlements along the northern coast. They say many more are coming. They wish to move further in-land to spread out. Why don't we propose an alliance? They will help us fight the Israelites and we will divide the land between us."

Jabin stroked his long black beard. Ever since the palace was rebuilt, he vowed never to cut his beard until all the Israelites were exterminated.

"Adan, send messengers to these newcomers. Make the offer to them. If they fight with us, they can have their choice of land to live in and farm. This territory will finally be ours."

Weeks later, the Sherden's response was delivered to the king.

Peace unto you. We will hear your terms.

Our leader Sisera travels to meet with you.

Jabin had heard that there were thousands of Sea Peoples. He was excited. Now he could fight the Israelites, defeat them, and then in time kill them off. He would then be king of Israel, king of Canaan! Jabin smiled. Then he would send out his army and conquer Egypt to the south and the old Hittite Empire to the north. He would be king of the world!

Jabin remembered the first time he met Sisera. The Sherden leader strutted into his palace. His deep brown hair was cut short to his scalp and his face had sharp angular lines. Even as he walked, he emanated power. Sisera's eyes narrowed when he first addressed Jabin.

"Your majesty," Sisera barely nodded his head toward Jabin on his throne. "My people have overcome many perils to arrive at this land. We are interested in your offer but are unable to wait for land allotment. We require coin, animals, and grain in exchange for military support. However, when we completely decimate the Israelites, we expect the final payment to be the best grazing land."

Jabin stood up with his black beard reaching to his waist. A brilliant red turban rested on his head. The Sherden commander didn't move as the two men faced one another in silence.

Jabin slowly smiled. "Sisera, I believe we understand one another. I can give you, for now, two barrels of dried barley, three oxen, five horses, ten lambs, and twenty sheep as a token of good will. More payment will come to you from your raids on Israelites towns and villages. We only expect fifty percent of your gains. The rest, you keep for yourself."

Sisera stared at Jabin.

"When all the Israelite towns and villages have been conquered," Jabin continued, "and their people are driven into the sea, then you can have the entire coast line and your choice of towns in the hillside for you and your people."

Sisera grunted his agreement.

"Excellent!" Jabin declared. "Let's have a meal to celebrate." Jabin clapped his hands together and four male servants brought out a wooden table and set it in the middle of the room. Bowls with almonds, pistachios, and figs were brought out. Sisera and Jabin sat together sampling the nuts and fruit as women brought out jugs of wine and filled their cups to the brim. Freshly baked wheat bread was passed to the men. It was lighter than barley and was soft to the touch. A servant then brought out roasted pigeons on large bronze serving trays with small cups of grape vinegar for dipping both meat and bread.

By the third cup of wine, Sisera relaxed and laughed with his partner. "I must admit, your majesty, nothing brings me greater pleasure than the thrill of battle. I am happy to work with you and for the good of my people."

Jabin raised a cup. "Then to your people and to mine. May our descendants be as numerous as the stars in heaven and may we prosper in this land!"

They drank and drank.

Jabin never regretted his alliance of twenty years with Sisera and the Sherden. They proved to be true warriors. He delighted in news of their raids and the spoils they brought back. In the meantime, he had arranged his own army. For the last couple of years, his men attacked more and more Israelite towns. Zonar was one of his favorites. Just last year, he took over the towns of Kinneret and Ramah in Naphtali, and Bethlehem and Taanach in Zebulun. By now, Sisera and Jabin had conquered most of Israel. There were only the tribes of Ephraim and Benjamin that still resisted. Yes, they paid tribute, but it was not enough. It was just a matter of time before the entire land was his. Times were good and they were only going to get better.

A Canaanite shepherd wearing a torn and soiled robe banged on the door of the palace. A servant led the man in.

"Shalom! I'm sure you have good tidings for me," replied the king, sitting on his damaged wooden throne.

The messenger was an emaciated man who looked ready to faint. King Jabin yelled out, "Water, bring the man some water!" A servant ran over with a cup filled with cool liquid. After draining the cup, the man began.

"Sir, I'm sorry to tell you of this but you must know. Zonar in Beth El, well…"

Jabin scowled, "Zonar what?"

"Zonar w…was…" the messenger stuttered. "K…killed, sir, along with his army. The Israelites have banded together."

"What? I thought they were beaten into submission!" erupted Jabin. "How dare they? How dare they attack Zonar and my men?" Jabin's face flushed red. "Who commands them? I'll have his head on a platter before winter!"

The messenger was shaking and sputtered out, "Sir, your majesty, they say it's not a man that commands them but… a woman."

Jabin stared at him in disbelief. He couldn't believe what he heard.

"What did you say?" Jabin asked.

"I…I…" the thin man looked like he was going to pass out.

"Get the man a chair!" bellowed the king.

A servant ran with a chair and the exhausted messenger collapsed into it. A cup of date juice was pressed into his hand and he drank. Jabin sat watching him quietly.

Collecting himself, the king said, "I think I may have misheard you. You told me that Israelites attacked one of my best generals and killed him and his soldiers? Also that the enemy is led by a female?"

The messenger exhaled and spoke slowly, "Yes, yes, your majesty."

"Well, this must end immediately," declared Jabin. "Rest up, young man. I'm sending you back south with a message for her. We will fight this out once and for all!"

Jabin summoned his servant Dothin and instructed him to send a message to Heber the Kenite.

Friend Heber,

Tell me, how many Kenites have you persuaded to join me in battle?

Know that there will be grievous punishment to those who refuse me, but also generous rewards to those who assist.

Bring them at once to me in Hazor.

A battle is coming at the Wadi Kishon next month.

King Jabin sent another servant to Sisera in Haroseth Hagoim.

To the greatest warrior of them all, Sisera.

I'm sure you heard about the Israelite uprising.

I have set a date and place for a battle to finally end their rebellion.

I need you at the head. Know that I will reward you handsomely for your victory.

You will have your choices of gems, animals, maidens, and land.

Assemble your men, chariots, and horses! Glorious victory awaits you!

CHAPTER 25
SISERA AT HAROSETH HAGOIIM

It was overcast on this last day of summer. Sisera stretched out on a bench in his olive grove behind his large stone house. He stared at the clouds above and gave a bored yawn.

"Miri! Miri!" he called out lying on his back. "Bring me some wine! Wine!"

Within moments, a young woman half ran, half stumbled to him, with a cup filled with red liquid. She tripped on a rock and some of the contents spilled on her white robe.

"I'm sorry, sir. I'm sorry," she said fearfully as she bowed before him holding up the cup two thirds filled.

"Stupid girl," snarled Sisera as he grabbed the cup from her shaking hand.

Drinking the wine in one gulp, Sisera stared at the girl on her knees. He stood up and lifted his robe and tunic up to his waist.

"Suck! Suck like a baby on her mother's teat!"

The girl bent down on one knee until her head was level with his now fully erect yerech. She sucked as hard as she could. As his breathing increased, she went faster as he thrust into the back of her throat. After a few seconds, her stomach heaved. Gruel from her breakfast spewed out of her mouth and ran down his yerech. Her eyes grew wide in panic as he looked at her angrily.

"Please, sir!" she pleaded as she wiped his yerech on her robe and then continued to fellate him. Sisera let out a moan before he exploded in her mouth. Pulling away, he lowered his tunic.

"You disgust me. You are nothing but a filthy Israelite. Go back and work in the kitchen before I give you away to the townsmen."

The girl nodded, got up, and ran towards the house.

Sisera laid back down on the wooden bench studying the cloud formations above. He was bored. There was no other way to put it. It had been weeks since his last raid. He just didn't know what to do with himself.

"Sisera," called out a middle aged woman wearing a pink silk robe cinched at the shoulder with an iron clasp in the shape of a lion. "I think we should plan an end of summer celebration. I can summon out the town elders. It can be Sisera's day; in honor of you, of course. We can have the prettiest slaves dance for you and the fattest pig roasted."

"Quiet, old woman," sneered Sisera. "Leave me." Sisera closed his eyes.

"Er, my apologies," the middle aged woman softly stated as she took a few steps backward and returned to the house.

Sisera was irritated by everyone, especially his own mother. If she was any other woman, he would have her executed. He didn't know why he even let her live with him. Well, she did manage the household. Soon there would be another raid, another adventure.

Sisera dozed off as a cool afternoon breeze blew through the olive trees.

"Sisera! Sisera!" his mother called out.

"What? What do you want, woman?" Sisera stirred.

"It's Renu, one of King Jabin's men, he is in the house and wants to talk with you. The servants have already brought him some goat cheese, bread, grapes, and ale."

Sitting up reluctantly, Sisera stretched, belched, and walked into his stone house through the back door.

At the wooden table, in the middle of the room, sat a man. Gray and brown curls peeked out from the white turban covering his head. He wore a faded ruby mantle.

"Renu! I haven't seen you in years," Sisera called out as he took a seat opposite Renu. "I assume King Jabin has been happy with my conquests?"

Swallowing his fermented barley beverage, Renu smiled towards Sisera.

"Our majesty has been happy to hear of your success on the northern coast. We understand that the tribe of Asher is completely subjugated. Excellent work."

Sisera grabbed a handful of purple grapes and stuffed them into his mouth. Chewing with juice trickling out over his bottom lip, he spit out the seeds onto the floor.

"So," Sisera said after wiping his mouth on his sleeve. "What brings you here?"

Renu put his ale down. "It's the Israelites down south. The tribe of Ephraim. They are banding together. Just weeks ago, they retook Beth El and killed Jabin's captain Zonar and his men. Jabin has challenged them to fight him up in the north. He wants you in the lead. There is no one he trusts more than you."

Sisera's face showed no emotion but his eyes opened wider. "Is that so?"

Renu continued, "It's hard to believe but it appears a woman leads the Israelites. She is called Deborah."

"A woman?" Sisera let out a loud belly laugh picturing in his mind what he would do to such a female. With a big smile, he said, "I find it hard to imagine that she is any threat." Sisera grabbed a thick slice of bread and bit his teeth fiercely into it.

"More Israelites are joining her army," Renu warned. "King Jabin wants you to lead the battle."

Sisera's mouth was full of chunks of bread. "So, when do we fight?"

"Very soon," Renu said, "very soon."

That night, Sisera summoned the leaders of his people. The Sherden council men gathered outside in the village square around a fire. The sun set moments ago.

"Sisera," said a balding man called Horer. "We haven't seen you in days. New looms arrived yesterday and the fields are full of wheat."

Sisera rolled his eyes. "I care little about the administrative details of this town. I'm here because a battle is coming. King Jabin has sent word that the Israelites are amassing an army. He needs his best soldiers to defeat them."

Kalir, a hefty younger man, with light tawny hair called out, "Finally! I've been waiting for the next raid."

Horer replied sternly, "No! No more battles."

Sisera turned his head to face the elder. "What? What did you say, Horer?"

"You heard me," the hairless man said. "Our people endured much. I have heard from the women and men that they want only to live off the land, fish in the sea, and raise their children. They desire no more land. They are content to keep what they have. We have fought many battles for Jabin. It's time we cease and beat our swords into ploughshares. There is no need for war anymore."

Sisera was shocked to hear this dissent. He studied the faces of the seven remaining elders. Most of them were young like Sisera himself. What did the other men think? Not that it mattered, he could kill them all. Sisera looked at Horer, so sure of himself. He observed Kalir's excitement but what about the others?

"What say the rest of you?" Sisera asked.

Kalir spoke again. "War will always be with us as long as there are Israelites. I favor continuing our fight until every Israelite is killed."

The other men lifted their fists into the air in agreement with Sisera and Kalir

Horer saw that he was outnumbered. "Do as you wish, Sisera, but we should offer our men a choice this time. I'm sure you don't want any deserters, right?"

"You are a coward, Horer," Sisera scoffed derisively. "There is no greater honor than battle. Yes, I will take voluntarily recruits but you will be surprised what men will do for plunder, women, and glory."

"I think you will regret this, Sisera," said Horer quietly.

CHAPTER 26

The next day the mood in Beth El was subdued. The people went to the fields, set up the market, and took care of their homes. The revelry of the night dissipated with the light of a new day.

Deborah was in the market early that morning. Many of her soldiers, including Barak, were sleeping through the fog left by drink and merriment. The town people gathered around her.

Shelah spoke first. "We are grateful to you, Deborah. You saved us, but for how long?"

"Do you think Jabin will send a bigger army to invade us?" inquired auburn haired Binah.

There were about ten men and women surrounding Deborah. She shifted from foot to foot as she looked at each person's face. Straightening her shoulders, Deborah spoke slowly, "I hear your concerns. I, too, share them. I do not believe this is the end. Defeating one of Jabin's captains does not defeat him, his army, nor his commander Sisera."

A lone man on horseback galloped towards Beth El. The townspeople stopped talking and put down their wares. The horseman wore a plated iron breast plate and was surely one of the king's men. Within moments, he was at the northern entrance to the market. Binah stood frozen as a statue.

"Who is your leader?" bellowed the Canaanite soldier from his horse. The people stared mutely at him. "I said, WHO is your leader?"

The people glanced at Deborah with uncertainty. Three Israelite men moved in front of her. Old man Shelah with his cane croaked out, "I am the leader! I am the one responsible for the upheaval yesterday!"

Another man decades younger than Shelah yelled out, "No, I am the leader."

The soldier sat astride his horse without moving. "I have a message for your judge, your leader. It is for no one else's eyes."

Deborah nudged her way through the three men shielding her until she was standing in front of the horse. "I am Deborah." Her legs were slightly shaking. "These are my people. What is your message?"

The Canaanite looked down in surprise at Deborah. He had heard rumors of a woman but this isn't what he expected. She was beautiful; a prize for any man to marry. Confusion spread over his face. "Are you really the female warrior?" he asked in disbelief.

"Are you here to kill me?" Deborah's shoulder muscles tensed as she reached for her bow.

Startled, the soldier replied, "Not today, woman. Here." He reached into his pouch and took out a rolled up scroll. Leaning from his horse, he held it out until one of the townsmen took it and handed it over to Deborah.

"We will meet again in the north," he said as he trotted out of Beth El.

When he left, one of the people asked, "Deborah, do you need a reader? I believe one of the youth has learned the alphabet."

Shaking her head, she replied, "No, I can read." Deborah unfurled the parchment and silently read the scroll.

Whoever you are, whatever you purport to be, know this,

I have begun to murder every Israelite baby, woman, and man in my towns and will continue unless you agree to face me with your army.

Let us fight up north.

Meet me at the Wadi Kishon at Japhia

on the first day of the seventh month.

If you refuse my challenge

then know that the rivers will flow with the blood of your people.

Your majesty and ruler King Jabin

Deborah's hands shook as she finished.

"What does it say?" one of women asked impatiently.

"It's…" Deborah swallowed her saliva. "It's a call for a battle."

Deborah looked at the people around her. "Well, at the very least, the fight will take place up north. Beth El will have peace for the time being."

A sigh of relief went through the small crowd.

She spoke again, "Wake up all my men and women immediately! Tell them to meet me by the palm trees. We have only four weeks to prepare."

The rest of the day was a blur. Her men and women arrived at the oasis bleary eyed. Deborah stood before hundreds of dazed people.

"I know you still feel the effects of wine but there is much work to be done. We must prepare for war," Deborah cajoled.

Stretching luxuriously, Barak reached his arms up over his head and yawned as he approached Deborah. "It feels rather early to be doing this. I was in the bed of a warm voluptuous woman. This is an unpleasant awakening."

"There is no time for joviality, Barak. You know as well as I do the challenges ahead," rebuked Deborah. They assembled their amateur soldiers. Barak took the men with the most experience as his 'elite' fighting squad. They went through maneuvers of efficient sword and battle ax techniques. Yoram reviewed the use of dagger and raising and lowering the shield with another group. Asher selected people to make more spear heads and knives. And Deborah worked with those with good aim to practice archery and sling shots.

By the time the sun began to set, everyone was tired. A camp fire was lit and women began to bake flat bread and cook stew to feed the army before them.

The days went by and the training grew more intense. Word had it that Jabin was amassing all the chariots he had under Sisera's leadership. The days for the Israelites were long and tiring. At night, though, when the sun went down, they allowed themselves to relax.

The full moon of the Hebrew month of Elul was shining brightly tonight. There was no more work to do other than to eat, drink, and converse. Dinner that night was a savory lentil stew with fresh chunks of garlic and onions. Men and women sopped up the broth with thick slices of barley bread and enjoyed sweet dates for dessert. Barak's friend Maon sat beside Deborah for a while.

"Our men are improving. Barak was impressed with how strong they have become. In a few months, they will be excellent soldiers."

Deborah noticed Maon's well-developed sinewy arms before looking back at the fire and sighed. "If only we had months. Time is running short."

"I didn't mean to dishearten you," Maon consoled. "Just wanted you to know that we are advancing."

A hearty laugh erupted on the other side of the fire. Barak was merry. Deborah glanced at his handsome face as he gestured dramatically before a few men and women. He was telling a good tale. Those around him broke into laughter as well. Then his eyes met Deborah's through the vapors of smoke from the fire. He stopped speaking, looked intently at her, and smiled. Deborah could feel heat race up to her cheeks. Thankfully, it was dark and no one could notice.

Was he getting up? He's not coming over, she thought. But he was. Barak waved to his admirers and walked around the fire pit to Deborah. "May I sit with you?" he asked in his deep voice.

"I…I…was just getting ready for sleep," Deborah said hurriedly.

"Only a few moments, it's all I ask." Barak sat down a bit too close to her.

Turning his head slightly to look at the woman by his side, he asked, "How are you faring, our Queen bee?"

Deborah looked toward the flames in front of her. "As bad or well as any of us could be."

"None of us have it easy," nodded Barak. "What do you fight for Deborah?"

"What?" she turned to him in puzzlement.

"None of us takes on this kind of trouble without a reason," Barak offered.

Deborah turned towards him. She had never verbalized how she came to be where she was. She thought of that last night of

Sukkot, the raid, the loss of Yael, her father, people she knew, and the loss of her childhood. Tilting her head down, she felt a pain rising up within her. It felt like a wave rising, getting higher, towering over her and within her.

Then a warm hand rested on her shoulder. The waters receded.

"I've had my own loss," conceded Barak with a pained look to his eyes. "My brother was murdered by these Canaanites."

Deborah sat upright and stared at Barak. Despite working closely for weeks, they never really shared their past with one another. "Tell me what happened," she gently inquired.

"My brother, Saad, was an amazing man." Barak stared into the flames. "Even though we were only fifteen months apart, he looked after me. He was my counsel. He was my laughter. He was my best friend." Kicking the dirt with his foot, a small cloud of dust flew into the air. "Saad was married and the proud father of a baby boy. He would tell me, 'Barakele, you will be next. I will drink so many cups of joy when you marry.'

"The Canaanites' invasion of Kadesh caught us by surprise. I was out in the hills with my sheep. I was in search of greener pasture and intended on having the evening meal at my brother's home." Barak's body froze as his jaw clenched. "He was just in the courtyard, grinding wheat, when the Canaanite men came upon him. He didn't even have time to grab a weapon. He was slaughtered as quickly as a goat! As though that wasn't enough, those Canaanite bastards chopped his body into pieces. Pieces!" Barak spit out these words furiously. "When I came back, half of the town was murdered and my, my brother…was…"

Barak fell silent. Deborah could feel his pain radiating through the air between them. "Well," he looked at her with fire in his eyes. "I wasn't going to be a shepherd anymore. I decided to be a warrior. I worked hard to make my body strong, master fighting, so I could expel these demons from my land and life!"

Deborah tentatively extended her hand and softy stroked his back. She could feel the strength of his tensed muscles. They sat there quietly.

Barak then turned towards Deborah and asked her once again how she came to be here. With a sigh, she spoke of the raid, her father, and to her surprise, she found herself telling him about Lappidoth. She felt ashamed to admit that she no longer knew her husband intimately and thus she would be childless and live with disgrace. Deborah never spoke so candidly but it felt safe to share. Barak nodded encouragement.

"Then, I realized in the past year," Deborah stated staring ahead, "that there was something I could do to help. Maybe everything has happened for a reason. I…cannot bring life to the dead but maybe I can throw off the yoke of Jabin."

Her forehead furrowed as she continued, "and give my people a life to look forward to." Deborah ceased speaking as an image of her sweet Aba came to her. He was smiling. Maybe, he'll be proud of me, she thought and shivered.

Suddenly, she felt exposed, vulnerable. Deborah stood up straight and abruptly stated, "We have a lot of work in the days ahead." Barak looked up gazing at her tenderly. He stood up and leaned towards her. His breath felt warm against her cheek. The smell of his skin was musky and alluring. Barak gently touched his lips to her forehead for a few long seconds. "Sleep well, Deborah," he said affectionately.

That night as Deborah laid on tops of palm fronds, she gazed at the big bright moon above her. She couldn't stop thinking about Barak. The sound of his voice, his aromatic smell, the look in his eyes, and the power of his body. She wished she could be close to him and feel his heart beat next to hers. And what would it be like to kiss him? Her hands traversed her body as she lay looking at the moon above.

The next morning, women set pots of water over hot coals to cook barley and dates for the morning meal.

Lanky Ner conversed with Shmuel. "Did I hear Shelah right that he wanted Deborah to stay back in Beth El?"

"He said he wanted to have some good men and women in case there's another attack," answered his friend.

Helon had just walked by on his way to the cooking pots. As he poured some of the hot cereal into his bowl, he said to his friend, Maon, "Some are staying in Beth El with Deborah to protect the villagers."

Maon shook his head, "I hope not too many. We will need as many as possible to fight Jabin."

Conversations created more conversations until Helon informed Barak that Deborah would be staying behind.

"That is outrageous!" Barak exclaimed. "Where is she? I must speak with her. Find her and tell her to meet me by the palm tree!"

Barak was pacing under the tree by the time Deborah arrived. He was wearing a waist skirt that revealed his deeply tanned chest. Deborah steered her eyes to his face.

"What is wrong, Barak?" she inquired confused.

"How do you explain yourself?" Barak roared. "Just so we are clear, I am not going up North without you. There will be no battle. The people have much trust in you."

Deborah stepped back in surprise. “I don’t know what you are talking about Barak. I…I, of course, I am coming. Everything in my life leads to this moment.”

Now it was Barak’s turn to be confused. “So you are not staying back in Beth El?”

Shaking her head, Deborah replied, “No, no…”

“But,” Barak said. “Helon told me that Shelah had asked you to stay and you agreed.

Deborah nodded her head. “I understand that he requested a handful of men and women to defend the town but rest assured, I am traveling with you and our people.”

Barak breathed a sigh of relief.

Deborah nodded. “We are in this together. I am unsure of what will happen. We certainly don’t have enough people to fight but, God willing, we will save not just the people of Beth El but all of Israel.”

Barak met her gaze. “I will see if we can increase our numbers. Perhaps the other tribes will join our battle. I am with you to the end.”

CHAPTER 27

Deborah stood on a large boulder as a warm breeze blew through her hair, in front of five hundred people by the oasis between Beth El and Ramah.

"Children of Israel, descendants of Abraham, Isaac, and Jacob," she called out. "We are on the cusp of war against the cruel King Jabin and his commander Sisera. You have been training for well over a year. We have made great progress."

Deborah paused and looked at the people in front of her. They were farmers, shepherds, metal workers, bakers, and weavers. Their expressions were serious but peaceful. It was hard to believe that they were capable of fighting. Yes, many had learned to use the bow and arrow, sling shot, ax, sword, and dagger but most lacked any experience of war.

Deborah continued. "The battle against our enemy will take place up north at the Wadi Kishon by Mount Tabor. We have training. We have God on our side. We only need more men and women to ensure our victory." Her voice was strong and steady. The crowd of Israelites listened attentively.

"Barak and his friends sent messages to the tribes of Naphtali and Zebulun in the north. I am rallying the people of Ephraim and Benjamin. Do any of you have relations with the other tribes of Israel? Now is the time to ask them to join us. Now is the time we will break off the Canaanite shackles as we did to the Egyptians." Deborah's voice grew stronger as she declared, "We will live as a free people in our land."

A loud spontaneous cheer rose from the people before her.

"Deborah! Deborah!" called out a young male with a closely cropped black beard. "I am from Menasheh. I have family who are Machir; it's a tribe from within Menasheh. I'll go and rally all I know."

Deborah looked at the young male, “Yarom, start out immediately. Thank you.”

Maon, one of Barak’s fighters, spoke out. “I will send messengers to Asher on the northern coast and Meroz.”

More people began to murmur and yell out offers to Deborah. It became so much that she couldn’t even hear their individual voices.

“If any of you have contacts with the rest of the tribes, meet me under the big palm tree,” she instructed. “In the meantime, go back to your training groups. We leave in one week.”

Ten men were already waiting for Deborah by the tree.

Ner, still thin but now sporting lean muscles, spoke first. “My sister-in-law lives in the hills to the east of the Jordan river. With your permission, I’d like to go immediately and talk to the leaders of Gad and Reuben.”

“Don’t you mean Gilead?” Deborah asked.

Ner shook his head, “It’s the same tribe. Some call them Gilead and others call them Gad.”

“Go at once, my friend,” responded Deborah.

Deborah rode a donkey back to her childhood home in Ramah. As the sun rose further in the sky, she wrapped a white scarf over her head and took a sip of water from her leather pouch. She hadn’t seen her mother in many months. Did Tamar even know what she was doing? As the hills grew higher and the rocky ground expanded, Deborah knew that by nightfall she would be face to face with her Ima. She looked up at the light blue sky.

"Please, God, let my mother understand. I don't want to upset her. Help me. Help me with my family. Help me with my people." Deborah closed her eyes for a moment and took in a long, deep breath.

After a few hours, her donkey labored up one of the largest hills in Ephraim. Deborah saw a large cave carved out of rock. There, she knew, laid her father, grandmother, and other family members she never met. Descending from the donkey, she walked over to its entrance. Little flecks of white limestone glistened on the huge rock blocking the entrance. Seeing that there was still another hour of sun light, Deborah put her hands on the stone and strained to move it.

Gradually, it gave way and Deborah successfully pushed it to the side. A rush of pungent air escaped the dark cavern. Slowly, Deborah walked in. To the right, laid her grandmother under a white linen cloth. This was the source of the odor, thought Deborah. On the left was the skeletal remains of her father.

Stepping between the dead, Deborah collapsed on her knees.

"Father! Aba! I miss you. I wish you were here. You would know what to do."

Her voice echoed in the cave.

After many minutes, she peered into the darkness. "Hineni, here I am! I am about to lead our people to war. I'm scared, Aba! I'm not sure how to do this. You taught me so much but I don't know if it's enough. Please guide me."

Turning her head to the right, she said, "Dear Savta, thank you for the love you have given me. I'm sorry, I didn't become a mother. Please forgive me."

Deborah sat in the dark cave. The outdoor sky was turning dark. She rose up and continued on to her home.

Her childhood home was one of five that were part of her father David's family compound. It was the first one after passing through the stone wall. Deborah studied the familiar stones in the walls and the well-worn wooden door. She ran her fingers over its rough grain. It all felt strange. There were so many memories growing up here. There was laughter, joy, and hardship. How odd it was to feel the passage of time with a simple wooden door.

Deborah stood there wondering if her mother was home or not. She secretly hoped that she wasn't, then she could send a message later. I've got to at least knock, she thought glumly to herself. Raising up her hand, Deborah rapped her knuckles on the aged door.

"Just a moment, Milcah! I'm coming," called out Tamar.

"Ima, it's me," Deborah replied as an old woman with gray hair opened the door.

In shock, Tamar asked, "Is it really you?"

Deborah closed the distance between them quickly and hugged her mother.

"Ima, were you going somewhere?"

Tamar said nothing as she held Deborah tightly.

With her eyes glistening with tears, Tamar looked at Deborah and said, "I was just getting ready to move some things into aunt Milcah's house temporarily until your brother is ready to move in. I was just packing a few things."

Suddenly quiet, Tamar inspected her daughter. "Deborah, how did your skin turn so dark?" Tamar touched her daughter's arms and then met her eyes. "You look different, serious."

Deborah stood silently in front of her mother.

Then the old woman offered, "Would you like some sweet bread?" as she pointed towards the table.

Deborah sat as Tamar grabbed a round loaf of bread, removed the cloth, and brought over cups of watered down wine.

Her mother started to cut the bread with a rust colored knife, but her hand was shaking.

"Here, let me help you," Deborah said as she took the knife from her mother.

"How are you, Ima?" asked Deborah as she put her hand over her mother's to try to still the quivers.

"I'm all right. I have tremors in my hands. The herbs aren't working."

"I am sorry not to have seen you sooner, Ima," her daughter offered. "There has been much for me to do."

"Of course, Deborah. You have to take care of your husband and…"Tamar scrutinized her daughter's figure. "No child yet?"

With a sigh, Deborah replied, "Ima, I'm here to tell you something. It's hard. I don't know if you will understand." Pausing, Deborah looked directly at her mother.

"You realize that King Jabin has only become crueler with time. His raids are more devastating. Our people are raped, kidnapped, and murdered."

Tamar's eyes grew sad. "Yes, yes, I know. We all know."

"Ima, we are going to war. We are going to fight for our freedom, for our lives, and for our future."

Confused, Tamar asked, "Who is going to fight? Shlomi cannot fight. He is in the first year of his marriage and he must stay home and fulfill his obligation."

"Ima, not him…it is me…" Deborah started.

Furrowing her forehead, the old woman said, "What do you mean you are? You are a wife, Devash! War is for the leaders."

Gently, Deborah spoke, "Ima, we are all the victims of war and so we all must fight. These are my people. We've been training for a year. We evicted Jabin's men from Beth El only weeks ago. Now, we will face him and Sisera in the north."

Tamar's chest heaved. "What do you mean by 'we'? What are you doing?"

Deborah slowly stated, "I have been training men and women for a long time by the palm trees between Ramah and Beth El. Our army is now five hundred but I hope with additions from the other tribes that we will reach thousands by the end of this week. I'm our people's leader, Ima."

"What!" Tamar withdrew her hand quickly away from her daughter and stood up. "What is this you say? How c…can this be?" Tamar hesitated, "What about Lappidoth?"

Calmly, Deborah offered, "He knows that we live in desperate times. He knows what I do."

A knock was heard on the door.

With a frown, Tamar opened it.

"Tamar, I was expecting you at the house for dinner," said a portly woman wearing a lime green scarf.

Suddenly noticing Deborah, Milcah ran over exclaiming, "Deborah! Look at you!"

With a hand caressing her niece's cheeks, she declared, "You are so beautiful! I'm so glad to see you." Aunt Milcah kissed Deborah's face with moist lips repeatedly.

Milcah noticed the expression on Tamar. "What's wrong? Did somebody die?" she inquired, as she looked from Tamar to Deborah and back again.

Tamar stammered, "Deborah…says she's…she's…"

Aunt Milcah put her hands on her hips and sighed. "I'll say it. Deborah is the *shofet*. She is the judge of our people."

In disbelief, Tamar looked towards her sister in law. "You knew? You didn't try and stop her?" she asked incredulously.

Milcah shook her head. "I've known for many months. The young men speak of their gatherings."

Glancing at Deborah and then back to Tamar, Milcah said, "I didn't think you would want to know. I didn't want to upset you, Tamar." She placed her hand on her sister-in-law's quivering arm. "You've suffered much."

Tamar stared blankly ahead. Milcah with almost a whisper added, "They said that Deborah is well respected, that she is better than Ehud. Some say, she is like Joshua."

The color drained out of Tamar's face as she collapsed in her chair.

Milcah and Deborah went to her side. "Here, Ima," Deborah held out a cup of wine. "Drink, Ima. Drink."

Tamar was shaking now. "I need to rest. I need to lay down."

Deborah looked at Milcah. "If you wish, I can stay the night. I'll stay with Ima."

Deborah escorted her mother to a bed of hay in the corner.

"Deborah," Milcah said with an intense gaze, "May God be with you. May God grant you victory over our enemies."

The next morning, Deborah awoke to the smell of bread baking in the cooking hearth. The warm earthy aroma of barley cooking with oil and apricots filled the house. Deborah sat up in the loft. She knew that she must go down the rope ladder and confront her mother. After closing her eyes in concentration for a few moments, Deborah descended to the first floor.

Tamar was removing piping hot bread from the hot coals when she noticed her daughter. Setting it down on some rocks to cool, she stared at Deborah. The two faced one another silently. Deborah didn't know what to say. Her mother stood still with a stony expression.

And then Tamar's face relaxed.

"Would you like some drink with your breakfast, Deborah?"

"Yes, thank you," responded Deborah in relief.

Tamar brought cups of mint leaves steeped in hot water and sat down at the wooden table. Deborah moved her hand over the surface. There were little splinters coming up from the surface.

Silently, they sipped their hot drinks and nibbled on the apricot barley bread.

"I barely recognize you, Deborah." Tamar studied her daughter. "When I think of you, I remember you running through the hills and smiling at your reflection in the waters of the cistern. But now, who are you?" Tamar's eyes teared up.

Looking at her mother, Deborah blinked her eyes and felt the sting of exhaustion.

"I don't know," Tamar said as she shook her head back in forth looking down at the table. "I don't understand."

After a couple of minutes of silence, the old woman looked up wearily and spoke again. "But here we are and here you are. Who can understand God's plan for us?"

Deborah glanced hopefully at her mother.

Tamar took her hand. "Miriam was a prophetess and leader of our people. Maybe you are the Miriam of our generation.

Go forth my daughter." A tear ran down Tamar's face. "May the God of Sarah, Rebekah, Rachel and Leah guide you and protect you. May I see you again soon, healthy and well." Tamar smiled weakly towards her daughter.

Deborah overcome with emotion, exclaimed, "Thank you, Ima!" as she stood up and embraced her mother.

CHAPTER 28

Deborah spent the morning helping her mother move into aunt Milcah's house and then departed. She arrived at the palm tree in the afternoon as the sun blazed intensely overhead.

Striding towards her, wearing only a tan linen skirt, Barak's chest glistened in perspiration.

"Deborah! Good news!" he exclaimed. "Elon and Helon have brought news about the tribes of Naphtali and Zebulun. They will join our battle against King Jabin. They have each promised five hundred warriors."

Deborah wiped the beads of sweat from her forehead onto her sleeve. It was hot journeying from Ramah. Taking out her pouch, she drank the rest of the tepid water inside.

Facing Barak, she said, "Good, it's a beginning. We will need more. I hear Sisera already commands thousands."

Barak nodded, "More will join us. We have all lost too much to turn back."

Gripping her bow tightly, Deborah stated, "Go Barak. Count up those from Ephraim and Benjamin who are joining us."

That evening, Deborah would sleep the last night in her home. As she came through the door at sunset, a delicious aroma greeted her. A pot of lentils, onions, leeks, garlic, and thyme boiled on the cooking hearth. Mara rummaged through one of the storage jars by the wall. A plump baby was swaddled to her hip.

"Shalom, Mara," Deborah greeted her. "Oh, your baby looks healthy and you, you look well too."

Mara's cheeks were chubby and they dimpled as she smiled.

"Lappidoth will be home soon. I'm glad you are joining us tonight, Deborah."

That evening the three of them sat at the table dipping their bread into the savory lentil stew. Mara bounced her baby on her lap as she giggled. Lappidoth couldn't have looked happier. His tunic was stained with dirt from a long day in the field but he smiled and laughed whole heartedly. Deborah was going to battle soon and she was going to fight for him, for Mara, for their baby, and for all the Israelites. They all deserved to live in peace, have children, and dream that their children's children will live in the hills and farm the land.

Swallowing her wine, Deborah looked at Lappidoth and Mara and said, "I am going north in a couple of days. I'll be away for a while."

Lappidoth's smile disappeared. A frown of concern replaced it as he asked, "The battle? Already? I was hoping Jabin would change his mind and we could all go back to…"

Lappidoth couldn't even finish his own sentence. Go back to what? More raids, more taxes, more kidnappings?

Mara looked down at her baby who smiled back at her. She raised her eyes towards Deborah. "May the God of Abraham be with you," she said solemnly.

That next morning Deborah made her way back to her oasis. It used to be a place of refuge and now it was a place of training men and women to become soldiers. Different strategies and tactics were discussed and discarded. It was now the only source of hope for her people.

Greeting Deborah were eight hundred men and women by the palm trees. Her five hundred regulars were augmented by fifty who came from Benjamin, one hundred from Machir, and the remaining people came in from Ephraim.

"Deborah!" called out a woman with big curly hair.

"Shifra? What are you doing here?" Deborah asked astounded. Her friend had gray ringlets interspersed among her black strands.

"Even though you have my husband Asher here, I thought the more hands, the greater the strength," Shifra broadly grinned.

"But," Deborah's forehead creased. "What about your children?"

Shifra laughed, "They are cared for. Asher's mother would desire nothing else but to take care of her grandchildren."

The tension dissipated from her shoulders for a brief moment as Deborah said, "It's nice to see a friend."

A tall round-faced man ran up to Deborah.

"D...Deborah," he stammered out of breath.

"Yes, Ner. It's all right. Take your time." Deborah turned towards him.

"I've received this message from Gad and Reuven. I can't read it though. I think its good news." Ner handed to Deborah two rolled parchments. Deborah unrolled the first scroll.

To Judge Deborah, we send our greetings:

We hear of your expedition and of your request

However, our leaders, after much deliberation, decline.

We feel the risk to our people is too great.

We cannot be part of a defeat.

Our people will suffer too much.

With our regrets,

Tribal leaders of Gad.

Deborah with great disappointment tossed the scroll aside and opened the one from Reuben.

To our brothers and sisters on the other side of Jordan,

We, too, have suffered under the Canaanites.

Many of our crops have been stolen, animals killed,

and daughters kidnapped.

However, we have decided to stay and tend to our remaining flocks

We hope with care they will breed and we will survive.

Apologies, we cannot join you at this time.

Tribal leaders of Reuben.

As Deborah finished this last line, she wanted to tear the parchment to pieces. She didn't have enough fighters. Not even close! She started to crush the paper with her hand and then stopped. She looked at the five people surrounding her. She couldn't let them know she was afraid.

Releasing the scroll, Deborah stood up straight and proclaimed, "Reuben and Gad will miss out on a great victory! Performers will sing of their cowardice! We don't need faint hearted men and women. Our skill and faith in God will assure us of success. Spread the word. We leave tomorrow morning at dawn."

Deborah wanted to collapse. She felt light-headed. Turning slowly away from her listeners, she walked to the big palm tree and sank to the ground.

That night, she deliberated with Barak and Yoram as the stars twinkled in the dark sky.

"It is almost the new moon. We have to set out tomorrow," Deborah stated. "How long do you think it will take until we reach the Wadi Kishon?"

Barak was wearing an outer robe covering his chest as a concession against the colder nighttime air. "Three to five days," he responded. "We still need to arrange transport of food, tents, and weapons. We'll need more oxen to pull some carts. This will slow us down but hopefully not too much," he offered thoughtfully.

Yoram sat quietly staring at his hands clasped in his lap.

"So what do you have to say, Yoram?" inquired Deborah with some concern.

Yoram's short frame was hunched over but upon hearing his name, he looked up.

"Deborah, Barak, have you counted the number of men and women fighting with us?" he asked tentatively.

Barak straightened his shoulders. "Yes! We have eight hundred and we should have at least one thousand more from the tribes of Zebulun and Naphtali."

After a pause, Yoram spoke, "I hear that Sisera has nine hundred chariots. Nine hundred chariots, weapons made of iron, and thousands of battle hardened soldiers."

The words just hung out there. Barak and Deborah didn't say a word but both were thinking the same thing. We don't have the numbers. Defeat will be likely.

Grimacing, Deborah said, "So what would you have us do? Jabin has threatened to massacre our people town by town unless we face him up north." Looking back and forth between Barak and Yoram, she continued, "We don't have the luxury of time anymore. You both know the conditions under Jabin are horrible. Our people don't have a future."

Barak put his hand on Deborah's shoulder, "I have faced bad odds before and prevailed. I believe with good strategy and morale, we can be successful."

Deborah glanced at Barak gratefully. He seemed to really believe that it was possible. Yoram clearly believed otherwise.

"Let's get a good night sleep and tomorrow we journey north," said Deborah.

Deborah's sleep was fitful at best. She tossed and turned. Images of a river and bees dominated her dreams. As the darkness of night dissipated, waters swelled. They pooled at her ankles, then rose to her knees, then higher to her waist. The waters turned dark and menacing as they reached her neck. She couldn't breathe. She couldn't breathe! She was under water. She tried to cry out but no sound came from her lips. Eyes wide open in terror, her lungs began to burn.

"Awake, Awake, Deborah!" Yoram raised his voice above her. Deborah opened her eyes and began to gasp for breath. Her chest heaved as she breathed raggedly.

"What's wrong? Are you ill?" Yoram grabbed her shoulders.

Catching her breath, Deborah mumbled, "I…I am all right."

"Your face is ashen. Deborah, something is wrong."

Breathing evenly now, Deborah pushed his hands away from her shoulders and slowly stood up. "I'm all right, I said. How is the packing coming along? Are our people ready?"

"Yes, Deborah, they are almost ready to attack."

A bee buzzed close to Yoram's ear. He swatted it away.

CHAPTER 29
YAEL, HEBER, & KING JABIN

"You can't go, Heber!" Yael pleaded with her husband. "You are no longer a young man." Yael looked at her husband. His thinning hair swayed in the breeze.

"Yael, Yael," he said quietly grasping her hand. "If I refuse, King Jabin will certainly have me killed and our son as well." He glanced at their son playing with rocks on the ground. "And you, you will be taken captive and…"

Yael's face flushed in anger, and she erupted, "I know very well what happens to captive women but… your place is here… with your family. You…you cannot fight." Her eyes blazed as she continued, "It would also be a sin for you to kill Israelites, Heber. Jabin is going to war with my people."

"Y…Yael," stammered Heber with a pleading look to his eyes. "I promise not to hurt an Israelite. I don't want to kill anyone. I have to go. I have to go to King Jabin. He's already enraged that I was unable to convince the Kenites to join his battle."

Kicking the dirt floor with her foot, Yael said angrily, "Of course you were unsuccessful. For one, they don't consider the Israelites their enemies. Two, you separated yourself from the Kenites decades ago. You've always been on your own. Jabin should recognize that."

Heber shook his head, "You don't understand. I have to go, Yael. At least, I can protect you and Merar, and hopefully return to see him grow into a man." Heber smiled as he watched his red-haired son piling rocks a cubit high.

The next morning, Heber packed a pouch of water and a loaf of bread and journeyed to Hazor to meet up with the king.

In Hazor, hundreds of people filled the market area. A scarlet turbaned man with a long flowing purple robe stood on an elevated platform above them.

"Now is the time, oh people of Canaan. We have struggled to eradicate a fungus that has grown wildly in the hills. The Israelites must be destroyed once and for all. Their land is our land. Their grain is our grain. Their children will serve you as slaves and their women will be yours."

The crowd of people cheered loudly at their king.

"I have assembled the Sherden, the fiercest of the Sea Peoples. Sisera will command our army and he is undefeated. Who will join him? Who will help kill off this poisonous mold?"

Men down below shouted their agreement as they waved their swords in the air.

Heber stood behind King Jabin, meekly awaiting the king's instruction.

"Those who are strong and brave, you can meet up with Sisera at Japhia. May the gods of Baal and El protect you and give you victory!"

Men bellowed their agreement as the king turned away and faced Heber.

Quietly, the king said, "I'm very disappointed. I expected a Kenite army to accompany you."

Heber bowed his head. It glistened with beads of sweat. "I apologize, your majesty. I am your faithful servant."

Jabin curled his lips in disgust. "I expect a victory nevertheless even without the cowardly Kenites. You go to Sisera. There you can at least be useful."

“Yes, yes, your majesty. I am ready to travel,” said Heber as he walked away backwards with his head still bowed in the king’s direction.

In the meantime, it took four days for the eight hundred Israelites to traverse the hills and valleys all the way up north. Many had trained with Deborah for a year but others joined them at the last moment.

Deborah spoke to Barak as they left Beth El, “I’m not sure about some of these people going north with us. I fear they may be more of a burden than an asset in our battle.”

Shaking his head in agreement, Barak said, “Yes, some of them can’t fight a fly but if anything, they will make us look more numerous. We need numbers, if only for appearance. I’m hoping that once we arrive, they will have greater use.”

Deborah’s army walked miles every day but when the sun set, they made camp. The women filled pots with water and tossed in barley, beans, garlic, and salt until it reduced to a thick stew. Some nights they added wild bitter greens that they picked by the side of the road. Multiple fires with cooking pots were established throughout their nightly encampment. A flat bread baked within minutes directly on the hot pans. Men came to lift the pots and distribute a bowl and a piece of bread to everyone.

On the third night, Deborah’s Israelites passed through an orchard at the spring of Harod. Hanging from the trees were ripe pomegranates! With excitement, men and women plucked the heavy fruit from branches. After cutting open the thick skin, they took large bites and chewed the hard seeds as purple juice ran over their lips. It was deliciously sweet. That night almost all the people had violet fingers and chins stained from the juice.

It was now day four and the tall mountain of Tabor loomed in front of them. Down below a stream of water trickled over rocks.

As Deborah's army came around the curve of the path, she saw a thousand men and women before her. Haggai said fearfully,

"Is that them? Is that Sisera? They got here before us?"

Deborah studied the people. Many of them had swords or daggers affixed to their belts but she didn't notice any horned helmets or armor. This didn't look like Sisera's army.

"Barak!" she called out.

Barak made his way to the front of the Israelites. A thick rope cut diagonally across his back supporting a long sword. Two daggers hung from his leather belt. Barak's egg-shell covering was stained in sweat and dirt.

"Barak, who are the people before us? It doesn't look like an ambush," said Deborah.

With a knowing smile, Barak said, "They are my kinsmen. They are the people from Naphtali and Zebulun." Barak waved enthusiastically.

"Ahira!" Barak called out to an elderly man who was walking towards them. The man's outer robe was a faded shade of cherry and flapped in the northern breeze behind him. His hair was sparse on his head but he sported a lush white beard.

"Ba—arak! Come! I haven't seen you in ages," Ahira said with a grin that revealed few teeth.

Barak kissed the man on each cheek and said, "Thank you for coming. I see Zebulun is here as well?" Barak surveyed the people behind Ahira.

"Yes, yes, not only Zebulun but a couple hundred men from Isaachar are here as well."

Ahira's gaze moved to Barak's left as he studied the dark haired women by his side. "And who is this? Could this be Deborah?" Ahira slightly bowed his head.

"We are grateful to you, Ahira," Deborah nodded. "Thank you for bringing your men and women to fight with us."

"Well," Ahira continued. "We in the north have borne the brunt of King Jabin and his campaigns. Whenever he needed to prove his might, we were just a town or village away. Many of his prisoners are our men. He has taken our women and destroyed our livelihood. We pledge ourselves to the God, Adonai, and to your cause."

By this point, the rest of the Israelites had caught up with Deborah and Barak. They stared at the people from the tribes of Zebulun, Issachar, and Naphtali.

Barak declared, "Here we sleep."

Once carts were unpacked, tents pitched, and the people settled, Deborah met with Barak and the tribal leaders in the center of the camp. Deborah entered the big tent through its cow hide flaps.

"Deborah, come in," beckoned Barak. "You have already met Ahira, leader of Naphtali but let me introduce you to Eliab of the tribe of Zebulun and Nethaniel of Issachar."

Deborah couldn't help noticing that all three of the northern leaders were old men. She and Barak were at least three decades younger.

"Greetings to you," Deborah offered.

Eliab's hair was gray and closely cropped to his head. His gigantic nose protruded well beyond any Deborah had seen.

“We have a girl with us?” he said as his nose scrunched up. “Barak, are you sure this isn’t one of your night mistresses?”

Ahira looked at him in shock as Eliab elbowed Nethaniel by his side.

Deborah thought to herself, how many times must I go through this? She stood as tall as she could and stared at Eliab as he laughed.

Barak replied sternly, “She is not a girl. She is the judge of our people.”

Eliab became completely quiet and discomfort filled the tent.

“Do we have a count of how many men and women can fight with us?” Deborah finally broke the silence.

Ahira scratched his chin under the thick beard, “While Naphtali and Zebulun have a total of one thousand people, only eight hundred are equipped to fight.”

Nethaniel looked the oldest of the three and his voice was frail. “I’m sorry to say Issachar only has two hundred men to offer but they are all ready to lay down their lives to defeat the Canaanites.”

Deborah pondered this information. “We have eight hundred people with us but like you not all of ours are trained to fight.” Deborah thought to herself that was an understatement.

“We are still vastly outnumbered,” Barak warned.

Nethaniel asked weakly, “What about Reuben, Gad, Dan, and Asher? How many troops have they provided?”

Scowling, Barak barked, “None, zero. Reuben wants to keep mounting their sheep.”

Barak rhythmically jerked his hips. Ahira and Eliab burst into laughter.

Barak continued, "Gad is lethargic. And Dan and Asher are dreaming by their ships."

Nethaniel nervously rubbed his hand over his bald head. "We don't even have close to enough soldiers. I heard there was a tribe forming in the south. Is it Juah?"

Deborah nodded, "They call themselves Judah. They are only starting to come together as a tribe. They have no leader or organization. There isn't anyone to ask."

With his forehead creasing, Ahira turned to Barak. "I believe you asked us to join a suicide mission."

"No!" Barak said curtly. "We will not be defeated. This is not the first time the few have defeated the many. All of you," he said to the three tribal leaders before him. "You fought in the time of Joshua. We need you. We need your men and women.'

"There is no choice," Deborah chimed in. "What are we going to do? Go back and watch Jabin murder our people? How many more outrages must we witness? We must fight for our families, our children, and our future!" Deborah's voice got louder and its tone sharpened. "This is it. We have the people we could muster. Now we must have faith."

Ahira, Nethaniel, and Eliab looked at Deborah in disbelief. Barak stood silently by Deborah's side. Then Eliab wiped his enormous nostril on his hand and said defiantly, "We will battle and we will win. What do you suggest, judge Deborah?"

Looking at the men, Deborah said, "I think we should scale Mount Tabor. The ridge will disguise our meager numbers and give us the advantage of seeing what we are fighting against."

Barak nodded his agreement.

CHAPTER 30

Sisera was ecstatic to receive the message from King Jabin and immediately summoned the elders and all the men of the town to the market square. The sun was setting in the west with streaks of tangerine and honey radiating from the horizon.

Horer spoke first. His beard still had crumbs of bread imbedded in it from the morning, "Sisera, I…I beg you. Think of your people. We can't keep on fighting Jabin's battles. Your people want to settle down and have children. Please…"

"Quiet old man!" erupted Sisera. "You will get peace soon enough when you close your eyes and go down to Sheol."

More men arrived. At first only fifty but then hundreds assembled at the meeting place. Sisera looked at the crowd swelling around him and smiled with satisfaction.

"Oh, Sherden people,' he said with his voice projecting into the distance. "We have an opportunity for riches, for land, and for slaves. There is only one battle but with it will come glory. Whoever is ready, whoever is fierce, join me! Join me!" Sisera's voice bellowed.

Balir was now at Sisera's side and looked up in admiration at the commander. "I am with Sisera! I will fight!" he yelled out.

Soon there was a cacophony of voices. Men raised their spears, daggers, and walking sticks. They began to sing the Sherden battle cry.

We will fight for the gods of water and earth.

Give us glory!

We are the sons of demi gods and none can withstand us.

None can defeat us.

We are People of the Sea.

Destruction for our enemies!

Devastation to those who oppose us!

The elder Horer shook his head sadly and walked away. Sisera called out, "We leave at first light tomorrow morning!"

It took Sisera only two days to arrive at Japhia where thousands of Canaanites and Jabin's best chariots awaited him.

Heber the Kenite was the first to greet Sisera. "King Jabin extends greetings and friendship to his most powerful and loyal commander." Heber bowed his head.

Sisera was wearing a bronze helmet with horns protruding from the top. His breastplate reflected sunlight, almost blinding Heber. He had to shade his eyes from the glare. With stinging eyes, he turned his head towards the ground.

Sisera got off his horse and towered over Heber. The middle-aged man looked pathetic. He was better tossed into a river and drowned.

Sisera barked, "Help spread the message that I am taking command and we will arrive at Mount Tabor by tomorrow."

'Yes, Sisera, I am proud to serve." Heber scampered away from the Sherden commander as fast as possible.

In the meantime, on top of the mountain, Deborah's army set up tents for the night. Most of her people already ate dinner and were either sleeping or drinking by a fire. Deborah walked away from the people and looked up. The stars were shining radiantly in the too clear nighttime sky. This isn't good, Deborah thought to herself. We can't attack on a clear day. It will be too obvious that we are outnumbered. Deborah kept staring upward and noticed three stars arranged in semi-circle, the shape of a bow. Squinting towards the sky, Deborah wondered if this was a sign. She gripped her fingers around her wooden bow and stared at the one in the heavens.

"Deborah," a low male voice called out from the darkness.

"Yes, Barak."

It was a bit cool and Barak wore a cape clasped at his right shoulder, exposing his left arm to the nighttime air.

"Sisera is on his way," he somberly stated as he studied the constellations with her.

"Yes, it is almost time," she said sullenly.

"Deborah…" Barak grew silent.

Deborah looked at Barak. He was never at a loss for words. She found herself feeling nervous.

"Deborah," he turned towards her. His face looked gentle as his eyes met hers. "I don't want you in the battle. I want you to stay up here."

"That's absurd, Barak. Of course I have to be with our men and women. This is where I belong."

"I…we'll be fine," stammered Barak. His voice became sterner. "I will lead the battle. I will defeat Sisera."

Shaking her head, Deborah said, "I must be with our people, Barak. You also need to know that I dreamed that Sisera will fall by the hands of a woman."

"You?" Barak asked in surprise.

"No, I don't think so. But then again who knows the will of God, or our destiny." Deborah slipped her hand into Barak's.

His hand felt so strong. The warmth of his skin tingled up her arm.

Barak looked down at her. Her hair fell around her shoulders and even in light of the flickering stars, he could see the brilliant green of her eyes. He leaned down as though he was going to kiss her. Deborah jerked back. She knew they couldn't do this. She was married and a judge of the people. It would be shameful.

In a somber tone, Deborah said, "We have to get some sleep." Turning around, she walked briskly away from Barak. She had to put some distance between them. She could not allow herself to be weak. Her people were going to need all her strength in the coming days.

The next morning Deborah awoke to Yoram's voice. "Deborah," he whispered. "You are going to want to see this." She stood up and walked with Yoram to the edge of the mountain. She gasped.

Down below by the Kishon River were thousands of soldiers. Their horned helmets glittered in the sun. They must have just arrived because tents were in the process of being erected. Looking to the sides of the Sea People's army, Deborah saw several hundred chariots. There were numerous horses as well. Deborah felt her throat tighten. She stood transfixed, staring at the army below.

Yoram broke their silence, "It's worse seeing it." And he became quiet again.

Deborah backed away from the ridge still looking straight ahead as though she was in a trance.

"Yoram," she finally exhaled. "Gather Barak and the elders of Naphtali, Zebulun, and Issachar."

It was morning and her people were awake. Women baked flat bread on bronze pans and put out the remaining pomegranates for breakfast. Deborah met Ahira of Naphtali, Nethaniel of Issachar, and Eliab of Zebulun in the central tent. Ahira's long white beard was gnarly and unkempt. He had been up for some time and the way he looked at Deborah told her that he was aware of what lay at the foot of Mount Tabor. Nethaniel had morning stubble on his cheeks. He looked confused. Eliab just stood without expression.

"Where is Barak?" Deborah inquired.

Eliab snorted loudly and jutted his head toward Deborah. She looked behind her and saw Barak opening the tent flap. His eyes were blazing as he stepped quickly inside.

"Sisera's men have only just arrived," Barak said curtly. "They are more numerous than us. They have chariots and weapons of iron, but they could be caught off guard."

Nethaniel nervously scratched the stubble on his chin. "What do you mean they are more numerous? How many soldiers does Sisera have?"

Barak said stiffly, "I estimate around ten thousand."

"But, but," Eliab stuttered. "We have maybe two thousand if we count everyone. We don't have a prayer of..."

"As I was saying," Barak resumed speaking. "We can surprise them if we are strategic. Sisera has no idea how many troops we have. We can make it appear that we have more people fighting than we actually do."

Deborah was listening to Barak. He was a good army leader because he could think tactically and psychologically. Thank God for Barak.

"We need to know more," Deborah said softly.

"What?" Nethaniel said.

"We need to know who comprises Sisera's army. Why are they here? What are they fighting for? We need to send some scouts, spies, someone who can lose themselves in the crowd and listen to their words."

"We don't have time for such matters," burst Eliab. "Barak just said we need to surprise them. I think now is the time."

Yoram raised his hand. "I'll go with two other men to different parts of Sisera's camp. We can blend in. Give us one to two days and we'll report back to you."

"Are we scouting the land of Israel under Joshua?" Eliab said sarcastically. "I hate to tell you, we are already in the Promised Land."

"Eliab! Stop!" Barak commanded. "There are many ways to take an enemy by surprise but some information could be helpful. We need time to prepare our own men and women. Go, Yoram, and may the angels of God bring you success."

CHAPTER 31

Within two days, Sisera and his army were completely settled. There would be no surprise attack. Sisera knew that Deborah was on the mountain and that eventually she would have to come back down. He and his men drank sour wine and roasted lambs and pigs. They laughed, ate, and slept knowing that time was on their side.

Deborah and her people trained on top of the mountain. Between Barak and the elders of Zebulun, Isaachar, and Naphtali, no one was allowed to stand idle. Everyone assisted one way or another. The leaders were careful though not to scare the people. Barak told them that the battle ahead would be challenging but with work, they could prevail.

On the third morning, Yoram and his two men climbed up the back side of the mountain. Their clothes were sullied and they looked exhausted. When he saw Deborah, he weakly smiled. "Gather the elders," he said hoarsely. "We have much to share."

Yoram stood in the center of the tent with his two scouts Yonah and Ner. Facing them were Deborah, Barak, Ahira, Nethaniel, and Eliab.

Taking hold of his water pouch, Yoram took a long satisfying drink, and then began.

"Those Sherden are goat turds!" sputtered Yoram. "They are looking forward to hacking our people to bits! And Sisera, he is the biggest ass of them all."

"Go on. Continue," Barak encouraged.

"All Sisera talks about is you, Deborah." Yoram fell quiet.

Yonah erupted, "He says you will become his prized harlot, that you will be locked in his bed chambers, and…"

"That's enough!" Barak barked. "Give us the information Deborah asked you for. We don't care about a dead man's boast."

Yoram continued, "Yes, the point is they are confident. Sisera's men are here for war and booty. Jabin's men, on the other hand, are a different story."

Even though Ner had substantial height, his face still looked boyish. Quietly, he said, "Those who came on behalf of Jabin, don't want to fight. They feel coerced. Last night around one of the fires, I saw a Kenite. Can you imagine?"

"You mean one of Moses' father-in-law's people?" Deborah asked.

"Yes, yes," eagerly added Yonah. "But he didn't want to be there. He drank a lot of wine and said that he just wanted to get back home. He struck me as a gentle sort of man."

"Not just the Kenite but many of the Canaanites have no appetite for battle," Yoram added. "The only ones who really want to fight are the Sherden."

"Good, good," thoughtfully spoke Barak. "It looks like we have a morale advantage."

"Let's get a good night of slumber. Tomorrow, we fight for our people and our future," spoke Deborah.

In the morning, Deborah mournfully looked at the sky as glimmers of morning light streaked over the horizon. There wasn't a cloud! It was going to be that much harder to disguise themselves. Barak whistled in her direction. They all had to eat what they could, grab any useful weapons, and take up positions in three groups on the mountain ridge.

Deborah joined the men and women in front with their bows and arrows.

Yarom approached her. “Deborah, I’ll be with the fighters in the back of this unit. You need to be on the top of the mountain.”

Barak stepped closer to Deborah. He wore a woven leather breast piece over his chest. It was the closest thing to armor he had. A long sword was strapped diagonally across his back, and he had at least three daggers affixed to his waist belt. His curly hair moved in the breeze.

“Deborah, Yoram is right. Your place is on the high ground. Someone needs to see the movements of Sisera and any changing tactics. You have a good eye for this. We need you.” Barak looked at her imploringly.

Deborah looked from Barak and Yoram and couldn’t help feeling that they wanted her safe. However, Barak’s words did make sense.

Nodding her head, Deborah took one more glance at the clear blue sky and then she had an idea. “All right, Barak. I’ll stand on the top of the ridge. I believe we may have a way to disguise our numbers. I’ll use a few people to set fires and the winds should blow the smoke down the slope when you attack. And I’ll keep vigilant in case a messenger needs to bring you more information.”

The Israelites divided into three groups around the mountain ridge. The sun peeked over the horizon as most of Sisera’s soldiers slept off their hangover.

Barak took a long curved ram’s horn and brought it to his lips. Its high pitched sound rang out and echoed. The Israelites charged down the mountain.

In the first group, Shifra joined the women and men armed with bows and sling-shots. With hearts beating fast, they tried not to focus on the size of the army below. They scampered over stones and picked up speed as they sprinted down the mountain side. As they approached Sisera's encampment, they stopped, and caught their breath. Holding their bows in the air, they took aim. The arrows flew through the air.

The second and third groups of Israelites approached Sisera's encampment from different directions and their archers did the same. A fusillade of arrows hit the Sea People and Canaanites tents.

A cry of rage erupted from the encampment. Men scurried out of the tents, grabbed their spears and swords. There were so many of them. Deborah could see from above that the arrows hit a number of soldiers but they were scampering out of their tents like a myriad of ants. She didn't have enough arrows or people shooting at them to even the odds.

Sisera's men scrambled to the horses and on to the chariots. Others donned their armor and metal helmets and walked towards the archers brandishing shining iron spears and swords.

On the mountain slope, smoke billowed out from wet rags. Deborah hoped it would be enough to give the appearance of more fighters. Through the smoke, her men broke through and brazenly charged Sisera's first soldiers.

Sisera's chariots rolled forward pulled by strong horses. Israelite men jumped out of the way. They screamed as their flesh tore. One man's torso completely separated from his legs. Blood and guts spilled out. And then another Israelite was torn into two. Were there iron blades attached to the sides of the chariots? Incoming Israelites soldiers looked bewildered in front of their severed comrades.

Deborah sent two young messengers to the archers. "Tell them to target the chariot riders and horses." They darted down the mountain.

The ram's horn sounded again. Deborah's men and women sought higher ground and shot at the chariots. Very few arrows hit their target because the chariots moved too fast. Sisera's men charged into the Israelites.

Deborah could see Barak in the middle of a group of their best warriors. His sword rose high gaining energy and forcefully decapitated one of Sisera's soldiers. The man's horned helmet flew off and hit the ground. At Barak's side was Maon. As small as he was, he moved rapidly through the soldiers thrusting his sword into their abdomen. Then he darted to the side to avoid retaliation. The other groups of Israelites faced Sisera's soldiers within the encampment. Sisera sat on top of his biggest chariot and hollered, "Kill the swarming locusts! Fight on! Glory to us!"

Shifra, from behind one of the boulders, stood up. She had a direct shot at Sisera. This was her chance. Pulling back on the string, she closed her right eye and took aim. Sisera turned his head in her direction. He then smirked.

The very next moment, Shifra felt something sharp and cold pierce her violently from behind. She couldn't breathe. Searing pain radiated from her chest. Looking down, she saw a spear head poking out between her breasts. With her eyes frozen in shock, her mouth opened in a cry. Her body tumbled to the ground. A soldier with a horned helmet stood over her. Looking toward Sisera, he bowed his head mockingly.

"No, not Shifra!" Deborah cried in anguish.

The chariots continued to slice and maim any Israelites in their way. Men and women were dying. Barak's dear friend Maon was surrounded by three soldiers. He forcefully swung his sword in front of him trying to keep two attackers at bay.

"Look behind you! Look behind you!" Barak yelled but his voice could not reach him. A third man approached Maon with an ax. The blade reflected the light of the sun. It crashed down into Maon's head, splitting his skull down the middle. Blood rushed over his body. Maon fell hard onto the ground.

Barak roared a primal scream. With his face tensed in rage, he savagely swung his sword, attacking every soldier within reach.

From the distance, Deborah could see the battle had to end. They had to stop fighting. They had to pull back. Deborah blew her horn in short static sounds.

Ahira, leader of Naphtali, took his horn and made the same short sounds. Nethaniel of Isaachar followed suit and then Eliab did likewise. The Israelites began to retreat. Archers walked backwards shooting arrows to slow down Sisera's soldiers. Deborah's men and women, those who survived, laboriously climbed back up the mountain.

In the meantime, Sisera sent a signal to his troops to remain where they were. He knew that what went up, even the filthy Israelite insects, would have to come back down again. In the next day or two, the battle would be over, and he would take great pleasure in the capture of the Israelite woman.

CHAPTER 32

Great despair blanketed the top of Mount Tabor that evening. They lost over five hundred people that day! And there were hundreds of people injured. Yoram sat on the ground as a woman sewed up a deep gash in his arm. He winced, but didn't let on how much it hurt. Ner laid on the ground moaning. A bloodied cloth clung to his head. Eliab, elder of Zebulun, wrapped up his foot tightly to stem the bleeding.

Deborah walked through the camp. She saw Barak sharpening the blade of his sword on a rock. His eyes were fixed on the sharp edge in deep concentration. When he looked up, his eyes met hers blankly. Neither of them said anything.

Ahira approached them both. His long beard was so grimy that it was no longer white. "I think it's over. We should all retreat to our homes and pray that Sisera will be merciful."

"Merciful?" Barak awoke from his reverie. "That's not something Sisera is known for. His mercy is a quick killing. I'm sure our people will not be so lucky."

"We can't win this war," Ahira stated gloomily.

"We are all upset," Deborah offered. "Let's care for the wounded, eat some bread, and rest. We need time to figure out what to do."

Ahira returned to his tent. Barak numbly returned to repetitively whetting his metal blade against the smooth stone.

Deborah walked briskly away. In one hour, she was on the eastern side of the mountain. No one was around as she sat down on a flat white rock. She kept seeing the spear pierce her childhood friend. The blood running down her chest. Her body lying lifeless on the ground.

"Oh, Shifra! I'm sorry!" whispered Deborah. "I failed you. And I failed our people." Deborah slumped over a rock and closed her eyes.

Down below at the foot of the mountain, the atmosphere at Sisera's camp was jovial. Wine and beer were passed out among the men. Meat from some of the dead horses roasted over the fire. Kalir, one of Sisera's comrades, from Haroseth Hagoim broke into song. Men laughed with meat stuck in between their teeth. One husky Canaanite played on his flute while others danced around them.

Kalir stopped singing when Sisera approached.

"Dear commander, the battle went well."

Sisera beamed in his direction. Unclasping his iron breastplate and helmet, they dropped to the ground as he stood in front of his men.

"Today was a victory for us! We sent the insects running. Tomorrow we will squash them all! Let us drink to the mighty Sherden and the friends of King Jabin." He raised his pouch and drank the wine in a single gulp.

Heber, the Kenite, looked around the encampment. He raised his cup of wine but found he couldn't drink it. He badly wanted to run away but knew very well what would happen to him. He would only get a few cubits away before an arrow would impale him through the back. Just as he was swirling his wine in his cup, Sisera walked up to him.

"There is good news for King Jabin, indeed!" He slapped his hand on Heber's back. With a confused look, Sisera added, "Why so glum, Heber? If you miss a woman, know that within a day," Sisera gestured to the mountain top, "we will all have fun with our new conquests."

Heber weakly smiled at Sisera and mumbled, "Yes, yes, my lord." Then he looked away quickly.

"Get some rest, friend," Sisera winked. "You'll need your energy tomorrow night."

The sun set and a refreshing cool air blew across the mountain. Deborah scrutinized the sky. Were those clouds forming? She wondered as she squinted. The moon was shrouded behind a thick gray cloud. Inhaling the sweet air, Deborah's heart beat a little faster. Maybe, just maybe, rain will come. She got up and found Barak. He was nibbling some bread.

"Barak."

He looked up at Deborah. His eyes were devoid of expression. "Barak, I think we may have a chance."

"What do you mean, Deborah?"

Pointing to the sky, Deborah continued, "If the rain comes, their chariots won't be able to move."

Barak shook his head, "That's a big if."

"Yes, I know. Barak…" she touched his shoulder. The knots of muscles were rock hard. "Today was terrible. But if we don't fight, we all know what will happen to us."

Barak nodded his head in agreement and then looked up with bloodshot eyes. "I would always rather go down in battle. As I told you before, I'm here to the end."

With a gentle squeeze of his shoulder, Deborah said, "Let's get a few hours of sleep and then assess the sky before the first light."

Barak stood up. They were both weary. He bent over and kissed her cheek. "Let's sleep."

It was an hour before the sun rose over the horizon when Deborah opened her eyes. She barely slept at all. Throughout the night, she kept waking up, not wanting to sleep past the sunrise. Glancing up, the sky was dark, very dark. Could there be rain today? Deborah could only hope.

She found Barak under an oak tree and shook him awake. "Barak, Barak. The heavens are on our side."

Barak opened his eyes, stood up and studied the clouds. Then silently, he walked to the ridge. For many minutes, he studied Sisera's quiet camp by the narrow Kishon River.

"Deborah," he said with eyes wide. "I'm thinking of bringing our army down the side of the mountain, behind Sisera's camp. I believe we can surprise them across the river."

Deborah's heart started to race. "They won't be expecting us there and if the rain comes, their chariots will be useless. And Barak…"

He looked at her.

"I'm coming this time."

"No, no you're not," he shook his head.

"Yes, I am. These are my people. I will not stand back again. Their fate is my fate. Their life is my life, and their death will be my death," Deborah stated.

Barak was quiet.

"Are you ready to bring our people together?" she said resolutely. "I have some things to say to them."

Barak and Deborah sent men and women to wake up the people. This time, there would be no ram horns blown. They must be quiet and quick. The Israelites gathered together as the dark sky began to show some initial rays of light.

“Children of Israel!” Deborah began. She could see their exhaustion. Some looked directly at her with eyes puffy and red. Others stared at the ground beneath their feet. “We have all experienced terrible loss. Yesterday, we lost friends and family. We suffered at the hands of the Canaanites and Sea People.”

Yoram placed his hand over his injured arm. Most of the Israelites met her gaze tentatively.

Deborah’s voice rose in volume, “And yet we know that wasn’t unusual. Our children, spouses, and parents have been terrorized for decades by our enemies. We can’t grow our crops in peace without robbery. We can’t raise our daughters without fear of abduction. Our children live without hope.” Some people nodded their heads.

“We cannot lose this fight!” Deborah looked pleadingly towards her people.

Even louder, she shouted, “We must fight! We must fight for our families! We must fight for our lives!”

The Israelites stood straighter.

“Adonai, the God of Sinai, is with our people. Just as God heard our people’s cry in Egypt, God hears our plea right now.”

A roar of agreement erupted from the crowd.

Barak stood by Deborah’s side in his leather outerwear grasping a sharp sword. He barked, “We are going down the eastern side of the mountain. Gather your weapons, water, and bread.”

“Wait!” called out Calir. “Isn’t that going to take hours?”

Barak looked at the blemished man in the midst of the Israelites. “Yes, but I believe it will give us the best chance.”

The morning sun barely penetrated the thick clouds as fifteen hundred Israelites climbed down the backside of Mount

Tabor. When they were half way down, tiny droplets of rain fell on them. Deborah looked up and felt the cool beads hit her face. She smiled. It was mid-morning when they arrived on the other side of the Kishon River. From bank to bank, it was barely ten arm widths.

Sisera and a few of his men were awake and studying Mt. Tabor. Deborah and Barak could see their backs from the distance.

Barak motioned for his troop leaders to approach him. Looking at Yoram, Ahira, Nethaniel, and Eliab, he said, "I want small groups of no more than a hundred people surrounding the perimeter of the camp. We must be utterly silent. Surprise is the only advantage we have. They won't expect us from this direction."

The rain trickled down Barak's face. Deborah looked with both fear and admiration at him. Then she noticed the river bed slightly swelling with new water.

"Barak! Barak!" she pointed at the flow of water. What if we ambush Sisera with our smaller groups and then immediately flee across the river? He would think we have panicked and chase us. Then we can attack again."

Yoram said, "The water bed is narrow. Sisera will cross it easily."

Glancing at the river, Barak replied, "We'll see. This may just work out well for us."

With a wave of his hand, Barak signaled that it was time. Fifteen groups of Israelites spread out. Ahira's men darted around rocks and hid behind some bushes. A Canaanite was urinating on an oak tree. Sneaking up behind him, Ahira's sword pierced his chest. With eyes wide and liquid still trickling from his yerech, he fell to the ground.

Nethaniel's group approached some Sea People boiling water over a fire. Smoke obscured their approach. The men laughed as they stretched by the fire. The Israelites stormed out of the bushes with swords and daggers. The Sea People soldiers looked up in shock without even a moment to stand. Nethaniel's men stabbed them in quick succession. Bloodied bodies now surrounded the fire pit.

Barak targeted some of Sisera's men by the chariots. Three men were idly looking at the fog above. The others were joking with one another. Two of his men pulled back on the strings of their bows and the arrows hit two of Sisera's soldiers. Barak darted out from behind a tree with ten men with him. The soldiers fumbled for their weapons. Barak's men skewered them with their sharpened swords. Their bodies fell with a thud.

Sisera stared at the mountain in confusion. Why didn't he see any Israelites on it? A man hollered from behind him. Turning around, Sisera saw hordes of Israelites swarming through his camp. They ran through the tents, knocking over supply jars with swords held high. One of Sisera's men yelled to alert the others to grab their weapons.

Ahira's group attacked. They struck so swiftly that Sisera's men didn't have time to don their helmets. Men fell to the ground moaning. Swords clashed in midair. Deborah and those with bows shot their arrows into Sisera's charging soldiers.

Sisera put on his helmet and rushed into his camp. In a fury, he swung his sword in a big arc. Within minutes, he killed ten Israelite men. The Sherden and Caaananite soldiers sliced with their iron blades through the Israelite leather armor like butter. Ahira's men screamed in agony as the swords cut into their necks, chests, and abdomen. An ax crashed down and struck Ahira in the head. He collapsed immediately.

Barak was in the second attack group. A spear soared pass his ear as he dodged out of the way. His sweat mingled with the rain dripping down his neck. Barak lifted up his sword and skewered two Sherden soldiers in front of him.

Deborah and the archers hid behind the tents. A horned-helmet soldier was in clear view. Deborah pulled back her string and let the arrow fly. It hit the man right in his neck. Blood spurted out.

Sisera roared. He plunged his dagger into Ner's abdomen. When he pulled out his blade out, Ner's intestines spilled out like snakes. Deborah could see her men and women losing. She took the curved ram's horn to her lips and blew it as loud as she could. Short, staccato bursts alerted her people to retreat. Retreat!

The Israelites turned on their heels and ran. They ran towards the river as the rain came down harder and harder. The Kishon River was double in size as men and women ran knee deep through it. It now took twenty minutes to cross. Sisera gave the signal to chase them. His men jumped into the chariots and raced toward the Israelites on the other side of the river.

"Hold your ground!" yelled Deborah when her Israelites made it across the water. "Face the Canaanites!"

Barak was in the last group to cross. Behind him were Sisera's chariots and his soldiers. However, as the chariots approached the river, they slowed down and then completely stopped moving. Their wheels were stuck in mud.

Sisera yelled, "On the ground, cross the river. Attack!"

The rain was coming down hard now. It felt like tiny thorns as it hit any exposed skin. Visibility was limited as the clouds turned from gray to charcoal black. Deborah and Barak could barely see through the sheets of rain. Everyone was drenched down to their inner tunics.

Sisera and his men leapt into the river. It was thigh high as they moved through the swirling water. As Sisera approached the opposite bank, the water rose up to his waist. He pulled himself out of the river accompanied by sixty of his men. Hundreds of soldiers, however, were still in the river when they heard the sound of rushing water. Then a roar. The Canaanites and Sea Peoples looked up and saw a wall of water coming towards them.

Heber, the Kenite, was at the very back of Sisera's army as he saw the huge wave coming from the northern bend of the river. Did a dam break? The water was like a towering mountain and they were all like mice in its shadow. Heber stopped breathing as he saw the water surge towards the men in the river. They screamed. Horses neighed. The water crashed on them. Surging, bubbling liquid forced its way down river.

Minutes went by. The water slowed. Chariots floated on the surface and then sunk. Heber stood away from the bank with eyes open in shock. There were no more screams of man or beast. Dead bodies, horse carcasses, and chariots flowed down the river,

Deborah watched in astonishment. "Barak! It's a miracle!"

Barak signaled for the Israelites to attack. Sisera slowly turned his gaze away from the river. Seeing Barak with raised sword, Sisera yelled, "Attack them! Kill them!"

His men ran toward Barak with their swords and daggers raised.

Sisera, however, turned to his right and ran. He ran away from his men. He ran away from the river. He ran through bushes, over rocks, and didn't look even once behind him. He kept running and running without concern of those he left behind.

CHAPTER 33

The morning sun rose over the eastern mountains. It was three weeks since Heber left to join King Jabin's army. Yael stood in front of the tent staring towards the west. An elderly traveler told her that the battle was at Mt. Tabor. Squinting, she could just barely make out the outline of Mount Tabor. How could that be? The mountain looked peaceful as the clouds covered its summit in a blanket. How was Heber? What of the war?

"Ima!" called out a youth with ruddy cheeks. "I want to go to the sea and fish like father."

Yael studied her son as she tucked a loose strand of red hair behind her ear. "Well, Merar, it is only an hour walk from here." Leaning down, she kissed him on his cheek. "Go ahead. If you bring back a fish, I'll cook it for you."

The boy grinned and scampered off with a basket and fishing rod.

Yael walked through the lush willow trees and began to survey the remainder of the summer crops. There were yellow and orange bumpy squash, cucumbers, and a few melons. Vines with ripe black-purplish grapes rested on a wooden fence. Yael picked one of the grapes and brought it to her lips. The sweetness exploded in her mouth as she swallowed the fruit with the tiny hard seeds.

As she was reaching for another one, she saw someone approaching from the distance. He was running with a limp. Who was this man? He was towering in height but also clearly injured. Was he was wearing a metal breastplate? Was he one of the Sea People? Yael thought in a panic. As he came closer, Yael saw the strong definition of his chin, his cheekbones, and… her heart stopped beating.

In mere minutes, Sisera would be upon her. What should she do? Yael looked back towards the tent and the tiny wood dwelling. There was nowhere to hide. She could run, but what about her son? Merar would come back to find a monster awaiting him. No, no she would face him. She survived him once before. Maybe after he took whatever it is that he came for, he would leave and her son would be safe.

Yael stood by the vine trembling as Sisera drew near. His short hair, encrusted in dirt and blood, was matted down to his forehead. His leg had a severe gash in the thigh.

"Wife of Heber, friend of King Jabin!" he uttered in exhaustion. "I seek shelter. I need water."

He ordered it as though it were nothing. Did he not remember all that he had done to her years ago? He likely did, reasoned Yael. He just didn't care. It meant nothing to him. Despite raping her and terrorizing her people, he expected that she would just help him. Yael looked around. "Do you have any soldiers with you? How many of your men need water and nourishment?"

Sisera dropped to his knees in exhaustion. "Only myself. I need water and rest right now."

Yael realized that it was only Sisera and herself. Sisera! The cruel man kneeling in front of her. "Come into the tent," she beckoned.

Opening up the animal flap, she pointed to a sheep skin on the ground. "You can rest there."

Yael went outside to draw water from the well. As she stared at the water below, she grew angrier thinking of all the things he did to her. How she tried to forget the pain and humiliation. How many others were like her? How many more women will he rape? How many men will he kill?

"I am thirsty!" the injured man hollered.

"The well is dry," called out Yael. "Don't worry, I'm getting you something to drink as fast as possible."

I've got to think. Yael's mind raced. What about Valerian root? That should make him sleep deeply. Could it kill him? Yael pulled up one of the pink, white flowering plants on the other side of the house. After cleaning its root, she chopped it up finely. I'm going to need to boil it. Yael heard one of her goats bleating. That's it! She milked the goat, put the milk in a pot with the Valerian root, and boiled it.

"You stupid whore! Where is my drink?" bellowed Sisera.

Yael poured the milk into a cup. "Sorry, I'm coming."

Once it was cool enough, Yael proclaimed, "Here, Lord Sisera." She entered the tent with the cup brimming with milk and slivers of valerian root.

"I said, I wanted water!" Sisera grabbed the cup angrily and stared at its contents. He then drank it in two gulps. "If anyone asks if I'm here, say no." He looked menacingly at Yael. Sisera then collapsed on his side with his back to Yael. Within minutes, he was deeply asleep.

Yael stood over the injured commander. The stench of blood and sweat filled the tent. I've got to get some air, thought Yael. She stepped outside. The sun was moving toward the west. Within a couple of hours, Merar would come home. What would happen then? How would Sisera act towards her when he regained his strength?

Yael shuddered. I can't let anything happen to Merar. I can't let that beast hurt me or anyone again. Yael took a sharp bronze tent peg and mallet. She could feel the weight of the mallet in her hand.

She opened the tent flap. Sisera hadn't budged at all. He was in deep slumber. She walked over to him. Her hand shook as she held the bronze peg but she forced herself to remember.

To remember that day years ago at the festival of Sukkot. How he killed her father. How he brutally raped her.

She lined up the metal point on his head. The cold metal touched his temple. Sisera's eyes opened in surprise. Yael lifted the mallet with all her might and struck the head of the peg. Crack!

Blood flowed over his face. Sisera's hand lurched towards her but she slammed the mallet down on the metal over and over again as she screamed. The peg pierced his skull and sank into the soft tissue of his head. Sisera's eyes froze open staring at Yael.

She was breathing hard as she stood up. Blood was all over Sisera's head, the sheep skin, and the ground. Taking two steps backward, she couldn't take her eyes off him. Yael's body shook and tears fell over her cheeks.

And then, she smiled.

Yael grinned. And then she laughed.

Sisera was dead! He was dead!

Stepping out of the tent, the sunlight was disappearing in the west.

"Ima," called out her son. "Look what I have! Three fish!" The boy held up three fish the size of two hands by the fins.

Yael turned toward her son.

"Ima," the boy eyes widened, "Are you all right? There's blood. Did you slaughter a lamb?"

Yael started to giggle. She couldn't stop. "Yes, yes, I did. We'll celebrate tonight. Go clean up the fish."

Merar looked puzzled at his mother and walked to the side of the house.

The sun was disappearing over the horizon, when Yael saw another man approaching their home on a horse. He was wearing only a goat skin around his waist. There was no armor or helmet. This clearly wasn't one of the Sea Peoples or Canaanites.

"Excuse me," called out the man as he dismounted. He was glistening in sweat and a bit out of breath. "I was chasing Sisera of the Sherden, the Sea People. Has he come through here?"

Barak stood in front of Yael and noticed the dried blood on her hand and tunic.

"Who are you?" Yael asked.

Wiping the sweat from his forehead on his arm, he replied, "I am Barak, of the tribe of Naphtali. I am with the Israelites, fighting for freedom under Deborah."

Deborah? It couldn't be her old friend. Yael blinked and stared incredulously at Barak.

"We just fought Sisera and the Canaanites at Mount Tabor. Sisera ran. I want to finish this. Do you understand?"

Yael still stood silently. Barak was starting to think of her as simple-minded.

And then she spoke again. "He's here."

Barak's body tensed and reached for his sword.

"In the tent." Yael motioned towards the animal skin flaps.

Barak charged in with his sword drawn.

A man's body was surrounded by a pool of blood. Could this be Sisera? Barak wondered. He kicked the body on to its back. He scrutinized the clothing and remnants of a face. It was unmistakable. Barak gasped.

It was Sisera. But how? How did this happen? He glanced towards the entrance of the tent and then back to his enemy lying before him. Sisera's head had a gaping hole. What did the woman do? How did she do this? It takes a lot of strength to pierce a skull. How did she overpower the greatest warrior of them all? The man who terrorized the Israelites for years. Sisera was clearly dead.

Barak stepped outside. He couldn't take his eyes off the red-haired woman. Yael pridefully met his gaze and then straightened the folds of her skirt that were saturated with Sisera's blood.

CHAPTER 34

Heber finally stood up. After the battle cries, clashing of swords, and rush of water subsided, he straightened his legs. His knees felt stiff from crouching so long behind a prickly bush. Heber observed how the Kishon River was still surging past its banks. On the other side, were hundreds of Israelites. A woman stood in front. Her long date-brown hair blew in the breeze as she clasped a bow. Heber waved to the woman across the river, raising his empty hands high. Hopefully, she could see that he had no weapons on him. The Israelites laid logs across the water as it started to calm.

"Shalom!" he waved and shouted. "I'm Heber, the Kenite. I mean you no harm. I didn't fight in the battle. I hid because I am here against my will."

Eight Israelites and the woman hopped over the logs to his side. Heber looked around him. The camp was abandoned. Was everyone killed or captured? Or did they retreat?

"Please," he approached the woman, "I am unarmed and at your service."

Her emerald eyes studied him. "If you didn't want to fight, then why are you here?"

Heber nervously ran his hand over his bald head. "King Jabin insisted. I didn't want him to harm my family. The Kenites and I bear you no ill will."

Yoram was listening to the conversation. "The Kenites are related to the Midianites, aren't they? You are a descendant of Jethro, Moses's father-in-law?"

"Yes!" Heber nodded emphatically. "We are your friends. I can offer you assistance. I know where Jabin lives. I know his city. Let me help you end this war. I only want peace for my family."

From the east, a man galloped on his horse. His dark curly hair waving in the wind.

Looking up from Heber, Deborah exclaimed, “Barak!”

In moments, Barak dismounted from his horse. He was breathing hard from the ride.

“It’s Sisera.” He stopped to catch his breath.

“Did you catch him?” Deborah asked.

“He’s dead. A red haired woman at Elon-bezaanannim killed him.”

Heber’s eyes widened. “What? Sisera was at Elon-bezaannim?” He shakily stepped towards Barak.

“The red haired woman,” his eyes started to fill with tears. “Is she all right? Is she injured? What about the boy?”

“Who is this?” Barak asked Deborah pointing to the bald man with tears running down his cheeks.

“It’s Heber, the Kenite,” Deborah explained. “He says he was forced to join Jabin’s army but he didn’t raise a sword against us. He’s been hiding in his tent.”

“Please!” Heber got down on his knees before Barak. “Is she all right? Did he hurt her? Is my son alive?”

“Yes,” Barak looked down on the man, “She is very well. So well that she took a mallet and killed Sisera with her own hand. She looked…” Barak paused for a moment. “She looked exultant. Your son was playing outside when I left.”

“Thank all the gods!” exclaimed Heber. “Thank the God of Israel, Adonai, of all the gods that are worshiped for looking out for Yael and Merar.”

“Yael,” Deborah asked. Her eyes grew wide. “Is your wife, Yael, the Israelite from Ephraim?” She clasped her hands together.

Heber rose to his feet and wiped the tears from his face. "Yes, Yael was Sisera's captive, but she is now my wife and the mother of our son. She is the most beautiful, loving woman I have ever known."

Deborah eyes started to water. Could it be? Was Yael alive? Was she happily married?

"I want to go back with you to see her," Deborah blurted out.

"Deborah," Barak placed his hand on her shoulder. "We have to finish what we started. We must capture Jabin."

"Yes," nodded Deborah. "You are right."

"The best way to enter Hazor is from the north. The entrance is barely guarded," Heber offered Deborah. "And there will be very few soldiers in the city. Jabin sent most of his men to Mount Tabor."

King Jabin sat on his broken throne with the carved bulls. It had been days since any news reached him. The last he heard was Sisera defeating those damned Israelites at Mount Tabor. He was eager for Sisera's return and all the bounty he would carry with him.

A man with dried blood on his face thrust open the doors of his palace. Jabin looked up hopefully. Two of Jabin's guards extended their swords in front of him.

"I must, I must, speak with the king," the man stuttered.

"Let him approach." Jabin waved his hand.

The man wore broken remnants of his breast plate and his legs were caked in mud. "The battle, your majesty," he said falling on his knees.

"Yes, yes, I've been awaiting word from Sisera." Jabin stroked his beard. "How quickly did you defeat the Israelites? Did you take many slaves?"

The man stared at the floor.

"Speak up," barked Jabin. "Tell me what happened."

"Your majesty, the battle didn't go well." The man's face was streaked with dried blood. "The river surged. We were caught unaware. Many drowned. The Israelites fought hard. We didn't expect them to be so fierce."

Jabin looked at him dumbfounded. "What about Sisera? Where is he?" roared Jabin.

"I...I...don't know. He ran off."

"Restrain him," yelled Jabin as he jolted up. Two of his guards took hold of the man.

"Here." Heber pointed to a tall cracked wooden door. It was only as high as two men. "The northern gate is never guarded. Hazor has only been attacked from the south or east."

Deborah and Barak stood in front of a thousand Israelites. They took a longer route to Hazor just to arrive at this small entrance. They even crossed the Jordan River twice where it flowed from Lake Huleh.

"Now is the time." Barak straightened his back as he grabbed hold of his sword. "Let's go!"

Barak and fifteen men struck the door with a thick log. The wood strained and began to crack. With one final ram, it crashed down. Barak peered at the stone dwellings in close proximity to one another. Clothes flapped on ropes outside of the homes. Townsmen looked up in shock. One woman dropped her jar.

As it shattered on the ground, the people of Hazor began to scream and run for cover.

Nethaniel blew the shofar horn loudly.

In the palace, Jabin cried out, "Curses! What is going on here?"

Another guard entered the room with a panicked look. "Your majesty, we are under attack. We must run. You must hide."

Jabin took a step closer to the messenger from the battle of Mount Tabor and drew his sword. The poor man couldn't comprehend what was happening. Jabin held his sword up high and then slammed it down, slicing through the man's neck. Blood gushed from the half severed head.

Jabin's guard took two quick steps toward the door.

Deborah followed the wave of men, leading the archers through the gateway. "Don't kill unnecessarily!" she warned. "We only want Jabin!"

Women of Hazor grabbed their children and hid in rooms. Children cowered in large jars or under hay. Men hid or ran. A ram's horn screeched again.

"Where is your king?" Barak yelled at the first man he encountered. The male seemed to be about twenty but was as skinny as a stick. The man trembled. "Please, don't hurt me," he said and then golden liquid ran down his legs.

"Tell me, where is your king!" Barak grabbed him by his tunic and shook him.

"He's...he's likely at the palace, over there." The terrified man pointed to a large column building in the center of the city.

Barak and his men raced to the ornate wooden door. Helon kicked it in. The door crashed to the floor. To their surprise, King Jabin stood there next to his wooden throne smiling in a crazed manner. His dead messenger laid at his feet in a pool of blood. Jabin's turban and robe were on the floor soaking in crimson liquid. He stood in his undergarment with his long black hair splayed out wildly over his shoulders.

"This ends nothing! You think killing me will end your battle?" King Jabin's crazy grin widened. "My descendants will avenge me. You, your children, and grandchildren will pay for what you have done. They will torture your babies, rape your wives, and…"

Barak plunged his dagger directly into Jabin's heart. Blood sprayed from the wound. Jabin's mouth filled with blood and he collapsed to the ground with a gurgled laugh.

Deborah and her men stared at the once great Canaanite king as he took his last breath.

CHAPTER 35

Deborah traveled with Heber and five Israelites to Elon-bezaanannim. Deborah wondered if she would recognize her old friend. How things have changed. The hours passed quickly until Deborah noticed a tent in front of a small wooden house. Heber ran ahead.

'Yael! It's me! I'm back. Merar!" the bald man cried out.

A messy haired boy ran from the house. "Father! You are home." He threw his arms around Heber. "I fished just like you. I brought home fishes and mother cooked them."

"You did well!" Heber's eyes filled with tears as he tousled the boy's hair.

Slowly the door to the house opened and Yael stepped out. She saw Heber and cautiously smiled.

"Yael," Heber released his son and closed the distance quickly between them. "Are you all right?"

Yael could barely move but as soon as Heber embraced her, she began to shake.

Deborah was a little further back. She watched as their son wrapped his arms around the two of them.

"Yael," Heber pulled back a little. "A friend of yours is here."

Yael looked over his shoulder and saw a woman with dark brown hair pulled back. "Who is this?" she asked.

Withdrawing from Heber, she took two steps towards the woman. She was muscular with long dark hair. Then their gaze met one another. "Those eyes!" Yael exclaimed as she sharply inhaled. "Devash? Is that you?"

Deborah smiled as her eyes teared up. “Yael, I thought you were, I thought...”

Yael ran towards her and hugged her so hard that she took Deborah’s breath away.

“Let me look at you,” Yael said as she pulled away. “You are different Devash. You are a grown woman. How did you get here?” Yael’s eyes misted.

Deborah shrugged her shoulders. How could Deborah possibly recount the events from that last day of Sukkot on the hill top over ten years ago? The death of her father, her marriage to Lappidoth, the training of the men and women at the palm trees, the battles against the Canaanites and Sea peoples.

Yael and Deborah held each other tightly. Heber, Barak, and Merar looked at them in bewilderment.

And then the women spontaneously laughed. What they were laughing at, neither of them knew, but within minutes their midsections hurt. They looked at one another and embraced once again.

Deborah ran her hands through Yael’s hair. “And you, you still have hair the color of fire.” Then she looked down in amazement at the boy at Yael’s side. “And you have a son.”

“Yes,” Yael reached her hand toward her son. “His name is Merar.”

Heber nodded his agreement.

“We are heading back home,” Deborah said in relief. “Come back with us. You’ve been away for long enough.”

“Home?” Yael looked at her in confusion. Heber stood by silently but his face was full of dismay. Yael turned her head towards her husband.

“I’ve been living here for almost ten years.”

Heber tentatively stepped forward and gingerly took Yael's hand. She smiled.

"Deborah, I am home."

Deborah looked at Yael in surprise. Heber and Yael looked at one another as their son gripped Yael's robe.

"I didn't think I would see you again, Yael." Deborah spoke slowly. "I'm happy that you are alive."

Yael let go of Heber and hugged her childhood friend tightly one last time.

After a few moments, Deborah regained her composure. "It's all right. We will tell your family that you are alive and well and that they should visit you. Now that the Canaanites and Sea People are defeated, we can freely travel to Northern Israel. We will see each other again."

"Yes," Yael approached Deborah. "You defeated them."

"Barak and our people did." Deborah pursed her lips. Tentatively, she asked, "Is it true Yael, that you, you..." She didn't know how to phrase it. "I mean Sisera, he's..."

Yael's eyes narrowed and anger passed over her face. "He will never harm another woman, man, or child again." She pointed to a mound by an oak tree. "I buried him there and with him, all of my pain." Yael smiled as Heber put his arm around her waist. "Go back home, Deborah. We will see each other in the future."

Deborah departed with her men. As she looked back at Yael, Heber, and Merar, she felt content.

Deborah, Barak, and the Israelites took their time heading south. It was a bittersweet journey. Deborah felt immense relief that they finally defeated King Jabin but she couldn't help feeling sad as well. Asher walked in the back of the group. His head hung low. He lost his wife, Shifra, the mother of his children. Deborah lost a friend, a confidant, someone who always spoke honestly with her.

Oh Shifra, you would've been so proud of all of us, Deborah thought to herself.

As sad as she was, though, she knew that everyone lost someone. Even Barak looked back at times with a heaviness. He lost his good friend Maon.

And yet they did it. They ended the war with the Canaanites and Sherden of the Sea People. Deborah knew that they saved lives and gave their children hope for a better life.

Along the way, people looked up from their fields to wave a hand in their direction. Women ran up to the Israelite soldiers and gave out handfuls of almonds, pouches of fresh goat milk, and bread made from wheat. The bystanders yelled out congratulations.

On the full moon of the Hebrew month of Tishrei, Deborah arrived back home. The Israelites packed up their belongings and animals and all headed to the plateau on the highest mountain. It was the Festival of Booths. Israelites traveled from the territories of Benjamin, Ephraim, Manasseh, and even some accompanied Barak from the northern tribes of Zebulun, Naphtali, and Issachar. They erected wooden frames and placed green palm fronds over the top. Children attached pomegranates, grapes, and crooked yellow and orange squash to its walls.

A fire roared on the altar. There were lambs and goats awaiting sacrifice.

"Deborah!" called out a woman wearing a beige scarf over her hair. "Deborah, you have returned." Her eyes watered.

"Ima," Deborah turned towards Tamar and hugged her.

"Look at you," Tamar studied her daughter. "I can't believe that my daughter is a chief."

Tamar shook her head in wonderment gazing at Deborah when an old man close by interrupted, "She isn't a chief. She's our judge."

Deborah and Tamar turned in surprise to Shelah.

Short blasts of the ram's horn sounded throughout the crowd.

The elderly priest stood by the blazing fire wearing his purple and crimson robe. His voice carried over the people. "We are here to thank God for the festival of Sukkot. Thank you for saving our people. Thank you for sending us Barak of Naphtali, the greatest commander of them all."

Cheers broke out but a younger male in the crowd yelled out, "What about Deborah?"

People began to call out the name. "Deborah! Deborah!"

The priest was confused but a younger man whispered in his ear. "Yes, I'm sorry. Thank you, God, for giving us Deborah, mother of our people, judge of Israel."

The crowd whistled, hooted, and clapped in loud applause. The priest continued, "We offer these animals in gratitude for our harvest and the peace in our land."

After the offerings, platters of juicy meat were passed out. Wine flowed unrestricted.

Shlomi's wife Yaakova led some women dancing around the perimeter of the gathering. Small camp fires lit up the night.

Shmuel took out a flute and played a melody as Haggai sang,

I will sing to Adonai, the God of Israel.

The earth trembled, heavens dripped water,

To those who didn't fight with us,

Shame on Reuben, Gilead, and Dan.

However, we praise the valor of Zebulun, Naphtali,

Issachar, Ephraim, and Benjamin.

The stars fought from heaven and the Kishon River overflowed.

Blessed be Yael who struck Sisera dead as he slept.

Arise Barak who took your captives.

Awake, Deborah as you delivered our people.

May all your enemies, O God, perish

And may we and our friends rise in might.

Barak listened to the chant with a smile and looked over at Deborah. She is so beautiful, so strong, he thought. He walked over to her and placed his hand on her shoulder.

"Deborah," he said huskily. "Now the war is over, I would like to court you."

Deborah's heart skipped a beat. She smelled his musky aroma mingled with the smoke of the fire. Oh, how she would like to live as husband and wife with Barak. It was with him she felt a connection unlike any other. There was attraction but something much deeper.

Deborah had never felt like this for any man, but, but she was married. Yes, she could ask Lappidoth for a divorce but the shame! Her people would likely reject her. Divorced women were shunned.

She stood there quietly thinking as Barak looked at her in puzzlement. She was a leader, a judge! She was using everything her Aba taught her, this is what she was meant to be. However, she looked up longingly at Barak. Why shouldn't she find joy in the arms of a man?

"Think about it, Deborah. I'll be over there by the oak trees. We can discuss more there." Barak took her hand, kissed it gently, and walked away.

Deborah's feet started to move in the direction of Barak but then Yoram approached.

"Judge Deborah," he said with pride. "The elders want to meet with you to discuss how the trade routes can be reopened. They are excited to plan our future." Yoram smiled wide. "You did it. We did it. They are over there at the tent." He pointed in the opposite direction of the oak grove.

Yoram walked away. Deborah stood in her place and watched Barak disappear into the trees. The Israelites sang and danced. Smoke wafted from the offering. And the full moon shined brightly in the night.

Nancy Rita Myers has been the rabbi of Temple Beth David in Orange County, California since the summer of 2004 where she brings her love of Jewish traditions, prayer, and community to both her writing and spiritual leadership. She has a B.A. in philosophy from Binghamton University, graduated from Hebrew Union College-Jewish Institute of Religion, and in 1997 was ordained as a rabbi. She is a past president of the Orange County Board of Rabbis and is active in the larger community. In 2022, she received her honorary Doctorate of Divinity from Hebrew Union College- Jewish Institute of Religion.

Rabbi Myers loves delving deeper into our people's ancient teachings and analyzing how they speak to us today, while challenging us to question ideas. She is the proud mother of Gabriel and Shane Myers Prunty.

Lightning Source UK Ltd.
Milton Keynes UK
UKHW041227010323
417854UK00001B/96

9 781678 164386